T0196314

Also by Michael Downing

FICTION
A Narrow Time
Mother of God

DRAMA
The Last Shaker

Perfect Agreement

Michael Downing

COUNTERPOINT
BERKELEY

Library of Congress Cataloging-in-Publication Data

Downing, Michael.
Perfect agreement / Michael Downing.
I. Title
PS3554.09346P47   1997
813'.54—dc21   97-25629

ISBN: 978-1-58243-538-1

Interior design by Wilsted & Taylor

Printed in the United States of America

COUNTERPOINT
2560 Ninth Street, Suite 318
Berkeley, CA 94710
www.counterpointpress.com

for Peter Bryant,

of course

The purpose of education, finally, is to create in a person the ability to look at the world for himself, to make his own decisions, to say to himself this is black or this is white, to decide for himself whether there is a God in heaven or not.

—JAMES BALDWIN

Perfect Agreement

Michael Downing

The Present
Monday, 10 June

standard usage

THIS STORY HAS already cost me my father. It was a loss of the worst kind, a loss I can live with. This distinguishes it from the loss of my job as director of the writing programs at McClintock College at the close of the 1996 academic year. I have to replace the job; I can't live without one of those. Fortunately, I will not have to conduct a search. My qualifications and my experience, along with the details of my dismissal, were broadcast in news stories and editorials throughout New England and New York during the last two weeks of May. You might have heard about me; my dead father did. I was the guy who refused to pass a so-called Black female student on the spelling portion of the Competency Achievement Test (CAT) and thus prevented her from entering her junior-year practice-teaching experience. It turned out all right in the end, in the World's terms: Rashelle was awarded a provisional pass by the college's academic dean, and I became the poster child of the angry so-called White people who are waging a campaign against political correctness. I found myself in bed with people who use the phrase "politically correct" as a white sheet. They use it to intimidate good people and to disguise their distaste for behaviors and institutional policies that acknowledge our place in history. They hate to be reminded of the past, which they treat like a corpse, rotten but hidden from view, memorialized with a headstone that records a few dates and a pious epitaph. Thus their outrage when someone starts digging it up. The past is dead; let it be. After a few years and a few bouquets of cut flowers, the smooth granite block is all we have, and it becomes a substitute for whatever lies beneath it. But the past is not a corpse. And the dead are not dead, as I have learned this month, this cool and breezy June. And though it makes a less effective epithet, could we suspend use of the term "politically correct" and accuse do-gooders instead of being morally correct? This is what is meant. After all, most of us know that we ought to bend over backward to help people whose lives are hard. When He was asked how often we are supposed to inconvenience ourselves, the White Jesus said, Not just seven times but seventy times seven times. (Don't do the math. He was a poet. He meant "Again. Always again.") Of course, there are fanatics everywhere, like germs, and they can infect a place. And college campuses are petri dishes for extremism. At McClintock, bending over to help became so fashionable that walking upright was deemed insensitive. Administrators and faculty scurried around like crabs, and the students got to like being bigger. I don't blame Rashelle for doing her best to avoid the spelling section of the CAT. What was I going to do, snap at her heels with my claw? Besides, as she explained in the letter she wrote under the guidance of a sociologist, "Mark has been showing his prejudgism to me." It sounded like a morals charge, but in her accompanying documentation, the sociologist explained that *"prejudgism* is a remarkable coinage, wherein Rashelle has conflated the behavioral inclination (the prejudice) with the sociopersonal causative (racism), and by importing the *g* to create a nonstandard spelling of the word (*prejudice* is the version more often recorded in English-language communities), Rashelle reconvenes the word with its literal cognate (*judge*). In short, Rashelle has been pre-judged, mis-judged." My judgment was and remains to this day a simple one: Rashelle can become an 80 percent speller. That's what I did for seven years at McClintock; I believed everyone could be literate—in the standard sense. I taught freshmen and sophomores how to spell and use rudimentary grammar. It was my work, not a cause. But publicity turned me into the Standard Bearer for Standards, and after I was fired, I was invited to apply for openings at three universities and four colleges in Boston, not one of them as progressive or innovative as McClintock, where I belong. I have my first interview this afternoon at Massachusetts Commonwealth University (MCU), pioneers in the policy of recruiting wealthy international students to bypass affirmative action quotas. (*Quota*: a great, plain word demonized by those who are inconvenienced by quotas and never spoken by those who know we need quotas, rather like the name Eugene McCarthy.) I do not belong at MCU. But before you entertain any gripes on my behalf, be aware that I will be named an associate professor of literature or the humanities (so that the students in my basic skills classes do not suspect they are being forced to do remedial work); I will be paid forty or fifty thousand dollars per academic year (not your standard year—classes meet two or three times a week and there are two fourteen-week semesters; do the math); and along with the attendant privileges, technology, support services, and benefits, I will be given parking rights in the city, where off-street spaces are otherwise sold or leased as condominiums. These conditions of employment, I have learned, constitute my "academic freedom"—another disguise, this one worn proudly, like regalia, by the conspirators better known as the Faculty. Don't misunderstand me; academic freedom remains a serious matter in higher education, but it is a matter of principal.

DICTION TIP
Principal/principle

A classic example of the dangers of "trick" teaching. You all remember that the head of your school is your "pal," and thus the spelling "principal." Yes? The problem is an odd one: the trick is too memorable. Young students immediately isolate the "pal" ending and reserve it for school administrators. So from now on, think of it this way: the princip<u>al</u> is the <u>main</u> person in a school, as books have <u>main</u> or principal characters, and you earn interest on the <u>main</u> amount of money, the principal, in your account. The other princip<u>le</u> means ru<u>le</u>; we use it for the rules of academic disciplines and for our ethical and moral rules or standards. Becoming people of principle ought to be our principal goal; we should not stand on our principles nor on our principals, no matter how crabby.

the measure of a man

FRED HOGWORTHY, CHAIR of English and American Literature at MCU, offered me a tenure-track job as associate professor of rhetoric before I sat down. He looked a little sad when I arrived, but it was June, and he must have regretted the time away from his boat and summer gardens, the standard research materials for senior faculty in the humanities. He was wearing a blue and white seersucker suit his wife had bought for him at Brooks Brothers about the time of the Kent State riots, before his blond hair had faded and his face had gone permanently red. He was old enough to be my father, and his shape was enough like mine to suggest a relationship. His eyes were blue, not a match with my eyes, but this difference was not definitive according to Mendel and his peas. I could not rule him out, except that I knew he wasn't my father because I had finally met my so-called father the week before. But I'd spent my whole life sizing up my elders, trying them on for size, and I didn't know how else to take the measure of a man. Despite my intention to despise MCU and all affiliated, I liked Fred Hogworthy immediately. His office was a modest ten-by-twelve desk-chair-shelving-the-window-doesn't-open-let-me-clear-off-a-chair-for-you place on the sixth floor of one of MCU's many concrete towers. He offered me a drink and then grimaced: summer, no staff. He was plagued by the idea of having to travel to an automated dispensary where he would find himself without the correct change. Instead, he cranked open a file drawer and pulled out a huge clot of paper, which he dumped into a plastic trash can. "Now I can say I've been through the résumés we have on file." Apparently, he and I had taken the same speed-reading course. That was how I got through the language-acquisition and semiotics journals every month. "Of course, we'll have to pretend to conduct a national search for someone with—what did you do at McClintock? Seven years? Someone with seven years' experience and—how many books have you done? Two? Two books on the teaching of language skills." He smiled and looked at his wrist, where his wife had forgot to attach his watch. "Before you leave campus, you should meet Eleanor—have you met her yet? Redhead? Knows everything about Cervantes, though she's still waiting for another human being to read *Quixote*. Eleanor Villegas. She will head up the search. She can round up the usual suspects in a week. She's awfully good at it. Bound to find us a Nigerian poetess with a linguistics degree from the Sorbonne on a postdoc at Yale." This alarmed him. If that poet didn't get the job, she'd have grounds for legal action. "We'll have to insert something administrative into the job description—tracking fluency rates or assessing second-language retention—so we can announce a

preference for candidates familiar with MCU systems and cur-
riculum. You must have picked up our way of doing things by
now. After all, McClintock is right around the corner from us."
He meant "in our shadow." He looked at his wrist again, then
at my face. "What time is it? President Derby wants to meet
you at four." He pronounced the president's name *Darby,* as if
to ally him with England and the horse race run at the Epsom
flats, not the Kentucky Derby. It was Hogworthy's only apparent affectation. Everyone in Massachusetts knew the man as
Nervy Derby, failed candidate for the U.S. Senate, who had returned to MCU but had not given up his public platform; I
mean, he literally had a platform built in his office. Derby was
remembered as a vicious debater with an impolitic knack for
articulating a crowd's deeply repressed hatreds and fears. But
he was best remembered for his obsession with his height.
Throughout the course of his campaign he was plagued by
questions about variations in the public record on this matter,
until one day a reporter challenged him to a test of the tape,
which he had kindly brought along. To that point in the campaign, Derby had called homeless people bums, referred to
working women as displaced moppers and shoppers, vowed to
turn public schools into sweatshops like the ones where the
Mexicans make our clothes, and promised to get the scary
African stuff out of Boston's African-American neighborhoods.
And he was at 60 percent in the polls and rising. But then he
called the reporter with the measuring tape to the stage, saying,
"Unless I've shrunk along with the brains of most Americans, I
stand five feet tall." He had wavered. Earlier in the campaign,
he'd gone on record at five foot one. The MCU public relations
people had him at five two. With cameras rolling, the reporter

tallied him up at four eleven, including his shoes. And Thomas
Derby lost his bid for the Senate by that inch or two. Massachusetts voters admired him, but they could no longer trust
him, even after a retired director of the Bureau of Standards
and Measures performed a "scientific calibration" in an MCU
physics lab with Derby on a stretcher. When he returned to
MCU, Thomas Derby had his office moved from the colonial
mansion where his predecessors had resided to the top floor of
Inifiti Towers, where the presidential desk and chair were installed on a foot-high dais near the windows overlooking his
kingdom and all that fell beneath its shadow. Visitors were
never invited onto the stage. And when Hogworthy and I got
there, the curtain was drawn. Beside the closed oak door, an
armed security guard with a West Indian accent said, "The
man is not here for you, man," and he tipped his nightstick in
its holster, directing us to a phalanx of young staff assistants
who responded to our request for a meeting with Derby by
huddling with their datebooks. After a lot of whispering and the
sound of a single page being torn from a book, a young woman
yelled, "July twenty-seventh at one-thirty," and the scrum broke
up. Hogworthy led me to his car in an underground garage. "I
hope you can make it. It's a Saturday, I think. Where did you
park?" He was evaporating. What did I expect? It was the tenth
day of June. The academic calendar ignores the principles of
nature; summer arrives weeks before the solstice. He'd offered
me a job. "Take some time to think it all over, Mark." He had
started his engine. I had to lean down and stick my head in the
window to hear him. "Right now, you're Joan of Arc. Derby
wants to be the one who pulls you out of the fire. But someone
else is getting broiled as we speak. You know how things are on

campuses now. The next political martyr is right behind you, and she might be a woman with a degree in a real discipline. I mean, take some time before you sign up with us. But remember, you're a white man who wants a job in the Boston market. You basically teach spelling." He was staring through his windshield at the cinder-block wall where the words "Faculty Only" were printed in yellow paint. But he was seeing blue, the smooth surface of a small bay bending beneath the bow of his boat. "It's a good life, Mark." I agreed, and I accepted the job. "And wear something better than what you've got on today when you meet him next month. There'll be a press conference." He fingered his lapel. "A dark suit? Anyway, something less poignant than this ingenuous artifact I wear." He waved, patted my elbow, and he was gone, rather like my father, I thought.

SPELLING TIP
Look for relationships among irregular words

Despite what you've heard, English spelling is not a nightmare of exceptions and inanities. Almost 90 percent of our commonly used words can be spelled according to the rules. But there are some oddities. Fortunately, they are rarely singular. Our job as spellers is to reunite these apparent strangers. For instance: *science* is easy to remember, right? So introduce <u>sci</u>ence to its knowledgeable relatives: <u>sci</u>ence/con<u>sci</u>ence/con<u>sci</u>ous/fa<u>sci</u>nating. You see, if you think about the words you often misspell, you will uncover commonalities. For example: independance or independence? tendancy or tendency? cemetary, cematery, cemetery? The truth is they are all *e* words, as if to remind us that we have a tendency to be independent, though we are only independent in the cemetery. And finally, for now, remember that we misspell some words because we misunderstand them. A classic problem for spellers: is it definetly? definately? definitly? definetely? What is the root word here? We assume it is "define," and we are wrong. The root is <u>finite</u>, limited, of certain measure. Add a prefix—use *de-* or *in-*—and then add the suffix *-ly* (which begins with a consonant, so we won't be dropping the final *e* of the root), and we are in<u>finite</u>ly more de<u>finite</u> than we were before. So, be con<u>sci</u>ous of, fa<u>sci</u>nated by, and con<u>sci</u>entious about the de<u>finite</u>ly infi<u>nite</u> connections we have yet to discover among words, which, like people, have a natural tendency toward interdependence.

o w n e r s h i p

FRED HOGWORTHY GAVE me the last line of my story: I got the
job! But I didn't understand a word of it, really. I was in the famous student position of trying to read between the lines or get
beneath the text and dredge up some deep meaning. This was
not a complaint. I got the job. I'd finally met my father. I had
everything I needed. But I was not looking forward to it, as if
my life was no longer ahead of me. No, on the afternoon of 10
June, I was only looking forward to dinner with Paul Pryor, who
would tell me that I didn't belong at MCU, which was just
what I didn't want to hear. I'd heard enough. I heard enough
during the first ten days of June to know that stories do not always end well and people do not always end up in agreement.
I will take you to dinner with Paul, but first, let's just stand at
the window and review the items on the menu. Are you with
me? The first thing you should see is my house. I bought my
house because it looks like a boat in dry dock. It is fifteen feet

wide and not quite twenty-five feet long. It is wooden and old, and when an apple orchard was divided and auctioned off in parcels in 1873, one of the house's owners liked it well enough to have it moved here from Center Street. The front of the house was jammed into this small hill, and its sides are bowed now, like gunwales, so clapboards occasionally pop off and the roof shingles buckle in winter and stand up like folded paper hats. The gabled back end is balanced high above the sloping lawn on a porous stack of stones, and sometimes I sit in the kitchen expecting a flood tide to sweep over the banks of the Ipswich River and take us away. We face the Atlantic, and we often smell it, but the distance to the open ocean is not navigable. There are several houses, the odd apple tree, a trafficky street, and a milk-and-beer store between the window and the river basin, and from there it is two miles of marsh as the egrets fly to the white dunes and vast tidal flats of the barrier beach. We are thirty miles north of Boston in this town of ten thousand. Ipswich is famous for its clams. Whenever I dig up a patch of my yard to plant a tree or move the perennials (which I treat like furniture, as if by rearranging my stock I can transform the disappointment I feel with my surroundings into happiness), I unearth evidence of clamshells, bone-white chips and ashy powder sifted deep into the soil. This was foretold by the wise Pest Inspector, who led me into the basement to examine evidence I'd discovered of termites in a beam, a few days after I'd bought the place in 1989. "Good news is the bugs walked outa this roadside diner fifty years ago and never came back," he said, and then he stuck his crowbar into the beam holding up the house and pried off a desiccated chunk. He banged the beam hard and smiled. "Like the sounda that. They left you plentya wood for a house this size." He was fat and small and his arms and neck and head were barnacled with whorls of white hair. Grandfather material. He pointed the pronged end of his crowbar at the floor like a divining rod, and then he dug up a divot of dirt and white dust. "Clamshells. They'll haunt ya here." He crushed the clot back into place. "It's what remains of the fortunes of most Ipswich families. See, diggin clams made us rich as boys. We were strong, and we could dig all day cause we wanted cars, and trips west to drink ourselves blind, and we didn't mind droppin a roll at the races. Dropped outa school makin more than our fathers, who'd done as we did till their backs went tender and their knees stiffened and they took up as postmen and pest inspectors. Wasn't a mother in town who could find fault with her son workin harder than a horse and buyin her hats, and besides, there was often a sister or two gonna need a weddin down the line. Our earnins broke our fathers' pride. In the end, broke our mothers' hearts with gamblin debts or drink. And usually married the sisters off to our clammin pals, keepin it all in the family." He wanted to get back above ground. "A man's family's nothing more than the foreseeable future." I led him out to the backyard, where there were four or five thousand bees living in a tar-paper toolshed. He told me his sister kept bees, and I was hoping he might send her by to collect a free gift. "In New Hampshire," he said. "She ran away in the forties to join the Shakers up in Canterbury. Then she died." It seemed a brutally efficient way to tell the story of a life. It was a defense; he didn't want to answer any questions about her or about the Shakers. I knew how he felt. The Shakers meant trouble to me, too. He expressed his gratitude for my silence by kicking in the walls of the toolshed. Then he grabbed my arm and rushed us into the cab of his truck. "Bees hate dirt." They'd tracked us to the truck, so he put on his windshield wipers and drove to the end of the block. "Give'm an hour or two. They'll move on. It's your house now, not theirs." Suddenly, I wanted to tell him about my father. He'd left his wife and kids for the Shakers twice. The first time he left was almost twenty years before I was born, in the late spring of 1941, about the time the sister of the future Pest Inspector packed her bag and the termites moved out of the house that was now mine. But what did this man want with one more broken shell of a family? So I jumped out of the truck and waved. Then I stood at the end of the street and stared at my unseaworthy hive of a home. The bees were buzzing like electrical wires in heat, but I could hear the familiar ring of my telephone—once, twice, machine engaged, message played, recording under way. Shore-to-ship communication. I wandered down to the river.

PUNCTUATION TIP
Solving the mystery of the apostrophe

Most Americans cannot use the apostrophe correctly. In fact, the government may have to step in soon and create a commission to install apostrophes in sentences, a logical extension of the Americans with Disabilities Act. Until then, forget everything you were told. It is not about ownership. Sure, the man's sweater belongs to the man, but does the man's wife? And is it the kid's father or the kids' father or the kids' fathers? And you all remember the problems with irregular plurals: is it the women's room or

the womens' room? The truth is, an apostrophe is always
a sign of something lost. For contractions, we use an
apostrophe to show a loss of letters: We're here! Where's
he going? Well, with nouns that are somehow related
(man/wife; kid/father), we can express the relationship
with "of" or "of the" and never need an apostrophe: the
wife of the man; the father of the kid, the father of the
kids, or the fathers of the kids. If you want to abbreviate
this, you make three changes: drop "of" or "of the," put an
apostrophe at the end of the second noun (and add an *s*
unless there is one before the apostrophe), and switch
the order of the two nouns: the man's wife; the kid's father; the kids' father; the kids' fathers. This will work for
most nouns. (People are the exceptions. Henry James's
novels might confound you, as can all of the Jameses'
tomes, but do not give up. Look again. You can avoid the
confusion by reading one of the short stories of Henry
James.) Don't let apostrophes defeat you; simply restore
the words to the order they were in before the loss occurred. The words of Jesus are exceptional because they
are Jesus' words; the room of the women is the women's
room; and the father of the children will be the children's
father. There is no mystery here. We must take possession of what was lost.

The Past

Saturday, 1 June,
Through Monday, 10 June

i m m e d i a t e   f a m i l y

"I WANT TO give you a picture of my life." It was Ellen, the good sister. She lived with my mother, who had been prostrate and speechless for nearly a year. "The picture was made this morning, this overcast first day of June, 1996, in the beautiful Berkshires." Ellen's word portraits were delivered without irony. They were not scripted, so she spoke slowly, and she often let fifteen or twenty seconds pass without a word—unnaturally long silences during which I could almost see the image developing. Once, many years ago, she had prepared a picture too big for my answering machine, and at the five-minute mark it was abruptly cropped. It never happened again. But whenever I replace my machine (usually twice a year; I drop things and knock them over), I avoid models with preset limits for individual calls. Otherwise, I would have no contact with my so-called family. Ellen did not mention my troubles at McClintock, though an unidentified supporter had clipped and sent a few favorable editorials from the daily Pittsfield news-paper, where Ellen worked mornings in Circulation. For almost twenty years, she had hired and overseen the paperboys and papergirls who got the news out to residents. Occasionally, she sent pictures from her office, and I especially loved the ones in-volving redrawn delivery routes, which always featured former homes of childhood friends, familiar storefronts being refur-bished or demolished, and other topographical changes in the landscape of my youth. Ellen was my nearest relative by far, but from the beginning even she was far away. When I was born, in 1960, she was already eighteen; Tommy was twenty-three, and Bridget was twenty-one. Ellen was the youngest of the three children who constituted the First Family. My parents, Nora McNab and Thomas Sternum, were both born in 1917, "the year America entered the First World War," my mother used to say. She, too, lacked irony. They met in high school and moved to the Berkshires to raise a family, again according to my mother. It's not that I doubted her on this point exactly, but she seemed to imply that only fools would have tried to keep kids in a city. My father was a photographer, and early on he made his living taking pictures of other people's kids and family cel-ebrations. He was good-natured and always had a lot of friends around, characteristics that my mother reported as personality disorders. They bought a huge stucco house in West Pittsfield from Dr. Shipton, a dentist who had built it with his sons. Maybe my parents hoped they'd have a dozen kids. Or maybe it was the I beams that appealed to them. In the clean, cool basement of the house you could look up and admire the two enormous steel I beams that ran beneath the wooden struts and joists. Every surface in that house is level, and every corner true; each section of the complicated slate roof reads like a sheet of graph paper. It must have looked like a dream come true to my father, who was apparently incapable of hammering a nail into a board. But he only stayed there for six years. In 1940, he made a portrait of Allen Cuthbert, an antiquarian. Cuthbert was the first ardent historian of the Shakers and the most ardent collector of all things Shaker. That summer, Cuthbert had installed himself at the Hancock Shaker Village, about two miles west of our stucco home, to document the artifacts and to stash a few chairs and highboys into his capacious pickup truck, though these losses were not registered for many years. Neither of my parents knew much about the Shakers beyond their round stone barn at Hancock and Christmas gifts of wild berry preserves stamped "Shaker Made." There was a village in Maine and one in New Hampshire, and there was the sprawling Central Ministry just a couple of miles west of Hancock, across the border in Lebanon, New York, but that village was being abandoned, and in the midforties it was sold off to the proprietors of a boarding school. Cuthbert wrote my father a note in October, inviting him to visit Hancock for "photographic opportunities untold." His note is still in our stucco house, in a drawer of the oak table we always referred to as "Dad's desk." I must have read Cuthbert's words a hundred times while I was growing up, trying to hear the untold story of my father's strange affiliation with the Shakers. My mother's version of the story was "all Swiss" (as the great woman who canned me at McClintock likes to say), more holes than cheese. I know that his contact with the Shakers altered my father's life. He tried to persuade my mother to spend some time with the few dozen Believers still residing at Hancock, but my mother only went once, in January of 1941. My father had been working at Hancock five or six days a week and spending a few nights there, too. Cuthbert had arranged a generous commission for him from the New England Historical Society, which was planning a major Shaker exhibition and a catalog. My mother was twenty-three. She left Tommy and Bridget at home with her brother, James, who was on leave from his post in the navy for a month. She did not know that she was pregnant with Ellen. She wore a black seal coat James had bought in Seattle and black button-up boots with heels. Her dark hair was curled and her skin was still smooth. She put on some lipstick, but she wiped it off before the taxi left her standing by the Visitors' Store. I can see her. She looks dark and handsome against the slate sky, but her mouth is closed, sealed tight, and her gaze does not wander past the clean lines of the gated fence into that strangely perfect world of wood and stone and hay and snow. A Shaker Sister emerged from the store with a broom and led my mother to the Ministry Shop, sweeping drifted snow from the brick path before them. My mother remembered her olive face and dark eyes framed by a gray bonnet. And her right hand, which was missing four fingers. My mother didn't want her sweeping with that hand, so she said her boots were waterproof, which they weren't. "Boots, Mrs. Sternum? Those are no boots to a Shaker. And the sweeping is a Gift." Years later, my mother read one of the books illustrated with my father's photographs of Hancock, and she understood what the Sister meant. Among the Shakers, having work to do was a Gift. She said this shamed her. She had misjudged the Shakers. At the Ministry Shop, my mother was left alone with my father. He had a kitchen, a reading room, and a bedroom on the first floor, and upstairs he had darkrooms and editing tables. The shop had been built as offices for the deacons and elders during the 1800s, when there were more than three hundred Believers at Hancock. My mother remembers the woodenness of the place—shiny wide pine floors, ash chairs with webbed cotton seats, cherry tables, built-in oak cabinets and closets, maple peg boards on every wall, and the six-over-six windows with wavy glass. It was the only place she'd ever been that was "as clean as the house I keep." And she told me more than once, "Your father looked strangely at ease there, and even while he begged me to bring the kids with me the next time, he was staring out through one of those windows, and I knew he expected to see me there, outside, in the world, where he never really belonged." When she got home, Tommy and Bridget were playing in an igloo Uncle James had built in the backyard. And James said, "He isn't coming home is he, Nora? The bastard." He knew how to read her face, which always made us eager for him to visit. He was a few years older than my mother, and his brush-cut hair was reddish, but with their dark eyes and Roman noses and their appealing overall tautness, they were often mistaken for twins. James managed to have his leave extended until the end of April, when he would ship out for Greenland on an icebreaker, the first of the American soldiers committed to the European war. My father visited a few times and tried to explain himself, occasionally asking my mother to come with him. She reminded him that the Shakers were celibate people. Eventually, he told her he was finished at Hancock and was going south, to photograph the abandoned village at Pleasant Hill in Kentucky. James threatened to have him drafted by the army. My father announced he was a pacifist.

James said, "That will please the Krauts no end." My mother asked my father if he was becoming a Shaker. He said he was all turned around, and could he leave his things in the house? "In case you turn around again, you mean?" was all my mother said. She didn't tell him or James about her pregnancy. And it was almost five years before she saw her brother again, and thirteen years more before she laid eyes on her husband. "We were all soldiers," she told me once. It was one of the few times I'd managed to make a direct request for information about my father. "Your uncle enlisted in the future, I was stationed in the present, and your father did battle with the past." I was nine, and I puzzled over her explanation for weeks. I finally cracked the code and drew myself a time line. But when I put myself into the picture, all three of them appeared to be in the past. Her meaning remained cryptic. My father became famous. After the publication of the catalog in 1943, his Hancock pictures appeared in national magazines, overseas newspapers, and finally in a book with a long essay by Allen Cuthbert. His Kentucky work extended to a second abandoned village, South Union, and north throughout the former haunts of the Western Shakers in Ohio and Indiana, though I believe his permanent home in those years before my birth was near or on the Pleasant Hill Shaker Village. His bio line in publications never varied: "Thomas Sternum's beloved wife and children reside in the Berkshires in a house built on two steel I beams." Of course, no one in town knew how my mother paid the mortgage. Had she ever told that husband of hers about the birth of little Ellen? Did Nora and Thomas Sternum exchange so much as a word after he went south? This was a secret shared only by my parents—until my brother Tommy spent an entire night and the morning of the next day eavesdropping in my father's clothes closet, and then my sister Bridget eventually got the story out of Tommy by blackmail, and Ellen listened at the door of Bridget's bedroom during the heated negotiations with Tommy, and Ellen memorized every detail which, many years later, she offered to tell me "verbatim" in exchange for my silence about her late-night trips over the mountain to Lebanon, New York. And I tell you all of this, and no more just now, because this is what came back to me during one gap in time, an especially languorous interlude in Ellen's word picture on the first day of June, 1996. When she resumed speaking, I could already see my mother, lying on her side, her blind eyes turned toward Ellen's calm voice. Ellen said, "She looks adorable. Her hair is too long probably, and I should tie it back or cut it. It is transparent, though, and where it covers her face I can still see her. I have just finished reading her *The French Lieutenant's Woman*. She is asleep. I had forgotten how long it is. The Fowles book. And her life. Mount Greylock is invisible today." I heard Ellen light a cigarette. Then I got distracted by three long blasts of a car horn somewhere near my house, and I went into the living room to see what was happening. It was Rachel Reed, the academic dean at McClintock. She drove a big blue van incautiously. She waved and pointed at my little hatchback as she passed it, and then eeeeech, she swerved and careened into the hill in front of my house, a classic demonstration of parallel parking, Boston style. Rachel was the woman who'd hired me and fired me at McClintock. I was charmed that she'd decided to spend her Saturday with me, and I hurried to the kitchen and put a bottle of wine into the freezer. I noticed the message light was blinking. Ellen had finished. I rewound her message and fast-forwarded until I got to the part about Mount Greylock obscured by clouds. Rachel was standing at the door, adjusting her hat. The rest of Ellen's brief word picture went like this: "Old as she is, Mom still has not acquired a taste for music. Whenever I play any of the disks you send, she winces, and this morning she cried during the Bach." Rachel said, "Who doesn't?"

PREFIXES
A guarantee

Unlike most of the rules of life, this spelling rule can be followed without exception. Prefixes never change the spelling of the root word. It is that simple. So, what do we do with this? First, get to know the common prefixes: *il-, im-, in-, non-, re-, pre-, dis-, mis-, un-*, and the like. Then, attach them to the front of words (pre-fix them) to alter the meaning. No need to wonder how many *s*'s are required for *misspell*; you would never spell *spell* without its initial *s*, and you know the prefix is *mis*. Nothing unnatural here; no weird dissimilarities or illogic; no unnecessary fuss. You can mediate your attachments, immediate and otherwise.

the least tern

RACHEL REED WAS the academic dean at McClintock and I was no longer the director of the writing programs, and what we discussed for two hours was whether her husband would approve of her decision to update the heating system in their five-story house in the city. I knew he'd rue the loss of the cast-iron kitchen radiators, which only warmed up to about sixty degrees (when the converted coal furnace was working) but made excellent benches when the house was crowded with guests. I said he wouldn't mind. And he wouldn't, for he certainly knew about the morning last February when Rachel had traveled down from her third-floor bedroom to the garden-level kitchen and taken a bad chill. Although she immediately spotted the problem—the long-term leak under the sink was feeding a sizable ice rink—it was another hour before she could bring herself to report this disaster to anyone. First, she left me a message: "Something very strange has happened here, and before I get someone to fix it, I was wondering if you own a pair of ice skates." Then she called the gas company. Then she found two neighborhood kids who skated in little circles while she drank coffee and discussed the furnace with her husband, Mark Reed, who was dead. He died in the winter of 1991 when he and Rachel were fifty—too young, or so we all said, pretending that time was a currency and we were owed more. I'd met Mark Reed a few times while he was alive, and I think I misunderstood him in just the way all of Rachel's admirers did. I thought he limited her life. He was an urban archaeologist, which is academy shorthand for a white leftist historian who didn't get tenure. He loved Boston and the people who'd built it, and that's why he and Rachel ended up in their vast brick townhouse between the Back Bay and Roxbury. In 1968, it was one of many salvageable dumps in a genuine neighborhood of working people—and it was on the market for twenty-thousand dollars. Mark also loved his two sons, and for years he biked with them around the city until they learned the name of every street and alley, every public building, every former industrial site. But he was censorious, too, and his commitment to authenticity often felt punitive. I didn't want him to see the vinyl windows I'd installed in Ipswich, for instance, though they were weather-tight and easy to clean, unlike the opaque wooden rattlers he and Rachel lined with plastic wrap every winter. His principles had matured into an archive of inconveniences—from an iron skillet seasoned by a century of use, which never let an egg go over easy, to prohibitions against restaurants with dress codes, all nonjug wines, and trust funds, like the small one Rachel had from her Presbyterian relatives who'd made a fortune in Iowa agribusiness. After he died,

Rachel told me Mark had been raised in safe houses all around the country because his parents were Reds, and then I knew him better. Communism hadn't taken with the kids born in the forties and fifties, but while they were young and impressionable, they had learned to see the rotten underside of the material world, like good Catholics. It's as if they were all fitted with phony X-ray glasses while they were infants. Long before they'd figured out that you couldn't even see through to a girl's breasts or your best friend's brain—never mind the Blood of the Masses or Satan—they'd acquired the habit of looking for the hidden danger, the concealed motive, the awful truth. "Those were his limits," Rachel told me once. "I bumped up against them all the time. How else do you ever touch a person? You find his limits and you memorize them eventually. Mark knew mine. And he loved them. It's where all of us meet the world, at our limits." She knew all of this, but she didn't know if he'd approve of the new furnace. I used to suspect that Rachel asked me to speak for her dead husband because he and I had the same first name. I worried that the affectionate trust she showed me was Freudian, or maybe just Pavlovian. But I no longer believe in the gospel of the social sciences. I don't believe our ambitions are the expression of mysterious market forces or ancient kinship rituals. I don't believe our desires are just sublimated urges and unconscious impulses festering like splinters in our hands and feet. I believe in the art of us, the impractical, unpredictable, and sometimes intolerable things Rachel and Mark and Ellen and Rashelle and the beekeeping sister of the pest inspector will do or say to be known and understood and loved. We are all artists, and we want to make a genuine impression on this world we must leave. So when it

came to questions about Mark, it wasn't that Rachel didn't
know what he would say. She was afraid that she was the only
one who knew what he would say, that she was all that was left
of him. I felt free to speak to the question of the radiators because I felt Mark too, and I had the distinct impression that he
wanted Rachel to be warm. Rachel and I achieved consensus
on the matter midway through a second bottle of wine, and
then we drove to the ocean. Normally, I put in a full day on the
beach, because it is my summer office and even I have my professional pride. But Rachel liked her skin white and wrinkle-
free, a preference I knew as one of her limits. It was six, and
shadows were starting to run long. Tide was coming in to meet
us and eventually forced us from the hard flats into the soft
sand berm, where we were introduced to the territorial habits
of the least tern. It is a small gray and white bird with a black
cap and yellow feet. The adults have pencil-sharp yellow bills.
They are prized and protected residents of North Shore
beaches because they are at the limit of their normal range up
here; most least terns summer along the warmer mid-Atlantic
coast. They nest in the sand in front of the dunes, so park
rangers string up barbed wire in the spring to protect the
chicks, which look like motes of dust scuttling underfoot,
where their chance of surviving is not great. This severely limits the high-tide beach, but most people don't mind. It's the
same spirit that keeps residents off Central Street during a bike
race or a marathon; you make room for unusual events. And by
mid-July, all the terns' bills are yellow, they know how to fly, the
wire comes down, and we have the run of the place. But in
June, the adult terns are wary of bipeds, and as Rachel and I
trudged through the soft sand, we heard some of them yapping

above us. We ignored them, much as we were ignoring the whole Spelling Tragedy, hoping it might just leave us alone. But the least tern is not a problem; it's more like a kingfisher. It will dive into the ocean for food, and it will dive into a woman's hat to protect its young. The birds above us began a series of strikes that drove us toward the water, and even as we waded up to our knees, they kept their sights on Rachel's straw hat, swooping and screaming until we had learned our lesson. The true-blue waters of the North Atlantic were running at about fifty-three degrees, and we were grateful for the breadth of the public beach when we got back. People were scarce. A few sun worshipers were still prostrated before the deity, and some older couples in windbreakers stared at the sea from the top of one of the wooden walkways that span the dunes, the fragile barrier between the beach and the rest of the world. And we were warm and safe because, like a tide, a problem will not always be with you. Everything goes away. The McClintock story had migrated back to the editorial page of the newspaper, the gateway to oblivion. The challenge ahead was the procurement of a perfect dinner. We had time. A little boy ran by and skidded down into the sand. Then he got up, shook himself off, and faced the water. It lapped at his bare legs and the sun turned his yellow hair silver. He was six or seven, and he stood still as a sentinel. He had no idea, but he was right there at the edge of it all, poised at the beginning and the end. He was at home in the whole world, on land and at sea. I assured myself that I had been there once. Everyone has. But it is an experience our memories cannot record, a page torn from our datebooks, a gap in time. It is where we are unmindful of our limits, or maybe there are no limits there. Maybe everything is inconclusive, irresolute, unprincipled, infinite. I have no idea. Sometimes I tell myself I will get back there, that each of us is on a journey home. But we're not birds, not even the least of us.

MORE DICTION ALREADY
More diction; all ready?

We can all spell *all*, but none of us is altogether certain when it is all right to spell *already* with one *l*. This uncertainty is sensible; we have watched *all right* turn into *alright* during our reading lifetimes. And many people do not accept *alright*, although they are altogether comfortable with almost all other *al* words. You can't be expected to guess the limits of other people's tolerance, but you can adopt a policy of your own so you can explain yourself when you bump up against them. If the word *all* can be eliminated from your sentence (my colleagues are all ready to lynch me), choose the two-word, a-l-l phrase; if the sentence does not make sense without it, use the one-word a-l form (my colleagues have already hung me out to dry). For instance, you wouldn't want to know that I am together confident about this policy; you would want to know that I am altogether confident. There will always be choices to make. And then it is time to move on, and that's alright by me.

b i n g o

I AM ONE of the last boom babies. But unlike most of my con-
temporaries, my birth cannot be blamed on the postwar eu-
phoria, industrial prosperity, or the tremendous number of
martinis consumed by fertile adults between 1945 and 1960.
No, I was conceived in August of 1959 as part of the strange
ceremonies conducted by Nora and Thomas Sternum to com-
memorate the end of Shakerism in the Berkshires. It all began
as a rumor after the Hancock Shakers donated half of their
considerable landholdings to the Commonwealth of Massachusetts for public recreation. The Pittsfield State Forest, a
wildlife refuge with spectacular stands of white azaleas in
spring and herds of campers in the summer, includes the
Shaker burial grounds. The bodies of all Believers who passed
at Hancock and Mount Lebanon are crowded into a few acres
marked by a single slab of granite bearing the word *Shakers* and
nothing else. This was their way. They didn't date their deaths,

dig discrete holes for their corpses, or plant geraniums. They went down together. The land grant to the state was a blow to several entrepreneurs, who then raised their bids on the remaining two hundred acres, where the last three Hancock Shakers resided surrounded by their beautiful buildings. Some of them had stood since 1790—the buildings, not the Believers—when the first Berkshire Family gathered, inspired by the opening of the Shaker Gospel in America in 1774 in Watervliet, New York. But in the late 1950s, architecture had not yet been put on the endangered species list, and any talk of preserving the round stone barn and the white wood Dwelling House was dismissed by Pittsfield natives as idle chatter from the ivory towers of Williamstown and Amherst. In the factories and kitchens of Pittsfield, people were talking a satellite plant for the vast General Electric Naval Ordnance facility, or a Ford factory, and how about a commercial airport? In the midst of this windstorm of speculation, Thomas Sternum blew back into town. Everyone was happy to see him. "Everyone was always happy to see your father," my mother used to say, indicting herself as well as her friends and neighbors. "He was pathologically likable. Like your sister Ellen, only worse. Even the priests who'd given sermons from the altar about his abandoning three children wanted to buy him a beer when he got back, and they asked him to come to their parishes to hear them preach on the Prodigal Son. Your father dined out on that parable until you were born." If asked why he came back, my mother would only say, "Your father was an honorable man. He paid his debts." This was Deep Code. Ellen tried to explain it to me on my eighteenth birthday at the Tin Lizzy, a big bar over the mountain in Lebanon, New York, where the radios were tuned to the call of the nightly trifecta at Saratoga. Of the many contradictions in Ellen's character, none is more gratifying than her passion for the ponies. She's been playing them since she was sixteen, and she says she's up about seventy-three thousand and change, and that's after paying for five White Russians on every visit to the Tin Lizzy, plus whatever her companions are drinking. "You have to understand," Ellen began, waving off her bookie and leading me to a booth away from the action, "Mom never told us anything about Dad's life in Kentucky. At home, we acted like he was dead. In public, we were supposed to say he was away on business. Even our stupidest friends knew we were lying. When they'd accuse him of being a criminal or a drunk, the only defense Mom would offer us was her prenuptial vow: 'I told your father I would never marry a man who drank or gambled.' You know what that means." I did not. Ellen looked a little disappointed. She pulled back her long brown hair and tied it into a hasty knot, and suddenly her heavy face and smooth white skin made a picture of my father as he appeared in old black and white photos. "Well, listen carefully, then. You can hear it from me, or you can waste four years at college majoring in psychology. There is really only one thing you have to know about people. Whenever they tell you the truth about themselves, you can be certain that they're lying. That's how psychiatrists work. They get you to tell them the truth about a million different ways until you've eliminated all of the practical explanations for your insanity except the real one, which they have the pleasure of announcing. It can take years." Ellen then revealed the big secret our brother Tommy had discovered years before when he'd spent a night eavesdropping in one of the clothes closets in my mother's bedroom:

my father called my mother every night for eighteen years. Did they discuss the children? No. The weather? No. Were my parents the uncredited inventors of phone sex? No. They prayed. At one in the morning, my mother's windup alarm sounded briefly, and she plucked the telephone from its cradle almost before it was electrically bestirred, and she and my father said the Rosary, as they had since the day they were married. It was a vow my mother had made after her older sister entered the convent. The McNab family had produced no priest, their only chance for a First Order Dominican. Nuns were Dominicans of the Second Order. Married people could become Third Order Dominicans, and with her sister gone and her brother James itching to join the navy, my mother became the sole support for her mother, so she took what was left to her—a husband and a permanent place in the ecclesiastical chorus line. Among her obligations as a member of the Third Order was a nightly recitation of the Rosary at an ungodly hour. The idea was to establish a perpetual Rosary, with someone starting a new rendition every split second. Most Third Order Dominicans were married, and they paid for this privilege; they got the late shift. Childless Dominican nuns were given a slight break; they had the early morning and evening hours, before or after a full day's teaching or nursing. The men of the First Order, the brothers and priests, assigned themselves the prime golfing hours and could be seen praying in particular earnest when facing a long putt. Tommy had uncovered the secret, but he could not explain the mystery. Why? I've always stood as far away as possible from this fact about my parents, where I could admire it. From my uncomprehending distance, they look like spiritual athletes training for the Big Race. Even Ellen was mystified.

But she did illuminate my mother's private vow not to get herself hitched to a man of loose morals. Ellen told me that both
of our grandfathers had been hard drinkers and that my father's
father bet on everything from train arrival times to the length
and weight of babies born at the hospital where he worked as
an accountant. "Even after he'd retired, his pockets were always jammed with thermometers, nurses' caps, lollipops, and
other treats he'd nicked from Saint Vincent's. To get a prize,
you had to cut the cards with him. After Dad left, Grandpa
showed up with a carload of sheets and towels, which Mom
wouldn't let us keep, but he gave Tommy a lifetime supply of
rubber gloves and Bridget and I got magnifying mirrors. You
would've liked him." All the grandparents were dead by the
time my father came back to Pittsfield. Was that the unspeak-
able condition for his return? Ellen didn't think so. "It was the
racetrack that brought him back." In the summer of 1959, the
eldress at Hancock died, leaving only Sister Celia and Sister
Ruth. They were invited to join one of the two remaining Families. They had to choose between Canterbury, New Hampshire, and Sabbathday Lake, Maine; either way, they had to
leave their Hancock home. The highest bid on the Hancock
property came from a group of businessmen and politicians
who wanted to "boost tourism" with "recreational opportunities." In fact, they were the only bidders. The coalition (Ellen
referred to them as "the syndicate") was headed up by the
Biondi brothers, the biggest contractors in Berkshire County,
whose crews also paved and maintained most of the Massachusetts turnpike. But the principal spokesman for the syndicate was Angus Mehan, bishop of Springfield, who ruled the
entire western end of the state. During his reign, there wasn't

a brick pointed in a Pittsfield parish before the green and white billboard was planted in the bushes: "Biondi Builders: At Home in God's House and Yours!" Mehan also introduced the faithful to the Polish, French, Italian, Canadian, and American Sweepstakes, variations on the Irish original, and once a week, every parish hall hosted Diocesan Bingo. The dedicated members of the many Third Order Rosary Sodalities were pressed into service as dealers and card counters. My mother resigned. And as if bingo wasn't bad enough, she'd heard that the bishop and the Biondis were planning to introduce pari-mutuel betting to the Berkshires. Ellen remembers her saying, "It will kill your father to know what's to become of the old Shaker place." That was in July. By August, my father was alive and at home. In the meantime, my mother brooked no bad words about the bishop or his minions. "Unless you intend to dedicate your life to the service of God and his church, you'll do well to pray for those who have." Ellen said everything would have been different if Uncle James had become a priest instead of enlisting in the navy; as it was, our only consolations were the weirdly smooth seal coat that hung in a cedar closet in the attic, and a free Europe. The hopes for a vocation of the First Order in the First Family hung on my brother Tommy, but during my father's stint in the South, Tommy had become a bad egg. Not only did he fail to hear the call; he flunked out of high school twice and had to attend special night classes to earn a diploma. It amazed people that Tom Sternum's son wasn't going to college. And after my father left the second time, some of his friends established a scholarship fund for Bridget, hoping to help her fulfill some of her father's promise, but Bridget left in the middle of her sophomore year to work with poor Indians in Manitoba. This always made sense to me. She was kind, and she loved to ski. Ellen also went to Regina College, on the banks of Lake Champlain, and was given the unused portion of Bridget's scholarship. She majored in psychology and figured out that Bridget had been kicked up to Canada by the nuns who ran the college when she turned up pregnant after a semester of intensely private ski lessons with a kid from Colorado. Someone probably should have had the sense to hate my father for everything that happened. But even his own wife and children remembered him fondly for things like the stash of photographs he left us with and especially the Easter Rebellion of 1960. After making my mother pregnant about two days after his return to our stucco house in August of 1959, my father spent most of the next eight months with the two elderly Shakers at Hancock, Sister Celia and Sister Ruth, taking pictures of them in every room in the empty village. He eventually made a book of these sad portraits, but no one would publish it. However, he left four leather satchels filled with pictures he'd made of the chairs, tools, desks, and clothing haunting the abandoned village, and my mother managed to support us on the proceeds for many years. But he didn't leave until June of 1960, a little more than a month after the Easter Sunday the bishop came to town to perform the Mass of the Resurrection for an SRO crowd at the new yellow brick Church of the Redeemer built by the Biondi brothers about half a mile from our house. In retrospect, my mother says, she should have known my father was up to something. He and Tommy had missed Holy Saturday services the night before, and when the First Family woke on Easter Sunday, the two of them were nursing a bottle of scotch in the kitchen, "though I had never seen your father take a drink."

And they were wearing tuxedos. They all walked to church together and sat near the front, except Tommy. He bolted up to the choir loft, but he did that every Sunday; his girlfriend was an auburn-haired soprano, and they made out during the sermons, as if they were in the balcony at the old Duchess Cinema. As was to be expected for such a solemn occasion, the special keepsake leaflet handed out by the ushers in the vestibule was printed on parchment paper. However, parishioners were surprised to find a bingo card stuffed inside. They ignored it until the bishop turned his mitered head to the congregation and strolled to the podium in his golden brocade to deliver the sermon, and my father stood up and yelled, "B-Seven. B-Seven." Bishop Mehan apparently mistook this for a hometown greeting, because he smiled and waved, showing off the thick gold ring with which he concussed young men when he delivered the ceremonial slap at their confirmations. My father yelled, "I-Three. I-Three. Mark it on your cards, everyone. And N-Six. N-Six." My mother was impressed. My father looked great in a tux. And before the bishop knew what was happening, husbands had their wives digging around in their clutch purses for lipstick, eyebrow pencils, and anything else they could use to keep up with the call. "G-Ten. G-Ten. Remember, the winner takes the bishop's crook." A woman near the back hollered, "I've got B-Six and N-Seven, or was it the other way around?" An old man near her stood up and recited the first four combinations, and then he told everyone to shut up. "And give us a winner, Thomas. It ain't easy livin on a schoolteacher's pension." Just to keep them in suspense, my father called, "I-Nine. I-Nine." Above the nervous moans of anticipation, the bishop barked, "Thomas Sternum, this is the holiest day on the church calendar and I will not have you turning it into—." My father shouted, "Excuse me, Your Excellency," as he slid by Bridget into the center aisle, "but where are your concelebrants for this splendid occasion? Or will the Brothers Biondi be passing the baskets, the better to make off with our Easter offerings?" Alice Wheeler yelled, "Bingo, Thomas." She was the fat school nurse who wrote medical excuses for all the troublemakers when they'd forgotten to study for a math test; she had basically been my brother Tommy's personal physician. Alice was wearing a broad-brimmed hat with a fresh pink carnation. She tipped it when she stood. "And, Thomas, inquire of His Holiness, if you would, how he pays for that limousine he drives." My father said, "Bingo again." Joe Krzcynkl, the good man who'd watched out for the First Family during snowstorms and blackouts while my father was away, stood up next. "Has any layperson ever actually won the annual sweepstakes? I read in the bulletin that the pastor takes two trips a year to Europe." This elicited another "Bingo!" from Thomas Sternum. Then the bishop banged his ring hand on the pulpit and called my father a heretic, adding, "This is a sacrilege." That was Tommy's cue. A thundering boom at the back of the church turned everyone around in their pews. A big plastic banner unfurled from the edge of the choir loft. "The Biondi Brothers and the Diocese of Springfield Invite You and Yours to the Ground-Breaking Ceremonies for Hancock Downs. Free Pony Rides for the Kids! Make it the First of Many Days at the Races." My father let his big moment just hang there for a while. Then he pointed to the sign and said, "*This* is a sacrilege, good Bishop Mehan. And this sign shall never hang above the sacred heritage left us by the Shakers. No

God-fearing Christian in Berkshire County will live to see the
Shaker legacy buried beneath a betting parlor. As I speak, the
deed for the Hancock Shaker Village is being signed over to
Bob and Dale Casper, two of the foremost preservationists in
New England and publishers of this city's hometown newspaper." This silenced the bishop, who never finished his sermon and gave the congregation a special dispensation for their
Easter obligations. Amen. Or so the story goes, as I heard many
people tell it while I was growing up. I believe it is how most
people remembered it, maybe even my mother; it was the way
she told it to me. It was Ellen who remembered the rest of the
story. She told it to me while I raised my third draft beer on the
occasion of my eighteenth birthday, right after she'd discussed
her options for the next race at Saratoga with a man half her
size whom everyone at the Tin Lizzy called "Jockey." Ellen had
a fresh drink by then, too, and she plunged her finger into the
pool of Kahlua and ice and stirred up the cream from the bottom. "If the bartender mixes it, you never really know the pro-
portions. They serve you in amber glasses to make it look
darker, unless they know you." She held one of her empty tum-
blers near the votive candle on our table. It was clear. "And
don't let them sell you anything with crushed ice. Save your
money for a real slurpy." I wondered if I should be taking notes;
one more beer and all of Ellen's advice would be history. "The
thing is," she continued, "the banner sort of backfired on Dad."
So had his speech. He had silenced Bishop Mehan, but he had
misjudged his audience. The parishioners were no more interested in my father's sermonizing about the Shakers than they
were in the bishop's rendition of the Resurrection. My father
was one of a handful of people in Pittsfield who had ever met

a living Shaker. He and the Caspers were probably the only three people in Pittsfield besides the Biondis who understood the significance of this moment in time. Shakerism was nearing the end of its life on earth. But most of my father's friends and neighbors thought the Shakers had died off at the turn of the century. The average citizen of Pittsfield thought Hancock Shaker Village had been a museum for thirty or forty years, and none of their visiting relatives, whom they regularly sent out to admire it, had come back with a different impression. So they were more than a little confused when my father asked them to turn to the back of their bingo cards, where they read about Bob and Dale Casper's heroic plan to purchase Hancock from the Shakers and "oversee its restoration and perpetual operation as a tribute to the Shaker way of life." Someone near the back of the church asked, "Do you think there'll be enough tourists for two museums out there, Thomas?" My father tried to explain: "Until today, there was no museum. That was their home." But Ellen remembers him stopping at that point, undoing his bow tie, and staring at his feet, as if he'd forgotten where he was. He was back in Pittsfield, but he didn't belong there. The Shakers were leaving. Ellen thinks he must have understood then that he couldn't stay, knowing as he did that his fervor about the Shakers hadn't spread so far as his own friends who'd lived for generations within shouting distance of the Hancock Family and never said so much as hello. "The truth is, whenever Dad dragged the Shakers into the picture, he forgot who he was. Before Allen Cuthbert set him up with a studio out in Hancock in the forties, he was just our father, the photographer. In those days, he snuck out with his friends once a week and drove past that round barn on the way to the Tin

Lizzy. He played the ponies. It was only good luck that he wasn't with Alice Wheeler's husband the night he drove off the road on his way back over the mountain. But Dad couldn't remember all that and bear the Shakers in mind. In church that day, Mrs. Wheeler wasn't alone in thinking a track in town would make everybody's life a little easier and maybe a little longer. Dad had forgotten who his friends were. Or maybe by then he wanted to believe he was the man Mom thought he was, a man who didn't gamble or drink." Ellen was pushing the ice cubes around in the bottom of her glass. I asked if she was counting them; I wanted to know every tip she had for the Smart Drinker. "No. I was just thinking about Mom, thinking how different we might be if she'd ever been able to talk about any of this." Ellen looked sad. I nursed my beer, worried now that I would have to drive us back over the mountain. I could see myself following Mr. Wheeler's tracks right off some dark height of land. I didn't even try to console Ellen or cheer her up. I wonder if anyone ever did. I think mostly people told her she had her father's disposition. And it's true; people tend to like Ellen. But we people, we have a funny way of showing it. "Dad reached his hand out toward the pew, and Mom took it and stood beside him." A free round from Jockey had restored Ellen to me. She looked like the photos of my father again. My father was still hoping to save the day, so he announced to the Easter congregation that for more than twenty years this good woman, his wife, and many women like her had been faithful Third Order Dominicans and Franciscans and Marists. They had kept their vows. And shouldn't the clergy of the Holy Roman Catholic Church respect the wishes of these women on this, the holiest of Holy Days? Did the women of this or any

Roman Catholic parish in all of Berkshire County want their young boys growing up with gambling as the neighborhood sport instead of baseball and hockey? At this point, Ellen remembers a number of women dragging their children into a line behind our father. He wasn't going to win every vote this way, but he had a moral majority, and he knew it. He bent down while my mother fixed his bow tie. Ellen looked more like him than ever when she recalled him yelling, "With Jesus as my Savior, I know there is only one Gospel read in the homes of Shaker and Catholic families alike. And I don't believe it needs printing on fancy parchment paper if it's to be paid for by the tolls the Biondi brothers collect every time one of us takes a ride on the Massachusetts turnpike. And I don't want the bishop and the Biondi brothers setting the odds against me on a racetrack built with the money my children drop into the basket every Sunday. Any horse could tell you that a racetrack built by a bishop is nothing but a crooked mile." Instead of leading an Easter Parade along West Street to Hancock as he had fondly planned, my father followed my mother back into the pew. She had said, "Alright, everyone. Thomas has saved the Shakers and spared us a racetrack in our backyards. Now let Bishop Mehan do his job." The bishop reeled off the prayers at record pace, and soon he was standing with his chalice full of hosts, waiting for the parishioners to kneel at his altar rail and receive Holy Communion. My father wouldn't budge, and Bridget and Ellen were attached to his two hands. My mother scooted by them all with her bulging belly and knelt to receive the Body of Christ, which she acknowledged with a firm "Amen." She walked straight out of the Church of the Redeemer and did not speak to anyone until she was safe in her solid home. Before her roast lamb was done, the house was crowded with happy Catholics who felt Thomas Sternum had struck a blow for their side, though they came from all sides, and most of them would spend more than they could afford in the coming years on school raffles, guessing how many beans were in a jar at the Boys' Club, Little League poker nights, Sunday football cards, the state lottery, and bets about who would win the next presidential election. But for a moment, in April of that year, it must have seemed that everyone, even the Shakers, had beaten the odds against them, because the bishop and the Biondi brothers had lost a sure bet.

SPELLING TIP
The cedes, ceeds, and sedes of discontent

Seed is a perfectly simple word to spell. And even when it becomes a root word—in nouns (<u>seed</u>ling) or verbs (He <u>seed</u>ed the lawn)—it does not vary; all forms of this word come true from *seed*. But there are three other *seed* soundalikes that make spellers miserable. By grouping the common prefixes, however, test takers and chalkboard writers can hedge their bets. All of the prefixes involving *re* or *er* spell alike: re<u>cede</u>; pre<u>cede</u>; inter<u>cede</u>. Reserve *ceed* for the *ex-* and *pro-* prefixes: The Easter pro<u>ceed</u>s ex<u>ceed</u>ed their expectations. You will be happy to learn that there is only one word in our language that accepts *sede*, and it is <u>super</u>sede, surpassing all others— that is, a sure bet.

m a i l   o n   s u n d a y

WHENEVER PEOPLE TALK, I consider their words a first draft. Not everyone gets around to revising everything, but that doesn't mean you should treat a drunken confession or a casual bit of sarcasm as if it had been carved in stone. This may be why I cannot abide radio and television talk shows. People open up their personal hydrants, and everything stuck in the pipeline spews out. By the end, I feel like I'm drowning in a stew of half-told stories, copious re-creations of innocuous conversations, criminal allegations, expressions of empathy for previous talk show guests, a mean word or two for each of the former spouses, and the summary comment about the importance of communication in relationships. Listening to these shows is like being a writing teacher of lazy and churlish students. They all want to express themselves in that fractured, inchoate, un-grammatical way that they refer to as "my true voice," and then they want to watch TV. If they happen to eat four bags of chips

while they do or later that evening sleep with the boy who delivered the pizza, well, there's an essay on eating disorders or
acquaintance rape for you: "He was, like, demanding the
money from me." The students I taught at McClintock were
devoted to talk shows. And why not? At Talk Show University,
each student is known by name, encouraged to speak, never
forced to provide a second or third draft, and everyone gets an
A just for showing up. But they knew better. They expected
more from themselves and from the college they had chosen.
They really didn't mind revising their essays or working on each
other's prose. In fact, students would often ask if they could
rewrite a paper or if they had time to start again in the middle
of an essay test. Many of my colleagues had firm policies that
anticipated such requests. One of the most elegant was "No."
It was also the stupidest. Abel Nagen, a historian with curly
black hair and a face like a fin who insisted on referring to himself as "an" historian, was a "No" man. When I told him I allowed for as many revisions as a student could generate as long
as there were evident substantial changes, he asked me if I
would accept seventy-five revisions of a single essay. Of course,
I'd never had to deal with double digits. "But that isn't the
point, Mark. That is not the point." Abel had a way of repeat-
ing himself that made you feel culpable, as if you hadn't reacted appropriately to the first iteration. "If someone wrote
them, would you read them?" I asked him if he'd ever listened
to the way students preface their questions. Abel paused like a
fish before bait. He said, "But we digress." I smiled, tugging the
line a little, knowing he could not resist a logical digression for
very long. "No, Mark, tell me. Tell me about students' prefatory
remarks." We were in his office, a den of ill will and anti-

Administration scheming lined with books by so-called subversives and equipped with a white-noise machine, which was black, one of the millions of arcane little ironies he put in your path—Abel's endless Rorschach test: What do you see? What does it mean? I told him I'd noticed that my students hardly ever spoke in class until they'd qualified their comments: "This is probably wrong, but . . . ," or "Maybe this isn't what you meant, but . . . ," or "I know this is going to sound crazy, but . . ." They were nervous; they were hedging their bets, but . . . they were also ready to revise. They wanted to get it right, and they suspected it would take some time. I had a policy about that. I asked students to try to lose the prefaces, not because I didn't credit them but because some things go without saying. The policy was this: Let's assume we all feel crazed and stupid when we first try to articulate anything. And let's bet we will not get it right, that we won't be satisfied. Abel was appalled. "What do you say when they do get it wrong? What do you do when a student says, 'I sort of think the coal miners should've been happy to have jobs. My boyfriend just got fired at the Gap'?" I knew what I would say: About those coal miners who couldn't feed their kids—say a little more. But in Abel's office, it sounded feeble—more white noise. Instead, I told him I needed a cigarette, so we'd have to talk about it outside. It was a tactical delay. Abel had quit smoking after our first year together at McClintock, but because he was a stickler about consistency and perversity, he'd become a virulent anti-antismoker. "You ought to light up right here." It was illegal in Boston. Abel produced an ashtray. I led him out to the parking lot. He harumphed. Abel hated to surrender his territorial advantage, but he was a good sport. Of the eighty-odd full-time faculty at

McClintock, Abel was one of only four or five who were still talking to me by the beginning of June. Most of my colleagues had reacted squeamishly to the Spelling Thing and the rift it caused, like prepubescent children subjected to a film about boys' and girls' blooming bodies. They didn't like either of the two available options. They said nothing. It was easy to condemn them. I assured myself that their refusal to side with me proved they were against me; that they were passive but guilty; that not to decide is to decide. But it is not. The effect of their cowardice, or indecision, or confusion was stasis, and by the middle of May, the campus was a swamp. I and a few members of the Administration stood on opposite sides from each other, on dry land, on high ground. Most everyone else was mucking around in the mess we had made of a few misspelled words. Rachel Reed had invented the Competency Achievement Test (CAT), and Rashelle Whippet was not the first undergraduate in its fifteen-year history to fail it. Ninety to 95 percent of all incoming freshmen failed two or more sections of the test, and more telling, the same percentage of sophomore and junior transfers failed it when they came to McClintock. It had three parts: (1) Spelling—a list of twenty words, most of them misspelled; the passing score was 15 out of 20. (2) Mechanics— ten diction sentences (circle the correct word, such as principal/principle); ten punctuation problems (add the missing punctuation: series comma, question mark, apostrophe, and punctuation for quotations); twenty sentence construction problems (identify and fix fragments, run-ons, comma splices, dangling and misplaced modifiers, and agreement mistakes); the passing score for Mechanics was 32 out of 40. (3) Essay— choose one of two 250- to 500-word passages (including a brief introduction and three questions for each) and write a short analytical essay (at least five independent paragraphs with direct references to the text); graded pass/fail. All students understood they had three chances to pass the test; they never had to retake a section that they passed. The first-year composition program prepared them to pass the CAT. And we offered seven-week workshops every semester for students who needed additional help; these carried one academic credit, but they were tuition-free classes, no matter how often a student enrolled. Students had to pass the test before they entered their practicum, the professional field experiences in education, social work, or health care for which they had come to McClintock College. During my first year, two sophomores flunked the test for the third time and had to appeal to the Academic Review Committee for permission to take it again. This seemed an unnecessarily scary and potentially whimsical way for such decisions to be made. I worked with Rachel to change it. Thereafter, as long as students had been in the workshops or meeting regularly with a peer tutor, the number of times they took the test was left to the discretion of the director of writing. This preserved the spirit of the old limit of three, which was to help students become fluent as quickly as possible. And students managed to pass the test. Students with dyslexia, anorexia, apoplexy, and wicked bad headaches—they all passed the CAT. Rashelle Whippet had transferred in as a junior. She was twenty-three. She had a son who was eight and two daughters, six and four. Her initial spelling result was 3/20; she scored 11/40 on mechanics; she'd skipped the essay. Those scores didn't surprise her, though before she came to McClintock she had been a sophomore in good standing at an accred-

ited, public, four-year college in Massachusetts. She had a sub-
urban high school diploma. When we reviewed her results, she
was suspicious of her correct answers. "Better double-check
that one there, Mark," she'd say. She told me she had never
read a whole book; in this she was not alone. She had chosen
McClintock. We had accepted her. She was with us now. She
never carried a full academic load, but she took at least sixteen
credits a year to keep her scholarship. She had a B — average.
She attended the workshops three times, missing only a few
classes. During her first two semesters, she met with me
weekly for an hour and never missed an appointment without
calling ahead to warn me. She had two peer tutors. When she
finally passed the essay portion of the test, I watched her read
the passage. It took her twenty minutes the first time, twenty
minutes the second time, and fifteen minutes the third time to
comprehend the three hundred words. She needed another
hour and ten minutes to write a first draft. "I still got some time
here, Mark?" She made a second draft in the next hour. She
had written five paragraphs, having finally memorized a formula that she and I had worked out for her to use when she
had to write essays in other classes: Topic Sentence—Evidence—Analysis (we called it "Opinion"); three sentences per
paragraph. Her essay was grammatically clear; she relied on
simple declarative sentences of seven words or less (not including quotations), and the apostrophe was still more ornamental than expressive in her work, but it was clear that she'd
retained a good portion of the mechanics she'd learned. She
asked if the author of the passage had written any books. I
showed her my collection of Zora Neale Hurston's prose, examination copies the publisher had sent free of charge, and

Rashelle chose one at random. "Maybe it'll be my first book, Mark, ya never know." She balked when she saw the word *Examination*, and she flipped to the back, scanning the Suggested Questions for Discussion. "You sposed to be able to answer every one of them questions when it's done?" I said they were more a way of recalling what you'd read. "Questions like you ask?" She smiled. Rashelle, the whole one, the all of her, only showed up occasionally. But she'd be there soon, I knew. She always lagged a few minutes behind her smile. "What you think about maybe I start readin to my kids? I know, I know, Mark, I can't count no books with pictures. This one, this Zora book, it'll still be my first book." She was eyeing me, figuring out what I would say next, then saying it. "Yeah, yeah, yeah. Will be if I read it. I know." In her third semester, Rashelle flunked the spelling section in September, October, and twice in December of 1995. Her practicum was scheduled to begin in January. She'd been assigned to a second-grade classroom in a public school in Cambridge. She'd missed all but two of her weekly meetings with me that semester, and she had not contacted a peer tutor. In October, I spoke to her adviser, the sociologist Gillian Cherbourg, who told me Rashelle was "challenged but gifted." I still don't understand her "but." In November, I sent an official warning to Rashelle, with copies to Gillian and the dozen or so others who were involved in the bureaucracy of academic progress, policy, and placements. I had included a couple of suggested plans for dealing with the situation in advance of a crisis. At a college of one thousand students, such documents lagged well behind unofficial reporting. But to Gillian Cherbourg, the letter came as a shock. She rushed into my office, wagging my report. "She has privacy rights. She has every fucking right you have as a white man, even if this is a private institution. Who can spell anyway? I can't spell, and I have a fucking Ph.D., you asshole." Gillian would later refer to this as "my constant efforts to engage Mark Sternum in a careful review of the pedagogical and psychological implications of his unilateral decision to punish Rashelle Whippet for attempting to preserve her linguistic heritage." On her final attempt to pass the CAT, Rashelle scored 5 on spelling, down from her high of 11. Within a month, Gillian Cherbourg had helped Rashelle document my "prejudgism," and Rashelle was placed as the assistant teacher in the second grade of the Bennett School in Cambridge. But it took sociologist Gillian Cherbourg, Academic Dean Rachel Reed, Dean of the Faculty Marie Bond, President Agatha Kroll, and me five months to get me fired. Our meetings were torture. It is hard to invent academic requirements, and it is even harder to create humane policies for effecting them. I did my best. The other side was doing its best to abbreviate Gillian's sermons and to keep Agatha Kroll's wires uncrossed, though that was a job for a master electrician, and we must have all known she was going to short-circuit eventually. I wrote weekly draft proposals to represent our collective thinking on a new policy, which would eventually have to be shoved down the throats of the faculty. But as early as April, Rachel Reed had identified the sticking point. I wanted Rashelle out of her field placement until she passed the test. They wanted Rashelle to stay where she was. I argued that Rashelle could earn her teaching credential and a bachelor's degree without ever learning to spell at almost any other college or university in the United States. They argued that another setback of a semester or two in her academic career would defeat Rashelle. We were strung out around the table in the Third-Floor conference room (Administration territory; Abel had advised me to hold these meetings in my tiny underground office). Marie Bond turned her hand into a spider, pressing her fingertips on the table. "You see this as a writing issue" (the spider drew its legs into a smaller circle), "a spelling thing" (smaller), "a skill test" (tiny; the spider's legs were folded beneath its body). She let my insectivorous concern sit there until I and everyone else in the room were wishing she'd shoo it away or crush it. "I see a moral obligation." She flipped her hand over and showed us her pink palm. I saw her life line. It was deep and dark, and it ran right up into her brown forearm, where it seemed to disappear, but you could tell it went on forever. Marie was born in the Deep South, and between Biloxi and Boston she had seen more than we had. She was the most potent thinker on campus, and she had never taught a class at the college, preferring to give the occasional seminar in Cultural Studies or Ethical Imperatives at the local branch of the Ivy network, where she could assume her students knew how to spell "principles," having paid thirty thousand dollars a year to learn how to stand on them. "The moral issue I see is this, Mark. One day, we got a letter of application from a poor woman who has never been given a chance in school. She wanted one real chance. We accepted her. We made her a member of the McClintock Family. Now, no one, not even you, is suggesting she's unfit to raise three black kids. She's just not ready to assist a certified teacher in a classroom full of whites and Asians. Am I right?" Alone in a room with Marie Bond, I could've answered directly. Indeed, I would have known she wanted an argument: prove me wrong; untangle my

illogic. But in public, "Am I right?" meant "The answer is always Race," which was a tautology since, in America, it is always a question of Race, as Marie Bond had taught me. Rachel
recognized the impasse, and she said, "I hope I don't sound
silly, but I wonder if now isn't the time to try to agree on the
wording of the revised requirement?" She walked over to the
open windows and sniffed the air. "Can you smell that, everyone? It's those Persian lilacs." She meant "It is almost May, the
students will be gone soon, and we are all people of goodwill,
aren't we?" But the prospect of time passing panicked Gillian
Cherbourg. She would be up for tenure in the fall. She hadn't
published a book yet, though she operated an Antiporn Home
Page on the Internet from which students could download photographs of mutilated women with excerpted bits of text from
Foucault. Gillian asked us to listen to something she had just
come across about language acquisition. She launched into a
long passage in her halting French, or some language spoken by
people who wear clothespins on their noses and store subway
tokens in their mouths. Rachel giggled but covered it by coughing. Marie Bond raised her hand to her head like a gun and
pulled the trigger. I said—I did say it—"Oh, for God's sake,
someone fire me, please." And Agatha Kroll began to twitch, as
if someone had finally had the sense to give her a good dose of
electroshock. She looked skinnier than ever, and her helmet of
white hair seemed to be shrinking, turning her face purple. She
stood up and screamed, "Fine. Fine. Nobody but me can make
any decisions around here. It all comes down to me anyway. It's
on my head. You're fired." She smiled, as if even she didn't believe she'd done it. Or maybe it was fun being on the loose. "I
mean it, Mark. Look for another job. Rachel will have to make

it official. That's her job. But we are done here." She paused
again and looked at everyone. Anxiety was her real juice. We
were producing it by the gallon. She screeched, "I don't want
to be dragged into court by some African-American teenage
mother. Our mission is to save children, not to squash them. I
haven't spent my career teaching in urban preschools and
squeezing money out of dead women on Beacon Hill so you
can run this college like your own private Spelling Bee! Rachel,
you heard me. He's fired. End of story. Period. I did it. Done."
Agatha shot out of the room. Two of her secretaries were quak-
ing by the door, ready to escort her to her office and, I hoped,
slip her into some restraints. Long before Rachel and Marie
could convince Agatha to revise her pronouncement, the story
leaked out of our confidential quarters, sped across campus,
and hit the local papers. It exploded. It was beyond repair. So
Rachel performed the unenviable task of firing the director of
writing who had succeeded her, who admired her, and who
knew they had all failed an important test. Final grade: F. No
opportunity to revise. The only lingering fallout in the Sunday
paper of 2 June appeared in the form of "Think Pieces" in the
Focus section about literacy rates and poverty, cultural bias in
marching-band music, and a charming little essay about a Sister Ruth, a Kentucky orphan who had moved to the Berkshires
in 1910 and had there become a productive Hancock Shaker,
though she'd lost four fingers in a childhood accident. It ended
with these words: "Her story came to mind in the midst of the
spelling brouhaha in Boston." It was signed as a letter, "Brother
Thomas S., Sabbathday Lake, Maine." I wasted most of the afternoon trying to decide if "S." was short for "Sternum." This
seemed unlikely. My father was dead, or so I had told myself

for many years, not least of all because my mother had sent us all announcements of his death in 1982, though I'd never seen an obituary or even a small-print death notice from a newspaper. Late that night, I logged onto the McClintock system and collected my e-mail for the first time in two weeks. I printed out fourteen missives from Abel for later reading. I wrote down Marie Bond's unpublished telephone number, which she'd sent with an offer to "talk things out before you move on." I deleted everything that began, "To All Members of the McClintock Family." I saved a couple of requests from students for letters of recommendation. And I wondered who had sent the following two sentences from a computer café in Boston: "She is your child. Do not leave her where she will not learn to spell."

DICTION TIP
A *distinction*

The choice between *accept* and *except* ought to be easy. One means to take, and the other means to leave out. But the difference is not always recognizable on first glance, particularly if you are under any pressure. Since the last four letters are identical, just remember that you were ac̲cepted to c̲ollege. No one put an x̲ through your name, which is what happens when everyone ex̲cept you is given a chance. Under pressure, people often choose to make an ex̲ception, and thereby make you an ex̲ception, even though they intended to offer you ac̲ceptance.

c a t s   a n d   d o g s

RAIN MAKES ME want to read. The pleasure of entering a book and wandering around in someone else's well-made world magnifies the gratitude I feel for my house. Reading in the rain, I am twice-sheltered from the storm. On Monday, the wet and windy third day of June, I sat on my blue sofa with all of my father's books open before me on the ten-dollar trunk I call a coffee table. I'd arranged his collections of photographs like a map of America, and I traveled from his first Shaker Village views, made in Hancock, to the other New England sites in Massachusetts, Maine, New Hampshire, and Connecticut, then west to New York, Ohio, and Indiana, and finally to Kentucky, where the grass is blue. It is easy to get lost in Kentucky. The stands of springtime magnolia, vast cultivated expanses of loose-leaf tobacco, and fallow fields of pennyroyal mint convince you that this is not the North, but the rivers freeze in February and snow drifts into the limestone caves and crevices of coal, and you are certainly not in the South. Most of my father's photographs are unpeopled. He worked in black and white, and he loved the Shaker line. He lets you stroll along a narrow path in Hancock, admiring the raised beds of herbs at either side, until you notice that the foundations of the rectangular frame houses and workshops are basically raised beds, too, and the windows are all rectangular white wooden frames within frames, and just when you think you understand the Shaker line, when you know its logic and its limits, you see the circular stone barn in the distance, and its weather vane is a shiny spot that makes you look up, where you can see beyond the gentle embrace of the Berkshire Hills to Mount Greylock, and you understand that this place goes on forever. It happens on the insides as well. In my father's photographs, you enter the massive white Dwelling House built by the Kentucky Shakers at Pleasant Hill first through the Sisters' door and then, on the facing page, through the Brothers' door. You go in twice through a paneled oak door set inside an arched entry, but before you are drawn into the spare and spacious rooms that run along either side of the building, you want to ascend and breathe the curved air above you in the apse. But then you remember that you are not an angel who can fly, and this is not a church where the likes of you are seen at such heights. You walk inside, in the Shaker way. And this way has its rewards. The floorboards shine, and they lead you like the throughline in a painting. Or you can go up, ascend the beautiful stairs. One flight rises on either side of the white hall, leading to the Sisters' and Brothers' bedrooms, and at that point the stairs turn toward each other and spiral up again, one side reflecting the other side, a double helix, a harmonic Shaker line. Given my father's admiration for the things they made, I should know more about the Shakers. But given my father's decision to leave my mother a few weeks after I was born, I have only the essays written by Allen Cuthbert and a few other so-called historians who befriended the last Shakers, scavenged shamelessly, and rewrote the Shaker story to boost the value of their booty. I have tried to read between the lines, but as my students would say, there are no words there. My father wrote his own captions, and I trusted him; I figured a man who had abandoned his family twice had no reason to lie. He was not a narrative captionist, but over the years, on rainy days, I have cobbled together my own word picture of the Shakers. In 1774, Ann Lee led eight fellow Shaking Quakers from persecution in England to New York, where she established the First Family of the United Society of Believers. Their ecstatic religious worship—tongues, trembling, turning—earned them the name Shakers. Mother Ann had four children. They all died young. This made her an ideal Spiritual Mother. The Shaker Family practiced celibacy, communal ownership of property, pacifism, and equality of the sexes and races in leadership and labor—a family unlike those we know and love. It was evident to me that the most radical of all their applied principles was the wisdom that work was a Gift. As far as I can tell, the romantic view of the Shakers as retiring, taciturn chair makers did not emerge until their membership began to decline in the late nineteenth century. In 1826, six thousand Shakers were living in eighteen villages. Mechanical and organizational innovations made them prosperous as farmers, ranchers, and manufacturers. Not surprisingly, they excited the envy and prejudices of many Americans. Shaker homes and barns were burned. Believers were physically attacked, and they were regularly brought up on false charges of illicit sexual practices, presumably because most Americans had no experience of celibate families. Lincoln admired them. Tolstoy corresponded with them. Friedrich Engels called them the world's first and only society to be organized on the basis of common property. Mary Baker Eddy studied them for years, but she flunked the big test by founding Christian Science, a sect the Shakers recognized as sanctified snake oil. In addition to their celebrated furniture and architecture, the Shakers gave the world the wooden clothespin, the flat broom, the automated washing machine, and the circular saw. They produced patented inventions at ten times the rate of the rest of the country. This is how I saw the Shakers as I flipped through my father's books in June of 1996. But growing up, I dwelt on the blank spaces, the empty rooms in the books of photographs. I was waiting for someone to enter the frame. I imagined the person from behind, just a hooded cape and black boots. That person—a Shaker? my father?—opened a window and then selected a chair from the many ladder-backs hanging from the rows of wooden pegs that ran around each room. I always chose the same chair. It had arms and a slightly bowed back and a woven reed seat. It was designed to be big enough for a big man, but it was short, kid-sized, because its legs had been cut to five or six inches. From the caption, I knew it was a gathering chair. A Shaker could sit in my chair and comfortably sort through harvested fruit, separating the pie and cider apples or the ripe peaches from the green. My mother sat in a chair when she read me stories at night. Hers was a wing chair. She arranged it near the side of my bed, as if I were a patient she visited in the hospital each night. She chose stories of saints who lived in Rome and Lima and Dublin. Most of them died young and painfully, and among my early career choices, alongside fireman and photographer, I often listed Christian martyr. When I learned to read, I chose books about sailors. I liked the hats. But what kept me reading was the ingenuity of their enterprise. Every detail of life at sea intrigued me. I had never given a thought to the preservation, storage, and preparation of food. The rudiments of plumbing were a revelation. I was fascinated by the design of habitable space. It was as if I had taken no notice of the work that went into the making of the world until I discovered the stories of men who had re-created it at sea. The idea, as I understood it, was to choose your mates carefully and build a home that could support you. Sailors did everything thoughtfully, economically, and cooperatively, because their lives depended on it. My ambitions were forever altered. I decided not to die young, which ruled out firefighting and martyrdom. I could not give up photography so easily. For three years running, I requested a camera for Christmas; I got an excellent bike, black hockey skates, and a twenty-six-volume encyclopedia with color illustrations that I read at night, from A to Z, before anyone bothered to inform me that it was not a regular book. I got my first camera when I graduated from college. I had a fellowship to live in England for a year. After a month abroad, I sent home dozens of photographs. They were not great pictures. Sometimes it was hard even for me to distinguish among Stonehenge, Winchester Cathedral, and the Tower of London. My mother wrote back and encouraged me to collect postcards. It was good advice. She was always in the unenviable position of telling her children what they needed to hear. This probably accounts for her peculiar choice of bedtime stories; with no man around the house, she was trying to scratch up some role models. I gave up photography. And I didn't become a sailor. I did write my undergraduate thesis on *Moby Dick*. Ishmael says that the sea was his Yale College and his Harvard. I felt the same was true for me, except it was all turned around: books were my boats. I sailed right into graduate school, my Doldrums. After wasting a few years in literature classes that were intense repetitions of my college education, I got blown off course entirely and might have been lost at sea forever. Unfortunately, I washed up on the shores of the Linguistics Department. There were a lot of former sailors in Linguistics. We sat around chewing on fish bones and sucking on shells, hoping we'd eventually spit out dissertations. I typed 270 pages about metaphors. I'd started with an actual question. When it is raining, and a child hears an adult say, "It is raining cats and dogs," how does the child know the adult is not lying? After a year of failed answers, my adviser told me "How?" is not an academic question. "The only thing less likely to get you a Ph.D. is a demonstration of any practical skill." Then she gave me a paper she'd written about the possibility of measuring the "metaphoricity" of various metaphors. I worked it out so that a high metaphoricity rating could be awarded the metaphors I liked. When the White Jesus called himself the Lamb of God, he scored well for relationship (son/lamb—one point), appearance (white/pure—one point), characteristics (innocence, youth, and appeal to children—three points), and fate (crucified/ slaughtered and roasted—one and a half points); this was an A+ metaphor. The business about raining cats and dogs didn't earn a single point, which in graduate school is the equivalent of a B. I got a doctorate. I lost the desire to live at sea. But I still had my father's books. And when I dove into them on this rainy Monday afternoon, I left the world behind. It was better where the Shakers were, better even than being on a boat. They had better beds, much better bread, and pantries stocked with homemade jam. It rained on the roofs and fields of Pleasant Hill, but it wasn't bad weather there. Rain was as welcome as the sun; it made the apples and the peaches grow. My telephone rang, and the noise brought me home. No message; none of my friends knew what to say anymore. The rainstorm was blowing out of town, heading out over the Atlantic. I went outside for the first time all day and walked around the corner to the store. I bought a sweating carton of milk, a frozen stick of butter, and a sad loaf of soft bread studded with a few compensatory raisins. For dessert, I bought two cartons of cigarettes. When I walked out of the store, I realized that the paper bag smelled better than the dinner ingredients. From down the street, I watched the lights go on in my house, room by room, as if I were inside, wandering around, looking for something to do. I heard the screen door on the other side slam shut, a sound that typically alerted my neighbors to my arrival on the deck, often wearing nothing but a pair of boxer shorts. I wanted to get home and I didn't, so I walked slowly, a cowardly and agonizing compromise. Before I climbed the three steps to the screen door, I peered in through the living room window. My father's books were closed and stacked like a chimney on the trunk. Someone said, "Mark? Is that you?" I saw a darkness at the screen door. He was big. I don't know if it was his deep voice, his size, or just the outline of his head and shoulders, but I knew he was my father. I was thirty-six years old. And I was happy in a way I had not been since I had learned to speak: all over, entirely at ease. I said, "Dad." The door swung open. "Dad? You idiot, I'm your goddamned brother." Tommy flicked on the porch light to prove his point. "Dad? Did Mom forget to tell you? Dad died ages ago. Where have you been?"

S P E L L I N G   T I P
Word endings

Every word in our language ends in one of two ways: with a vowel or with a consonant. There are no other options. (Long before we had computers, we had a binary spelling system.) The only task for spellers dealing with root words that end in consonants is to decide whether or not to double the final letter before adding a suffix that begins with a vowel (like *-ing*). If we are adding a suffix that begins with a consonant (say, *-ly or -ment*), we simply attach it to the root (glad<u>ly</u>; attach<u>ment</u>). But how do we know, for example, that we are not supposed to be leting on (but <u>letting</u> on) that we are <u>waiting</u> (not waitting) for something we have long been <u>wanting</u> (not wantting)? For root words of one syllable, it is simple: recognize the pattern. The last three letters determine your choice. *Let* is consonant-vowel-consonant (c-v-c); *wait* is v-v-c; *want* is v-c-c. You double the final letter only if the end of the root shows the pattern c-v-c. A more complicated version of the same rule applies for root words of more than one syllable. (This may seem a long way to go, but follow me here; we're getting to the root of every word in the language that ends with a consonant.) A multisyllabic word must meet two conditions before you double its final consonant. First, the root must end c-v-c. Thus, we are never becomming; we are always <u>becoming</u>. You are not expect-ted, no matter what you are <u>expecting</u>. I am not awaitting anything, but I have been known to spend decades <u>await-ing</u> a better ending. Second, if the root does end c-v-c (as in be<u>gin</u> and re<u>fer</u>), you add the suffix (use *-ing* and *-ence*), pronounce the whole word, and double the final consonant of the root *only* if you stress the c-v-c syllable. (Can it be this complicated? Yes. But remember, we have hundreds of thousands of root words ending in conso-nants, and we need only this one rule to spell them all correctly. Compare this to, say, the tax codes.) We do say beGINning, so we double the *n*. We say reFERring, and we double the *r*. But we do not stress *-FER-* when we say REFerence; though the root shows the pattern c-v-c, we do not double the *r*. I inFERred my father's presence in my home on the evening of the third of June. I reFERred to the screen door, and I recognized the shadow, the fa-miliar pattern of the man. But then I pronounced his name with DEFerence and discovered that my PREFer-ence was immaterial. It was not my father but my brother—apples and oranges; cats and dogs.

m o r e   s h e l l s

TOMMY FOUND SOME eggs in my refrigerator and made French
toast for our dinner, redeeming the raisin bread. As we sat
down on the deck, he looked disappointed. He went back into
the kitchen. I heard the chiming of glass, and from behind my
gift collection of flavored vinegars he extracted an unopened
bottle of maple syrup he and his wife had sent me as a Christmas present, which he set down on the little table between us.
We ate quickly because, as Tommy explained, "the difference
between French toast and milk toast is about five minutes." He
was as handsome as ever. A few years ago, as he approached his
midfifties, his dark hair had begun to whiten around the edges,
but his eyes were still as brown as coffee beans, and his skin
was beige and smooth as suede. He had my mother's colors.
"Black Irish," she liked to say, "because the Spaniards brought
more than their ships to those shores." When he finished eating, he sat back. He was as broad as the white Adirondack

chair. I felt small. "How are you, Mark?" I assured him that I was fine. I had forgotten that Tommy's questions were not questions; they were prefaces. He said, "I only ask because you look like shit. You oughta stop smoking." I lit up a cigarette while he cleared the table. If I could've, I would've stuck a whole carton in my mouth and smoked it like a cigar. Smoking was my hatch door; it gave me a sense of privacy in public. Tommy washed the dishes despite my feeble boasts about the dishwasher I'd installed and how well it worked. While he made coffee and set out mugs and spoons, he left me with a folder of business cards, letterhead, and signs prepared by people who worked for him. Each one carried a conspicuous error: promotional materials for electritions, plummers, a pubic accountant, the Berkshire Citys Mayors Conference, and Free Water Annalasis. Tommy's jobs were legion, but the latest was managing a photocopy franchise. "Those mistakes cost me a fortune every month." He poured the coffee. I noticed he had produced a beverage without an oil slick on top. And he had somehow omitted the burned rubber, a flavor I always included. I asked him how he'd done it. "Eggshells ground up with the beans. What do you think?" I raved about the coffee. Tommy said, "I only ask because I can't find anybody who can spell. I'll make you my assistant manager." My brother was cursed with an amazing capacity to invent practical solutions to almost any problem. It endeared him to many people, and it repelled as many others. My sister Bridget had cut off all communication with Tommy about ten years earlier. She was convinced he had a messiah complex. Of course, her disavowal came after years of courting him as marriage counselor, moral guide in matters of child rearing, and confessor. Ellen was at

the other extreme; she gladly ate Tommy's homemade onion
rings and pizza on Friday nights, even though they were served
up with admonitions about her trips to the Tin Lizzy, photo-
copies of fad diets, and dubious investment opportunities. He
was convinced that she lived at home with my mother because
she was overweight and financially insecure. The machinations
of the First Family happened above me, at a remove, like the
Administration politics on the Third Floor at McClintock. I
had adopted a compromise position. I didn't take Tommy's advice, and I didn't end up in either of the two positions available
to Tommy's intimates—infuriated or suffocated. But as happens with every compromise we make, I lost touch with
Tommy and with a part of myself. Tommy stood up. "I know
you think I'm a failure, Mark." Was that a question? His back
was to me. He was hugging the rail. I suppose we were both
thinking of his wife of thirty years, the soprano from the church
choir; their four children, all adopted with bruises and busted
bones and broken hearts that had begun to heal; his fifteen or
twenty thousand jobs; his slavish and complaining and sustain-
ing attention to our mother's needs. I did not count him a failure as a brother; he was no worse at it than I was. What failed
Tommy was his attention span. He could muster energy
enough to rescue a whole neighborhood from a zoning board
decision to allow strip clubs near a school, but he had no abid-
ing interest in his own life. Maybe it was too amorphous a challenge, or maybe he had found it resistant to practical remedies.
He could not solve it. "I love these chairs you have, Mark."
Tommy had turned around. He could see that I was not going
to accept his offer of a job in Pittsfield. I could see that he'd
known that before he'd jumped into his car and driven the

length of the turnpike. It was awkward, but he had come to my house and put it on the table anyway, and it was something new between us, something we could both feel. He braced himself on the back of the chair. "The chairs remind me of Dad. The way they're slung back and relaxed. They look as if someone just stood up from them." He should have come back, I thought. He should have sat down with you, Tommy, and taken a lifelong interest. "I noticed you still have all of his books." I thought of the tower he'd made of the books on the trunk. What problem did that solve? "I suppose you feel sort of at home with the Shakers, living the way you do." I misunderstood this as a compliment to my wooden house. "Mother Ann Lee and her bisexuality, I mean." There was so much meaning condensed into that contorted sentence that I actually admired it; I wouldn't have thought anyone but my mother capable of such a linguistic feat. Neither Ann Lee nor I was bisexual. The Shakers recognized the bisexual nature of the deity. They saw Mother Ann as a second manifestation of the Christ, the Female Jesus, whose appearance rectified the terrible rift that had opened between the genders. Her life made possible the equality of the sexes, a potential the Shakers put to work until it was second nature to them. I was monosexual historically, homosexual by desire, and asexual these days. But my mother thought *homosexual* was a term invented by gay men to make themselves sound normal; she thought it was conspiratorially easy to confuse with "Homo sapiens." She liked to call me a bisexual; she seemed to think it carried a sense of promiscuity. As Tommy led us down the deck stairs toward his car, I could see stars through the expended clouds. I wanted to thank him for his visit, but what I said was "I have a boyfriend," a phrase obviously uttered to make him squirm. I squirmed. Boyfriend? It was a term I would never apply to another man. All I could do was locate a star and wish he would not ask me any more questions. I located the bright and powerful Arcturus, and Tommy didn't ask. He didn't even flinch. "It won't last," he said. "You're just like Dad." I think he meant it disparagingly, though I am frequently stumped by the First Family's lexicon and its arcane usage rules. I had never before been compared to my father, so I took it in the same spirit as I had taken the compliment he hadn't given me about my Shaker-quality house. I took it to heart.

DICTION
Thn

Than and *then* are often confused in writing, though we all know what we mean when we say either one. In our speech, the words often sound alike. All we need here is a trick to remind ourselves of the literal distinction that we don't always enunciate. "Th<u>e</u>n" basically means "<u>ne</u>xt," and we use it to show sequence in time or place; "th<u>a</u>n" is reserved for comp<u>a</u>risons. You might be smaller and younger th<u>a</u>n your brother; you may be more or less like your father th<u>a</u>n you wish. It does not much matter. You still won't know what to do <u>ne</u>xt; so, th<u>e</u>n what?

the y chromosome

I PUT IN ten-hour days on Tuesday and Wednesday, timing my
arrival for an hour after high tide. I set up shop two miles down
the eastern shore on the shiny wet flats. At that end of the
beach the dunes were backed by acres of sandy trails and waxy
green patches of summer-sweet, which grew on knobby,
crooked limbs like olive trees and flowered in July. That was
something to look forward to, the lilac-scented week the
clethra on the beach would bloom. The terns liked it back
there in the shade, as did most of the men who walked this far
away and then felt they deserved a sexual favor for their efforts.
On the flats, I was on my own. On Tuesday, I brought Abel
Nagen with me in spirit; he was as rancorous as ever. His e-
mailed invectives about the McClintock Administration and
my former faculty colleagues ran to fourteen pages. In the final
letter of this batch, he promised to write again soon and to "fur-
nish evidence of the predictably inept and elaborate scheme to

reclassify the practicum failure of a certain so-called Inventive Speller." I did not conclude from this piece of cryptography that Rashelle Whippet had flunked her eight-credit stint as an assistant teacher at the Bennett School. I awaited the promised evidence. But it seemed grimly sensible to assume Rashelle had failed. I had failed her. Her adviser had failed her. The Administration had failed her. On whose shoulders might she have stood and reached her goal? In the first memo, dated 17 May, Abel had signed off with a simple, "Hope you are well." But as time wore on, he became more emotive. "Odd to think of you not here in September." "Wish you would take me with you." "I really miss you, Mark." It was endearing, and not least of all because it was unexpected. His emotions always seemed out of context, as if he kept his heart in a desk drawer and only uncovered it while he was searching for a lost file or a particularly hilarious student essay he'd socked away. I'd seen it happen in his home, too. He had a kitchen with an island in the middle, a design that precludes calm sailing in the most organized of homes, and the Nagens were sprung-seat-cushion people. I remember my first night at their home. Sarah was washing the dishes she intended to use for dinner along with a week's worth of fresh fruit for the kids' lunches. Ten-year-old Sam was sitting on a loaf of bread on the island, trying to get the blender to puree a fork. When he opened the cover and peeked inside, he looked disappointed, so he poured in the apple juice from his beer mug and tried again. Abel was on the phone, yelling at Rachel Reed about the hypocrisy of the college's multicultural requirement. Eight-year-old Donovan was sitting on a stool with his homework balanced before him on a windowsill; the telephone cord was loosely coiled around his neck. I was hugging the wall. I heard a voice in the wilderness: "Dad?" I would never have known who had spoken but for Abel's reaction. His head swung around and suddenly his attention was riveted on Donovan. He pressed the receiver to his chest. Donovan said, "Why are all the numbers afraid of number seven?" Abel tilted his head and smiled. He said, "Why, Donno?" The kitchen went quiet with Abel. Donovan pressed the eraser of his pencil into his cheek. He knew a joke was all in the delivery. He was staring at his father. "Because 7-8-9." Sam said, "7-8-9? I don't get it." Donovan said it again, slowly, so we all heard the punch line as "Seven ate nine." He and his father exchanged a nod. He went back to his arithmetic. Sam surrendered the blender to his mother. Abel immediately told Rachel the joke and then completed his tirade. Sarah brought me a fresh beer. We ate three hours later, and I knew Abel would be my friend. On the beach on Wednesday, I had nothing as interesting as Abel in my knapsack. I had a file full of requests from former students and a few other notes that I'd downloaded from my computer. I drafted fourteen letters of recommendation, which amounted to about five paragraphs of original prose suitable for shuffling. Each letter was formulaic but serviceable, a solid "Pass" on the essay section of the Competency Achievement Test. My dutiful work was rewarded. At the bottom of the day's file, I found another piece of e-mail from my anonymous adviser at the computer café in Boston. "You are on my mind again today. I wonder what you are thinking about. I wonder if the student you left behind will ever learn to spell. I wonder, too, if you have thought about the origin of her surname. It is easy to establish. Using your c-v-c rule, it is clear that the *p* was doubled before the suffix was added, right? The root word of Whippet is *whip*. I suspect the *-et* is a copying error, that the name originated in the speech of the Master: Whip it. That is her name. And until she learns to spell, to understand the derivation, the joke's on her." I had no way of establishing the identity of my adviser. The familiarity with the c-v-c rule pointed to a former student, but they numbered more than a thousand. I waited for the tide to come in and chase me out of my office. My skin had darkened considerably. My head was hot, which meant my hair would be reddish. When I got home, I showered and wished Tommy would drop in to make dinner again. Left to my own initiative, I'd be eating raisin toast with frozen butter chips. I wandered into the living room, where two of the three windows are oversized, the best spot in my house for air drying, as I suspect my neighbors knew as well as I did. I met a man there. He stood up from the sofa with my copy of *The Shaker Way* in his left hand. It was the first of my father's books, the one that had made him famous and launched him on his lifelong sabbatical. The man was old but sturdy, like a quality antique. He had a few long silver hairs hanging from the sides of his head. He looked a bit like Ben Franklin in a buttoned-up black trench coat. He was stout and no taller than I was in my bare feet, which were the least of my worries at the moment. He said, "You must be Mark." We shook hands. "I am Brother Thomas. I've come this afternoon from Maine. I wanted to speak to you. I let myself in." For clarity, he added, "From Sabbathday Lake." He was the author of the essay about the six-fingered Shaker Sister that had run in Sunday's paper. He held up my copy of *The Shaker Way*. "This is a bad book. When it still mattered, it was a dangerous book." I felt a little surge of defensiveness on my father's behalf, but it passed like a shiver. I asked him if he was a Shaker. He said, "Oh, Mark, there are no genuine Shakers left," and then he sat down. I liked his voice, which scratched like an old record. I also liked his contrariness: in less than two minutes he'd disputed my father's accomplishments and contradicted my understanding about the so-called Shakers who lived in Maine. His ease in my home was notable, given his technical status as an intruder, and I had to wonder about his use of the title "Brother." Whose brother was this Brother Thomas with the bass-drum belly and no socks to mediate the distance from the cuffs of his black trousers to the white rim of his running shoes? "Mark, I want to tell you about Sister Celia and Sister Ruth. It is a story of the Shaker way." He unbuttoned his coat, revealing a white shirt. "It is a story your father should have told you." I didn't do anything. I stood there, apparently waiting for someone to invent language and motor skills. "I would like to rest first, though," he said. He closed his eyes and his head tipped back. Then he said, "You know, Mark, you are naked. When we are a little better acquainted, I am going to have to ask you why."

SPELLING TIP
Other word endings

Words can end with vowels, and before you extend them with suffixes, you need to know a few rules. Because *e* is the most common, we'll deal with it separately. As for the others, here's the good news: so few words in our language end with *a*, *i*, and *u* that no special rules apply. We simply add the letters we need. That leaves *o* and *y*. We

have two kinds of words that end in *o*. Words that end
vowel-o (such as z<u>oo</u> and rat<u>io</u>) need no special care, but
those that end consonant-o (such as he<u>ro</u> and pota<u>to</u>) require a little assistance to become plural. Before you add
an *s* to consonant-o words, add an *e* to the root—toma-
to<u>es</u>. An old teachers' trick asks you to remember that in
addition to eyes, pota<u>toes</u> have <u>toes</u>. Our former vice
president Dan Quayle never ran into those old teachers.
There are some exceptions, but they tend to be words we
get directly from other languages. For instance, piano becomes *pianos*; as a sign of respect, we don't alter root
words imported from other cultures. This leaves us with
words that end in *y*. It is almost hereditary knowledge
that we change *y* to *i* before adding *-es, -er*, or *-ed*, which
is a compliment to our second-grade teachers. In fact,
unless we are adding *-ing*, we always change the *y* to *i* to
extend the root. *Beauty* becomes *beautiful; embody* becomes *embodiment*. It's second nature, right? Whether
we're looking at a wor<u>ri</u>some marr<u>ia</u>ge or a perfid<u>i</u>ous
seminar<u>ia</u>n, we know what happened. The Y became I.

the end

I AM A sensible dresser, and with my clothes on, I could not imagine why I had allowed the so-called Brother Thomas to commandeer my living room. Was it his essay in the Sunday paper that reassured me? Possibly. I wouldn't kick Herman Melville off my couch, and if James Baldwin stopped by unannounced, I wouldn't frisk him—not without his permission. Of course, the stout man asleep on my sofa had no such canonical credentials. And unlike my biological brother, who'd occupied the place two nights before, Brother Thomas had demonstrated no culinary flair. His only contribution to the household was his snoring. So I opened the freezer to pull out the butter for my toast, but then the telephone rang. "Hi, Mark." I sat on a stool to listen as the message was recorded. It was Rashelle. "I'm callin cause there's some problems comin up in my life. Don't call me this week. They wanna disconnect my phone again, I think, and I ain't home anyways. That Jilly lady"—Gillian Cherbourg?—"been on my case bout all the same old things you and me talked over before I flunked your spellin test last time. Jilly says—whas her name anyways, Mark? Sounds like Jelly to me. Aw, who cares? She talks so much woman shit that I gotta write down my real problems before I go see her, else I forget. You know, she can't spell the easiest words. Like my name. How'd she get to be my teacher? Did I mess you up bad, Mark? Anyways, call me next week. At night, but not late. Aw, any time, really. Where you workin at now?" Rashelle sounded worn out, which worked on me like a recrimination: the woman I'd flunked was raising three kids, usually had a couple of part-time jobs, could only afford her telephone for three weeks a month, and she was a permanent guest at the Gillian Cherbourg lecture series. Brother Thomas came into the kitchen and stopped behind me. He rubbed my back roughly and then patted my head, as if I were a dog. I felt grateful and pathetic. "Will you return her call, Mark?" I nodded. He moved around me and poked his head into the refrigerator. "What's for dinner? All I see in here is some raisin bread." I pointed to the butter. Thomas looked hurt, as if he suspected I was saving the good stuff for the next home invader. I tried to cheer him up with an offer of tuna fish or cereal. I didn't mention that the cereal was a risk. A friend who knew the limits of my larder had brought the granola with him when he'd come to visit the previous summer. About six months later, I opened the box and some moths flew out. Thomas said, "I could do without dinner, I suppose," and then he retreated into the living room. I followed. "Go ahead and smoke if you like," he said. "It won't bother me." I obliged him. He began to cough immediately, and then he scooted down to the far end of the sofa, where he managed to choke out the words, "Don't worry. Just slightly asthmatic." I ditched the cigarette. I asked him what he'd done with my copy of *The Shaker Way*, which was conspicuously absent from the tower of my father's books. "I put it downstairs. It's pleasant down there at ground level, what with the screened porch you built under the deck and that second bathroom. Is that your guest quarters? I suppose the couch unfolds. Do you have any bourbon?" I knew I had maple syrup and several jugs of an alcoholic beverage labeled "vin de table," which I'd found to be just as effective as white wine. I also had five or six reds from vineyards in Nantucket, New Zealand, and Bulgaria; these were part of a large collection of novelty wines that traveled among the homes of friends whenever we exchanged dinner invitations. I left Thomas in the living room and dug up four bottles of rum and several cans of coconut milk in a cabinet; at least once a year, some friend of a friend arrived with the world's best recipe for piña coladas only to discover I did not own a blender. I had my own recipe for all tropical drinks: another jug of wine. I had never heard anyone order a rum on the rocks, but I prepared a generous one and added a slice of rind from a dehydrated lemon. I also decided to let Thomas spend the night. This made me feel both kind and adventurous. I didn't know anything about him, but something about his appearance and demeanor had defeated my curiosity. It might have been his clothing. He dressed like a hand-me-down priest, and he reminded me of the facsimile faculty I'd seen in herringbone blazers asleep on the heat vents beside the Harvard residence houses. I didn't ask them questions, either; I offered them quarters and cigarettes. Thomas didn't smell bad, and I wasn't afraid of him; he was a literate asthmatic who didn't fuss about food. If he'd come with more hair and less belly, I might have changed the sheets on my bed. My powers of discrimination didn't extend beyond gender lately, which is what happens when you don't ever raise your antenna. I poured myself some wine and delivered his drink, which he sniffed and sipped with some trepidation, the way a kid approaches coffee. He grimaced, concerned but hopeful; it looked like he could live with it. When he leaned forward to put his drink on the trunk, the features of his face receded beneath a swell of skin, as if his head was a water balloon. He was older than he'd looked earlier, which struck me as deceitful. I didn't sit down; suddenly, I wanted him to leave, whoever he was. This was my house, he was a stranger, and I'd poured him enough rum for a week. I was particularly pissed off about his running shoes—one non sequitur too many. "Mark?" Thomas had registered my disapproval. His voice was apologetic, and his manners became retributive. He dug his handkerchief out of his trouser pocket and slid it under his sweaty drink, and then he folded his hands on his lap and stared at them. "I will have to leave soon. The others are expecting me at home tonight." What others? Other Brothers? "Maybe I was wrong to come here today, Mark. But when I read about you in the papers, I was moved. In one of the first reports, you were quoted as saying, 'This is not the end of the world.' And I knew what you meant. You meant 'I am in the middle of something I do not understand.' You meant 'I can see the end already; it's too late to turn this around.' You meant 'This *is* the end of the world as I know it.' Didn't you?" He'd obviously studied psychology with my sister Ellen. But I assured him that I had meant what I'd said. It was *not* the end of the world; I was bound to live through it. He said, "But can you live with it?" I said I would get over it, or get beyond it. He said, "It is your life." And I thought, No. It was an episode, an event, a strange moment in time. But, of course, that's life. Thomas said, "It might interest you to know that I was at Hancock Village in 1960, on the evening of the nineteenth day of May." His voice crackled with asthmatic interference, as if it was coming in over the wireless. "That was the day Sister Celia passed to the Other Side and Sister Ruth found herself alone." It was also the day I was born. Apparently, Brother Thomas knew this. How? He sipped his drink, content to let me make the connection. I had been trying to make this connection for years. From the start, the Shakers had been an irreconcilable part of my life, just as Hancock itself was not an independent city but a township within Pittsfield's boundaries, and just as my father's attention had been imperfectly divided between the First Family and the Shaker Family. I had been told more than once that my birth coincided with the death of Sister Celia. My mother had saved a paragraph from the local newspaper that publicized the coincidence under the headline, "Ships in the Night." My father's long association with the Shakers had provoked the ironic notice about "the timely birth of a son to Thomas Sternum, renowned photographer of *The Shaker Way*, and the peaceful death of the elder of the two Sisters living at the Old Shaker Village, which is soon to be opened to the public as a historical site and museum." The reporter did not know that my father would set sail within a month for parts unknown. Thirty-six years later, I finally made the connection. I imagined Brother Thomas with Ellen's hair, and then a tuxedo. It was a weirdly compelling image, a Diane Arbus photograph, and as he poked at the ice cubes in his rum, the round old man from Maine looked suspiciously like the man missing from the First Family portraits. Suddenly, it did interest me to know that he had been with Sister Celia and Sister Ruth on the nineteenth of May in 1960. I knew my father had not been at the hospital the night I was born, but I did not know he'd been at Hancock. My mother had often told the story of his bedraggled appearance in the maternity ward the following morning, and when anyone asked where he'd been all night, she'd say, "Pacing the floorboards." I'd assumed those floorboards underlaid the hospital Waiting Room. But she never said so. Her version of the story of my birth emphasized the joy she felt when she saw my father with me in his arms. During her labor, she'd worried he had left her, as he had left her expecting my sister Ellen in 1941. "And once I saw him hold you, once he had you in his arms, I thought he had finally learned to hold us all in his heart. I never saw what was coming," she told me apologetically, as if she should have. "He left us in June, just as the summer started, and it really knocked the heart out of me. A perfect sucker punch." I tried to picture Brother Thomas in another house, the stucco house in Pittsfield where my mother lay like Sleeping Beauty. Could he kiss and wake her? I had read many stories of sailors lost at sea for the better part of their lives. The lucky ones found faithful families. I knew the stucco house had stood the test of time; it was as solid as the day he left us in it, secure upon two steel I beams. But his children had not fared so well. Our foundation had been shaken when he pulled out of Pittsfield. We'd been propped up by a single mother. We had finally settled down, but like the plaster walls in my house, the stress showed on our once smooth surfaces, and no one could patch up all the gaps. "Mark?" I'd been staring out the window at a street lamp whose pale light was with me in bed every night, like a private moon. Thomas did remind me of my father, as did most men over sixty. But Brother Thomas was alive, which was more than could be said of Thomas Sternum. Whoever he was, this man before me, this ersatz Shaker, had taken the time to travel from Sabbathday Lake to Ipswich to tell me something of the story of my birth. I was still a little anxious around him, but I was also nervous every time I turned on an overhead light. As an electrician, I was a master of the short circuit, and I knew the illumination of every room was tenuous good luck based on many crossed wires. In my house, you risk a shock every time you make a connection. I asked Brother Thomas to tell me the story of Sister Ruth and Sister Celia. He was pleased. "As I said, the story ends on the nineteenth of May in 1960. When I arrived at Hancock, all of the buildings were dark but the Meeting House. This was strange." Thomas paused for a mouthful of rum. I thought it was strange that two Sisters would try to hold a Shaker meeting, but that was not the story. Thomas said, "The original Hancock Meeting House was not a classic. It was destroyed soon after Bob and Dale Casper purchased the place. At the abandoned Shaker Village in Shirley, Massachusetts, the Caspers had found one of the classic gambrel-roofed Meeting Houses designed by Moses Johnson, and they'd moved it up to the Berkshires in early May. It was museum quality, but when I got there, it was still sitting on a wooden pallet balanced on the old stone foundation. It was bright with candlelight inside, and I saw someone, an indefinite darkness at the window. I leaned on the fence across the street. I watched her move. Whoever she was, she was dancing, and when she twirled around I saw she had a partner. They traveled the length of the Meeting House, gone one minute, and then reappearing at the next window. Can you see her, Mark?" I said I couldn't quite, and Thomas said, "It takes time. I stood until she made another pass, and she was tall and slightly bent, and it was clearly Sister Celia, ninety-odd years old, and then I saw her partner was a broom, and she was sweeping. She had not wanted to be moved, and she didn't want to move on now—I mean, then—didn't want to move to New Hampshire or Maine, where there were still a few Shakers trying to believe in this world without end. There comes a time—that's what Sister Celia believed. Time comes, and you see that you will not be here forever. She had seen it all before. She had been the last Shaker to leave Kentucky. She'd left Pleasant Hill with Little Ruth and headed north to Hancock in 1910. Fifty years later, she must have known she had reached the end of her life. She'd told me years before that she suspected the end had always been with her, hovering like a moon, rising at night, a shining suggestion of the rounder, fuller life she desired. She stopped beside the chandelier. She turned around. Then she turned again, slowly, gazing into the middle distance. What on earth was she looking for? I wondered. She knew where she was. She was in the Meeting House." I sat down on an ottoman, and that stopped the story. I was in the way. I worried that anything I said to Thomas by way of encouragement would sound patronizing after my petulance, so I just slid back into the armchair and chugged some wine. Thomas took a hit of rum, then fished out the nasty chunk of lemon peel. I made a private vow to procure some fresh fruit. I had a vision of a big bin of cherries, but it was fleeting, unlike

Celia, who had been standing there the whole time, as Thomas said, "near the center of the Meeting House, with her broom," and I saw the black tin chandelier that was slung low, at reading height, hovering beside her like a halo. Thomas told me that Celia had swept the floor with a flat broom, which the Shakers had invented many years before her birth. Thomas looked at me and said, "Sweeping? Why? Because she was trying to recollect all the Shakers who were not with her—the Hancock Shakers, the Shirley Shakers, and her first Family at Pleasant Hill. She remembered when she was a child in Kentucky, surrounded by thousands of Shakers who were spread out across America. Her mother had left her among the Shakers, where she had stood for ninety-five years. Or was it ninety-four? Celia had long since stopped counting on years to give her life meaning. A year was an unreliable measure; like a cup of flour, its mass increased as you sifted through it." One week had been sufficient to the Creation. And, as Brother Thomas told it, everything that had ever happened to Celia had happened in one week, years ago, that one long week when she was at the middle of her age, the center of her life, where she could yet recall her mother's voice and where she might yet turn herself into a mother, a woman of the World. Everything had been within her reach, and everything she had made of herself had been made that week, at the Pleasant Hill, Kentucky, Shaker Village. And then the telephone rang, and Brother Thomas sat forward, ready to answer it. Before he got up, he remembered where he was. He took another drink. "Can you see her, Mark?" I said I could not quite; I still needed more words to flesh out the portrait. I told him I had visited Hancock, and I had seen pictures of Pleasant Hill, so I did know what it looked like, wherever she was. He smiled and said, "That's the question, of course. Where was she? In time?" Brother Thomas leaned forward and said, "Pleasant Hill had not been the first village to close. Hancock would not be the last. It must have been hard on Celia, but the Shakers were good at leaving." Brother Thomas hesitated, and I began to see Sister Celia. She had to leave Hancock. So, Sister Celia looked at the floor she had swept. The golden boards shone, and in the gassy candlelight they seemed to run away from her, like railroad tracks. They ran away, beyond the windowed walls, slanting like parallel lines in a painting, straining toward a distance where they might meet. Her work was done. This was the vanishing point. The Shakers swept clean. Beyond the deep wooden windowsills, beyond the patchwork panes of wavy glass, light was failing. She could still see the foursquare frames of the familiar buildings, the meadows stitched with stone paths and hemmed by painted fences. She could not see the running beds of chamomile and lavender blanketed by weeds. And the fallow fields and pastures where no sheep or cattle grazed were beyond her now. As Brother Thomas pointed out, "This might have been the late spring of 1910, the spring the Shakers set no seeds at Pleasant Hill. But it was the late spring of 1960, the spring the Shakers put up no preserves at Hancock. Darkness was evening the day. The village was disappearing with the light." Brother Thomas paused, as if it was up to me to finish the story. He said, "Can't you see her yet, Mark? Don't you see? You are in the dark. Well, so was I. It was nightfall in Hancock. But the Meeting House was lit from within. You can see her." And as he sat back and spoke to me, I saw. I saw that Sister Celia was expected to travel north, but

she must have known that she was going away, farther than
north. She would follow the floorboards to that point beyond
this illusory, painted space to the Other Side, where lines con-
verge. Sister Celia knew it was time. She latched the Brothers'
door. She latched the Sisters' door. This left the Visitors' door.
It seemed best to leave that way, to leave as she had never left
before. The Visitors' door would remain forever unlatched.
Never before had a Hancock Shaker needed an outside lock.
The Family had always been home, within, awaiting your return. She turned to go, and she saw someone standing just outside the window. It was a woman. It was Celia. She looked
shiny. And as she moved across the room, Celia saw herself reflected outside every window. She understood; she was gone
before she knew it. Outside, in the night, Celia tried to see inside the Meeting House. But the windows were higher than
normal, raised up a foot or so by the wooden pallet, so she
backed up until she saw the chandelier. The candle flames
were pale and perfect, like rosebuds, but their stems could not
last. Their light would never flower. Backing off again, she saw
her leaning broom. And after she backed away again, she could
see right through the room, through to the time when the
World's people would come to Hancock at last, not for the
Shakers but for the things they left behind. They would not see
a Shaker, for as far as Celia could see, the Shakers had left no
impression on the World. Even she was not reflected in the
Meeting House. Was it time? She moved in closer to the window, raising her hands to touch the sill. The window glass was
thick, and each pane was thickest at the bottom, as if it were
dripping and pooling up against its wooden frame. Was glass
liquid? Sister Celia stared, as if she might be able to detect the

imperceptible current. Was it time? There were footfalls coming from a distance down the road, and then the gate hinge whined, and when she turned herself around, Celia saw

Brother Thomas fell asleep and left me midsentence. His head tilted to one side, flattening his face against his shoulder. I finished my wine, and then I banged around a bit, hoping to rouse him. He started to snore. It was after ten. His glass was empty. I went downstairs and made up the guest bed. *The Shaker Way* fell out of a fold in the sofa. I paged through the pictures of Hancock. One of my favorites was a photograph of an endless white hall. On the left, daylight dropped in through the many doorways and lay on the floor like fallen headstones. The other wall, the right one, was lined with built-in cabinets and drawers, secret spaces I supposed my father had seen. As a kid, I'd wished my bed was a built-in, a cozy little hole in a wall with a door my father could secure after I was asleep. When I returned to the living room with my father's book in hand, Brother Thomas was awake. He slapped his face a few times, like a man applying aftershave in an advertisement. "So why weren't you wearing any clothes when we met, Mark?" I told him I often walked around my house naked after a shower. I explained that this was just one item in the comprehensive benefits package I enjoyed as a single adult. I also got to waste hot water, ignore nutrition and the telephone, refuse admission to all cats and dogs, throw out houseplants received as gifts, leave lights burning in unoccupied rooms, misdiagnose every hangover as a stress-related sickness, and host no holidays. "I un-

derstand," he said. He stood up. "A man wants some compensation when he finds himself alone. That's what drove me to
Kentucky, son." Son? I immediately generated another version
of the same sentence: *That's what drove me to Kentucky. Sun.*
But those were not his words, and I knew it. Then he said, "I'd
prefer you didn't tell anyone else that I'm here. Not yet. Your
brother and sisters, I mean, and your mother. I don't want them
to know you've seen me." He had said *son.* In a word, Brother
Thomas had turned into my father.

SPELLING TIP

The last of the suffix rules: the final e

Do you drop or keep the final *e* of a root word before you
add a suffix? The rule is clear. If you have a suffix that begins with a consonant (-*ly* or -*ment*), keep it: <u>sure</u>ly a simple <u>state</u>ment. If the suffix begins with a vowel (-*ing* or
-*able*), you drop it, <u>minimiz</u>ing confusion, although a few
words are <u>debat</u>able. Yes, the dreaded exceptions. Don't
despair. Memorize the common words that behave badly.
Here are three that ought to have the final *e* but don't:
<u>tru</u>ly, <u>du</u>ly, and <u>argu</u>ment. Oddities like these often enter
the language as printing errors in popular or influential
books, thus gaining credibility because someone wasn't
<u>eye</u>ing things carefully. But another set of exceptions
comes to us because of the two distinct sounds the letters
c and *g* are <u>able</u> to make. Unlike the other twenty-four letters, *c* and *g* have distinct hard and soft sounds. This capacity is not threatened by the addition of any suffix
except -*able*. Before a root word ending in -*ce* (noti<u>ce</u> or

embra*ce*) or *-ge* (chang*e* or mana*ge*) can accept an *-able* suffix, it must be allowed to keep its final *e*. Why? Because of tic, cable, chang, and nag. A turn of events may be <u>notice</u>able (not no<u>tic</u>able); we might notice that a particular man is <u>embrace</u>able (but not embra<u>cable</u>); after all, our hearts are <u>change</u>able (not <u>chang</u>able), and change in our lives ought to be <u>manage</u>able (not man<u>ag</u>able).

c a r r o t s

UNTIL I LEFT home at eighteen, Jimmy Krzcynkl was my best friend. He had blue eyes and dirty blond hair—I mean, his hair looked unwashed. Jimmy was always a big kid, broader and taller and heavier than I. He lived next door in a white house with his older sister and brother, and like me he had a mother, but Jimmy also had a father, and he shared him with me. Jimmy fell off his bike a lot, and his penmanship was so bad that the teachers in grammar school made his mother type all of his homework, even the math, and he flunked art almost every year. He had perfect aim, but he wore it lightly, as he did all of his talents; when we threw rocks together, he often credited me with a window he'd broken. No one could understand why we remained friends after we started school and had a better se-lection of companions than our neighborhood offered us. And from first grade on, we had no real friends in common. We both behaved badly when another kid was invited to join us after school or for a Saturday. Jimmy beat up a number of my guests, and I forced his friends to race me hundreds of times, because I knew I would win, and when they got cranky or winded, I could rely on Jimmy to threaten them and make them go home. As far as we knew, Jimmy was Polish and I was Irish, people whose ancestors ate cabbage. We had a few other things in common, but even our mothers called us polar opposites; however, Jimmy and I misunderstood this as a profound compliment, as if there was no friendship in the world so remarkable as ours. Until we went away to separate colleges, our differences meant nothing to me. He and I knew we were the same. We weren't stupid; we knew we weren't twins. And I never thought of him as a brother; we both had much older brothers who occupied more space in our lives than they'd earned. We liked each other, which to us meant we were alike. Love, and its attendant judges and jurors, never entered the picture, though I loved his last name as much as the nuns at the Saint Esprit grammar school hated it. Because she stumbled whenever she tried to pronounce "Krzcynkl," Sister Gerard Magellan called Jimmy "Mr. Sometimes Y," inferring that there was something provisional about his very existence because the only vowel in his last name was the y, which was a part-timer. She was the inventor of the typed-homework policy, which was her way of punishing his parents for producing "the only human being I have encountered who cannot acquire the Palmer Method." She saw to it that Jimmy would never write legibly. While the rest of us practiced our penmanship, she made Jimmy stand near the windows with his right hand in a pot of dirt. When we complained to Jimmy's father about this, Joe Krzcynkl said, "Just be sure to keep your fingers moving so you don't put down roots. You don't want to get stuck in second grade." Jimmy's father was constantly saying things I didn't understand. When he let us pick carrots from his garden, he'd have us brush them off on our jeans rather than rinsing off the dirt with the hose. He'd say, "Have to eat a peck of dirt before you die." For years, I thought this was a prescription, and to forestall my death, I was fastidious about rubbing my carrots clean. Though Jimmy and I never talked about it, I think one of the things that bound us together was other people's objections to our last names. I was alerted to my surname problem on the first day of first grade, when Sister Martin de Porres announced to the class that my name was weird. She said, "In all my years of teaching, I have never run across a boy who was named for a bone," and then she grinned and had a coughing fit and had to leave the room. We could all hear her laughing in the hallway. At home that afternoon, I was astonished to find *sternum* in *The Child's World View Encyclopedia* without a capital letter and horrified to discover that Sister Martin was right about its being a bone. Worse yet, I saw that my name meant "breastbone." I had been hoping it was something neutral, like an elbow or a thumb. All at once, I understood why my father had left town. I needed help. Desperation drove me to the First Family. Ellen was living at home again, teaching history at South Junior High. I found her in her bedroom, her sanctum, which I never entered, unless I couldn't scrounge up any decent cookies in the pantry. Ellen kept a private stash of snacks in her closet, all national brands. She wasn't stingy. After I burst in on her and handed her volume S of the encyclopedia, she dug me out a can of orange soda and some Mint Dreams. She let me lie on her double bed while she corrected a quiz her students had flunked; like all young teachers, Ellen expected kids to know everything she did. When she was done, she said she wanted to show me something downstairs, but we had to wait until I finished the soda. She had a strict rule about food not leaving her bedroom, just as my mother had a rule about food never entering a bedroom. Later, Ellen sat me down at the kitchen table and put the telephone book in front of me. She said, "I trust you, Mark. You can never use this information to hurt anybody." She asked me to find the doctors in the yellow pages, but I needed help with the spelling of "physicians." Then she asked if I remembered when she'd had the problems with her nose. It was just after she graduated from college, and it was memorable because her nose bled all the time, and she had to stuff cotton balls up her nostrils. Another rule of my mother's was No removing or adding cotton balls during dinner. "I had to go to an ear, nose, and throat specialist. His name is right there." She dragged her finger down the yellow page until it was poised beside *Foote, Samuel J*. She backed off and waited for me to get the irony. I said, "Dr. Foote?" And Ellen said, "Dr. Foote. And that's not the best one." She directed my attention to a small advertisement for Williamstown Podiatry Services, which was printed with a helpful illustration of a swollen foot. At the bottom, above his office telephone number, the doctor's name was printed in italics: *Benjamin Head, M.D.* I was impressed. This left Dr. Foote in the dust. Dr. Head's name was spelled exactly like the real thing, and unlike a sternum, every first-grader knew he had a head. Ellen left me with the phone book. Did she know what I would do with it? I closed it, opened it, found Dr. Head's ad, and closed it again. I looked him up in the white pages and found him there. I did it several times; it consoled me. I told no one else, not even Jimmy. But occasionally, I would call the office number and listen to the secretary say, "Dr. Head's line," as if it was just another name. Once, I called him at home. A woman answered. I said I wanted to speak to Dr. Head. The woman said, "He's at work. May I ask who is calling?" I told her my name, and she made a funny sound, like a grunt. Then she said, "Mark Sternum? Very funny, young man," and she hung up. I never called again. Or so I told my father on a humid Thursday morning, the sixth day of June, 1996. In truth, I took to calling Dr. Head's office at night, a habit I cultivated until I took up smoking in college. In those dark days before the advent of the answering machine, Head's office phone would ring endlessly, just how I liked it. I called that number to hear another hollowness, a dim ringing in my ear that approximated the feeling of having no father and, for a few moments, would serve as a substitute for him. But my father was happy to believe that I had made that call but once. I was happy that he had got out of bed early, long before I had, because he'd used the time to walk to the little store for orange juice and coffee, which he served with raisin toast on the screened porch. "I threw out your coffee," he said, refilling my mug. "Let's keep the new stuff in the freezer, where it won't go off." He was wearing a different white shirt, and I wondered where he was hiding his clothes. Had he called "the others" in Sabbathday Lake and told them not to expect him? Were there really more like him in Maine? Should I contact Ellen? I was having a speculative morning, to match the weather, I suppose: how humid could it get before it rained? But I kept my questions to myself, just as my father had not interrupted my story about Jimmy Krzcynkl and Dr. Head. I was happy to trade stories with him. His absence in my life had been an ever accumulating deficit, and like the national debt, it was so profound by 1996 that it seemed naive to think it could be remedied. He had his losses, too. He paid attention to my account of life with the First Family, and I paid attention to his Shaker Sisters. We had time, and we treated it like a currency; we paid some interest on our overwhelming debts. I know that other sons might have demanded explanations, and other fathers would have obliged them. But there are no words for making sense of what he did. *Why did you do it?* is just a preface to an accusation. I had no interest in his motive for abandoning me. It was wrong-headed, whatever it was, and his appearance in Ipswich was his confession. I could not bring him back when I wanted him to accompany me to a Father and Son Communion Breakfast. I could not hold him in the hospital in 1960. What could I do thirty-six years later? I could forgive him; in practical terms, this meant I could learn to live with him. And if my lack of histrionics disappointed him, if he'd been hoping for something operatic with a tearful conclusion to wipe the slate clean, he didn't burden me with it. I knew it must have been tempting for him to make a melodramatic declaration: Daddy's home! I gave him high marks for his restraint. He gave me a decent breakfast, which was more than I'd ever asked of my father. I also decided to give him some time before I notified Ellen of his existence. This was an act of loyalty, but the bow was to my mother, not to him. She had wanted him dead in 1982, perhaps because she considered longevity a consolation prize, and I didn't want to take away her trophy as she lay dying. I asked my father what Sister Celia had seen when she turned around in Hancock on the evening I was born. This pleased him. He said,

"Where was she when we saw her last?" I could see her standing outside the Meeting House window. The gate hinge had
just whined behind her. "She turned herself around," he said,
"and she saw that nothing turned but time." He was trying to
get comfortable in his wicker armchair; its barrel back left him
little room for maneuvering. He leaned on the table between
us. "She saw all the way back to Kentucky. It was 1903 and she
was thirty-seven or thirty-eight—your age, son—the middle
age, the center of a life. She was standing in the middle of the
Pleasant Hill Meeting House, surrounded by Shakers. It was
her job to raise the black tin chandelier before the dance
began. As she doused the candles, the Sisters and the Brothers
swiftly pushed the spindle-back benches against the walls and
stood in opposing rows, shuffling, swaying, swelled up with the
evening's prayers, and wavering with readiness. They wanted to
dance until they were dizzy. They wanted to spin until the
Spirit was drawn down among them. But as Celia walked toward the peg board to untie the lamp cord and hoist it up on
its pulley, she saw something in the window. It was dark, and it
moved when she did, so she told herself it was her own reflection. She started to unloop the long cord, and as she wound the
slack around her hand she saw a man's unblinking gaze below
her, in the bottom pane. His hot breath fogged the chilly glass,
obscuring his intentions. And thus began the week Celia found
herself, the week she found herself at the center of it all." The
telephone rang, and my father still had the habit of answering,
or starting to, so Celia and the Man were on hold until my machine kicked in. My father said, "I wonder who that could be."
It was a carrot of a comment; he hoped to lure me toward the
receiver. I'd seen better bait; some visitors to my house had of-

fered me cash to answer the telephone. "Not picking up," my friend Opal announced at the most recent of her spectacular dinner parties, "is Mark's way of asserting he might be reading Ovid or Voltaire." People hated my policy of never answering the phone. I was sympathetic to the annoyance my friends felt when they were calling me—not responsive but sympathetic. However, when they were with me, why did they want me to get up, sit with the receiver stuck to my ear, and talk to someone else? My father could not just sit there while I didn't answer the call, so he wandered out into my backyard. I wished he'd come sooner, while the crab apple trees were in flower. For three or four splendid days in May, they looked like white clouds, and the blue sky above them was within reach. I wished he'd come sooner for reasons as many as there had been days without him.

A FEW WORDS ABOUT
The language of language

Language is a currency, and many so-called teachers collect rare coins, which they like to show off to their students. English teachers will often pull something like "gerunds" or "ablatives" out of the drawer and pass them around. When the bell rings, these coins are returned to the teacher for safekeeping. This ensures that students will never learn the value of these words, and its keeps them out of general circulation. Of course, somehow the world manages to conduct its business without "phonemes" and "labial fricatives." But there are a few words stuck in display cases that we could really use.

"Preposition" is one. And despite your vague memory of being handed this coin in "prepositional phrases" and then passing it right back to the teacher, hold onto it. It is a simple compound: a prefix (<u>pre-</u>) and a root (<u>position</u>). *On, under, by, with, before, after*—these are <u>prepositions</u>; they come before (<u>pre</u>) you and other nouns in a sentence and establish your place (<u>position</u>) in space or time. "Participles" ought to be in our pockets, too. Whether in the present or the past tense, a <u>particip</u>le is the *-ing* form of a verb we use when we want to emphasize the doing, the <u>particip</u>ating. It is one thing to say, Celia turned; it is quite another to say, Celia was <u>turning</u>. Celia waits, and she does it alone. But if Celia is <u>waiting</u>, it's almost as if you are with her, or she is <u>waiting</u> for you. Everything we do is participial and prepositional; liv<u>ing</u> is find<u>ing</u> ourselves <u>in</u> the right place <u>at</u> the right time.

the book of j

WHY HADN'T SISTER Celia opened the window? That was the question I was left with on Thursday morning after my father had fallen asleep midsentence, as was his habit. I'd left him on the screened porch. I was leaning on my shopping cart in the excessively cool Stellar Food Market, staring at the Bing cherries, which were spread out in a vast flat like an edible Pebble Beach. I scooped a few handfuls into a bag as a woman sidled up beside me. She said, "You have to wash them with detergent, you know." She picked one up and held it under her nose. Sure, I thought, now you'll have to wash it. She picked up another cherry and shook her head: not quite. I understood: she was going to treat them like tomatoes. "I saw an interview with Meryl Streep," she said. "She uses dishwashing liquid." She smelled of suntan lotion and perfume, creamy sweet. Her hair was dyed yellow. Her fingernails were pale pink, and so were her lips. It was hard to see why she objected

to her fruit wearing makeup. I moved on to the plums. She
trailed me and said, "My name's Janice. I'm basically a vege-
tarian." I was starting to remember why I'd given up food shopping. The array of choices required too much self-definition:
Am I a red, black, or green plum man? Regular peas, snow
peas, or snap peas? I told her I was omnivorous. She said, "I
knew it. You're in such good shape, I knew you must be on a
special diet." Of course, it's true that I was devoted to the only
fad diet worth a damn: the cigarette; unlike the sensible alter-
natives—say, raw grains or exercise—lung tar did not noticeably increase my body weight. She picked up a plum and
smelled it. She said, "Mmmm." Then she offered it up to my
nose and said, "Where do you hang out when you're not shopping?" It's amazing what someone will do to get laid. Here was
a beautiful woman who had chemically altered her appearance, sworn off lamb chops and hot dogs, and performed a
one-act play for an unshaven stranger in the produce section.
What could she expect for her efforts? Maybe she hoped I
would produce act two: "What Do You Do for a Living?" Now
I know that other people must find this sort of thing romantic;
other people answer their telephones. But that wasn't my
problem. My problem—and I am open to advice—was eti-
quette. I take no pride in passing. And I don't want to waste
anybody's time, particularly if she's on the biological clock. But
my public declarations to strangers always sound like confes-
sions. I'm Mark and I'm gay. The first of twelve steps. And
then the implicit compliment fades into an apology: I'm sorry.
I didn't know. Janice was still holding the plum, which smelled
just like a plum. I told her I was unemployed, living with my
father, and I had—I did say it—a boyfriend. Three strikes. She

tossed the plum into the bin. "That's nothing," she said. "I'm married. Two kids. Think I'll try another aisle. Take it easy." She headed toward Prepared Foods. Since my last visit, the Stellar had created an Asian Specialties section. I don't think anyone in Ipswich purchased any of the stocked items; the bok choy, water chestnuts, and bamboo looked ancient and undisturbed, artifacts of the Tang dynasty. But like me, other shoppers seemed to appreciate the little museum. It was fun to try to guess which of the specimens were featured in your take-out tubs of moo shu. I left the store with seven bags of raw materials, but I wasn't sure they added up to a single co-herent meal. When I got home, a sea breeze was wearing away the cloud cover, and though the sun was still invisible, the sky was shiny white. My father was nowhere in sight. I figured he'd gone for a walk by the river. I knew he'd be back. He'd begun to feel at home in my house, though not without some effort. He had washed out the refrigerator. It smelled like bleach, and my collection of sprouted onions and desiccated lemons was in the trash. On the deck, he'd strung up four lengths of rope. Damp white pillow cases and sheets and wrin-kled white shirts were interspersed with several pairs of his black slacks and some shorts and T-shirts I thought I'd lost. I knelt in front of the refrigerator to put away the fresh food, and this made me mindful of Sister Celia and the Man at the Meeting House window. The truth is, I had nothing better to think about. I cultivated the connection to Celia and every correspondence between her story and my own. The Shakers had haunted my youth. I liked to think that my father and I shared an ancient, tragic history that superseded the history of the First Family. In my father's story, Sister Celia and the other

Kentucky Shakers seemed blissfully unaware of their fate, but I knew they were doomed. It was like discovering I had relatives on the Titanic. Celia did not open the window, I guessed, because she did not want to scare the Man away. She understood his wary gaze: to an outsider, the Shakers looked strange, as do most families. And my father had said that Celia herself felt weird whenever the Sisters spun in ecstasy and the Brothers growled out Greek and Babylonian prayers. Standing outside, at a remove, that Man stood for Celia, her vagrant thoughts, her disinclination to join the Family dance. I knew how she felt. And as I told myself her story, or as much of it as my father had told me, I began to understand her. At least that's how I saw it: Sister Celia unlooped the rest of the lamp cord from the peg slowly, ponderously, and painfully as far as everyone else in the room was concerned. She heard a few ahems from the Brothers, some sniffling among the Sisters, and then a lot of coughing; impatience was contagious. Celia noticed that her stillness had stilled the Man. Or was he the seer? Was Celia the image in his mirror, waiting to be moved? The Sisters and Brothers stared at Celia, but this did not dislodge her. They stared at the window, too, but from their angles they saw only their shining selves, ghostly Shakers hovering beyond the glass. Someone sneezed. Then someone else. Eldress Anna spoke before a plague broke out. "Do all your work as if you had a thousand years to live." This chided them into silence. "Yea," said Sister Louise, who knew it was up to her to complete the eldress's wisdom. "And work as if you must die tomorrow." Celia understood: get on with it. But as she moved, the Man shook his head desperately. He opened his mouth. No. Please. No. He was placing his fate in her hands, begging her to keep him a secret from the others, with whom she shared everything. His eyes were bloodshot and shadowed by too little sleep. Was he a Wanted Man? She turned to the exasperated Family. Had they not seen him? She turned to him again, and he backed off a bit. Celia did not move. She stayed where she was, right where she always found herself, between the Shakers and the World. She had been found here by the Shakers thirty years before. Sister Louise had been heading toward the kitchen with two steaming tins of milk. There was Celia, standing at the gate of Pleasant Hill, an unescorted girl of eight, an open suitcase at her feet. She was pressing wrinkles from a dozen silky slips and satin dresses hanging from the white fence that traced the limits of the Shaker land. Louise pointed to the Dwelling House and said, "Is your mother inside?" Celia stuck her hand into the banded cuff of a pink dress sleeve. Then she laid the dress down on the lawn and pressed the sleeves across the bodice. "My mother called me Celia. Will I get a new name?" Louise said, "You are safe here." The words worked. It was what her mother had said just before she left Celia on the Shaker's lawn. Sitting on the suitcase with Celia, her mother had said, "You will be safe here," but then she turned away and waved at the big man pacing beside their horse and carriage. He was the latest man-in-waiting. People waited on her mother, and so did Celia. Which dress should she wear tonight, was her hair coming undone in the back, did the man who brought those flowers leave his card, where were the gloves with the pearl buttons, who told the landlady we're leaving town tonight, did you bring Mummy back a bowl of whatever they were serving, was her hair coming undone, was the piano player a profes-

sional or another local church organist, how is she going to get
the rest of her dresses out of hock in Topeka if they leave
tonight for Roanoke, are you sure he didn't leave his card,
didn't she say pearls, did the landlady promise to look in on
you tonight, don't you know enough to ask a man for his card,
does she think we're paying full board for soup every night,
and does it have to rain every time she has her hair done?
Celia rarely had the answers. Her mother always found someone else to find the gloves, the man's name, the rent, and
rooms in the next city. Celia waited. After the questions were
answered, the songs sung, suitors entertained, arrangements
made, and promises broken, her mother might slide into the
slim bed beside her and kiss the back of her neck, draw Celia's
back against her bare breast, put a hand to her belly, and pull
them together until the warm weight of her thigh pinned
Celia's leg. The nearness, the bigness, the silence and softness
of being surrounded by her mother made Celia someone. It
gave her shape, and wherever they were going next, she knew
just where she was. Celia was right there. Then her mother
said, "Your momma loves you," and they fell apart, fell asleep,
and woke up among strangers and questions, and Celia was in
the way and out of place and she wished they were somewhere
else, not the last hotel and not the town before that, but somewhere better, a place she couldn't recall. "Your momma loves
you." Her mother stood up from the suitcase and looked at the
carriage again. Celia tried to stand, but her mother's hand was
heavy on her shoulder, and she understood. Her mother was
leaving without her, no question about it. This was amazing.
Celia was sure it would astonish people who found out about
it. It was as incredible as having a nameless father, attending

fourteen schools in one year, eating cake and pudding for breakfast, and sleeping with no clothes on. She watched her mother climb into the carriage. The horse nodded its head. Her mother didn't turn around until they were past the fence. She looked confused. The man yelled, "Whoa." Her mother stood up in her seat and yelled, "Look at me." She held up both hands, and her palms were dark at this distance. "Didn't I have a pair of blue gloves?" Celia hopped off the suitcase and flipped it open. She fished out a clump of bright green silk and shook it. No gloves. She grabbed something stiff. It was the corset of the blue dress, "for the saddest songs, the love songs," her mother liked to say. Long ago, her mother had sung those songs to Celia, but lately she said she had to save her voice. She said she was tired of singing for her supper. This had worried Celia; she knew they had to eat, and she'd heard her mother say she'd starve before she took to cooking. And now, Celia couldn't remember the songs, and she couldn't find any gloves in the suitcase, and she knew her mother wouldn't wait forever. Celia looked up. The man handed something to her mother. The man had found the gloves. Her mother forgot to wave good-bye. Celia had lost her mother, whom she began to remember right away, airing and folding and repacking the useless dresses, inching toward the Dwelling House as her trousseau was made. The Sisters and the Brothers bowed as they passed the fence festooned with fancy dresses on their way to breakfast. Sister Louise told them, "Her name is Celia." And they understood. She had come to them from among the World's people, who acted out their sad lives in such silly cos-tumes. When she finished, Celia told Louise the dresses were a gift, but my father didn't tell me if Celia meant they were a gift she wanted to keep or a gift she wanted to give away, maybe to secure her supper. Of course, this was immaterial to the Sisters, I suppose. They knew she had to be fed, and they didn't see any use for the dresses, so within the week, Celia's gift was put away, hidden in the generous eaves. History will tell you—as would my father if you poured him a bourbon— that the appearance of an orphan girl with ball gowns wasn't the most notable event that Shaker spring of 1873. Tecumseh, who'd been dead for sixty years, had been visiting the villages, often in the company of General Lafayette. At Hancock, Sister Frances received the Painting Gift. Spirits rapped on the walls and turned the tables in New York. At almost every village Foundress Mother Ann was speaking from the Other Side in Aramaic, Sanskrit, and in French. Pleasant Hill Shakers received 111 inspired poems and songs, and many of the Sisters had been taken on tours of the Celestial Space. Celia was not visited with Gifts. But then, what did she want? She had a bed of her own and five roommates, including two Bulgarian girls who called her "Cheely" and begged to braid her hair at night. She ate eggs every morning, learned to bake cookies that looked like farm animals, and when the Shakers served soup for supper it was studded with barley and chunks of chicken or turnip, and there was hot bread for dipping. She was asked questions about her mother, her father, her schooling, and her shoe size. The Sisters made her dresses and aprons and bonnets, and when she stood on their worktable and turned, they smiled and pulled pins from their mouths to mark the hems. It was just like being her mother. She had regular chores with Sister Louise in the physics garden and Sister Bertha in the laundry, and occasionally she and the other children were called into service for low-bush berrying. And like her mother, she had her night job. The Shakers called it Laboring—dancing and singing and calling out the name of Christ. She looked forward to evenings in the crowded Meeting House, where she got safely lost amid the spinning. And the Shaker songs were simple and joyful, easy to remember. She labored faithfully that first spring, but alone among Kentucky Shakers, Celia was not moved. Of course, I knew what it was like to be unmoved. Apparently, Rashelle Whippet had not moved me, nor had Rachel Reed's cajoling, Marie Bond's logic, or Gillian Cherbourg's hectoring. My brother Tommy had failed to lure me back to the Berkshires, as had Ellen's word pictures of my mother's approaching death. Even Janice had taken a shot with the plums. It was all more friends on the phone. It's not that I wouldn't return the call; I needed time. And when you take your time, you appear to be unmoved. I'd often been compared unfavorably to molasses, or maple syrup in the summer, so I liked this Sister Celia. I liked that she moved at the rate of window glass in a wooden frame. That takes time, which, like wavy glass, can distort things. The McClintock calamity had left me looking like the American Jeremiah, prophet of cultural doom. As for Celia, before the end of her first summer at Pleasant Hill, she found herself in a strange position, too. The Gifts that had showered down on the Shakers in the spring of 1873 turned into a monsoon. The angels grew garrulous. A Sister could not set a seed without attracting their attention, which led to protracted conversations in the shade and too few carrots. Winter damage to the fences and foundations went untended while the Brothers passed whole days in a Profound Recline. Nocturnal spirits roamed the Dwelling

House and roused the sleepers, occasioning more than one embarrassing collision of a Brother and a Sister. Soon Jesus took to waking up the children, which did not endear him to Celia. She had often dealt with noisy men in the bedroom. One night, the Bulgarian sisters raced around the room screaming and crying, which was interpreted by one of the older girls as an accusation of misconduct against one of the elders. Celia was impressed. She had seen the Bulgarians chase and wrestle and choke each other, but she'd always figured they were screaming things like "I hate you" or "You bit me first." At the same time, Celia began to dread public prayer meetings, where the velocity of the spinning and shaking had increased dangerously. She usually retreated to a corner bench beside big Sister Louise, who always packed some fruit or bread in her apron. From this vantage, the Shaker reverie resembled the revelry her mother and her friends used to instigate after a particularly successful concert. Public attendance at Shaker Meetings was breaking all previous records until the Central Ministry stepped in with a new Doctrine of Discernment. Meeting Houses all across the country were closed to the World's people. Elders at each village were advised to seek the Gift of Detachment. New dietary laws were drafted with stricter prohibitions against red meat. Pattern dances were invented and endorsed as the communitarian alternative to frenzied bouts of individual turning and shaking. Many Shakers had been through this before. Like Pentacostal revivals and Great Awakenings, the Shakers' Gift extravaganzas happened every thirty or forty years. But this time, they had not converted many of the World's people. Their numbers continued to decline. At ten of the remaining twenty villages, there were fewer than fifty Believers. The Shaker chair, seed, and clothing manufactories were suffering severe losses. The Era of Manifestations was over. In the years that followed, Gifts became rare and suspect. This gave Celia a peculiar status. Unlike the children who'd been misled and unlike her elders who confessed to faking a frenzy or two, Celia had nothing to retract. She acquired an identity by default. She became a symbol of the new skepticism, but she also stood for the hope of another renewal, the longing for genuine ecstasy. After all, they were called Shakers. One day, they believed, that unresponsive child would be suddenly filled; sober Celia would be overcome and—well, the Sisters and the Brothers were prepared to be delighted. Celia came of age. She signed the Covenant, ungifted and unshaken in her faith. No one was sure if this made her more or less a Shaker. It did make her a slowpoke at Meeting. They assumed Celia was always waiting for something to move her. It was not a pleasure, waiting for Celia to raise the chandelier, but they loved her, and there were compensations, including her amazing way with lemon pie. Of course, they couldn't wait forever, and this was why they coughed and sneezed so much the night she stood by the window twisting the lamp cord around her hand, the night in 1903 when no one but Celia saw the Man. Finally, old Sister Ethel clucked her tongue and said, "The lamp, Sister. Up with it." Celia obeyed. She wound the rest of the rope around her left hand. The Man at the window stiffened. She knelt to secure the rope to the wall, but she never completed that task because she had knelt to be near him, too. Eldress Anna thought she was genuflecting and whispered to Sister Louise, "I think she's gone Catholic!" The Man backed off a bit, and

Celia could see he was brown and bare to the waist. He floated like a sculpted bust above his invisible legs. Was she losing him? Eldress Anna stomped her foot. She sang, "Good evening, friends and fellows." The Man retreated from the noise, twisting toward the night. But he stopped and turned his face to Celia as she studied the strange topography of his back. He had been beaten. She said, "Dear God," and she leaned into the windowsill. This infuriated Brother Joseph, who thought Celia was conducting a private prayer session. In full basso profundo he sang, "The journey is a long one," and then he drummed his feet against the floor, rousing the others, and the thunderous clopping resolved into a metronomic march, the prelude to the dance. Celia felt the rhythm as a heartbeat. The Man raised the pink palm of his hand. This was sign language, the language of leaving, the sign her mother had made from the carriage. It meant "Say nothing. Words are of no use." It also meant "You are where you are. I am here." Eldress Anna tunelessly intoned, "Along the way the sky is fair, the wind rides from the North." Celia pressed her right palm against the glass. Did he understand? This meant "Wait." Brother Joseph's "Amen" was cut off by a yelp from Celia, who felt the whizzing rope uncoiling from her left hand and— Whack! The tin chandelier slammed down and clanged around like a snapped-off wagon wheel. The explosion caused a melee, scattering the marchers. Sister Louise steadied Eldress Anna, who was suddenly surrounded by Brothers ducking to retrieve the candles shot out from their stems. Sister Ethel planted her boot on the limp cord, as if it were a serpent. And as Brother Richard caught the rolling chandelier, the glass gave way to the pressure of Celia's hand, and she screamed as the pane exploded. The Man dropped to the ground, cradling his head, as if someone had shot at him. He slithered forward, then stood and looked one last time at Celia. He saw her hand. He shook his head and said, "Don't say you saw me," and he ran across the road and past the Dwelling House, and Celia could not forget his dark back—all purple ridges, blisters, swollen muscle cords, and traceries of blood—as he ran beneath the budded branches of the orchard and away, beyond the final run of fence. The Meeting House was weirdly warm with bodies excited and stilled by the siege. Eldress Anna raised her hand, and Sister Louise steered her toward the wreckage. From several feet away, the eldress spoke without inflection. "What is it, Sister?" Celia sat back on her heels. When she looked through the empty frame, she could not recall his face. He was gone, like a random thought. Celia closed her eyes, and she woke up twenty-two hours later. She couldn't see anything, and it occurred to her that she might be dead because she felt extraordinarily comfortable and she didn't seem to have any limbs. She said "What time is it?" The eldress answered, "It is Thursday, Sister. You were a long time gone." Celia wasn't sure, but the eldress seemed to be above her, possibly suspended from the ceiling, as if she'd acquired the Gift of Flight. The eldress said, "You are among us again," and she removed the blinder from Celia's eyes. "I wanted to prevent your being drawn back abruptly," she said. Celia asked after her legs. "It is the tea," said the eldress, "Emma's herbs. Your body will be back by morning. And your arms are unscathed. Sleep, Sister." Celia said, "The glass." It was a question. The eldress understood. She said, "Repaired. The Family is praying for the return of the Man." This woke Celia, but she could not

rouse her memory. "I betrayed him?" The eldress said, "The
World betrayed him, Sister. We will welcome him." She was
interrupted by a clattering of china. Something stank. It was
Sister Emma. She was carrying a steaming bowl of humus
soup on a tray. The eldress put her hand under Celia's neck
and tipped her head toward the bowl. "You are thirsty, Sister.
Drink. When you awake, you will tell us all about your meeting with the Negro Jesus." Celia's head swelled up to twice its
normal size. Her skull was straining to escape its skin. Emma
and her herbs were swept away. It was dark again. Celia felt
the eldress hovering above her, cooing and singing until she
evanesced, cool and gray, like morning mist. This is where my
father had left me, and when he returned from his walk he
seemed to be listing to one side, as if his hips weren't working
properly. He was tired, too tired to talk much. He started to
take down the laundry from the lines on the deck, but it was
still damp, so he agreed to leave it for me to deal with later. He
told me I ought to make some phone calls, and it was true that
the message light was blinking rapidly, like a distress signal.
Then he hobbled down the stairs to take a nap. I wondered if
he regretted time, all the time he had taken away from the
First Family, all the time he'd taken to find his way to me. I
was grateful he had come, and the interrupted story of Celia
made me feel like a child, eager for the next installment. But
I was not a child, and maybe it was too late for me and the
Negro Jesus. I had already closed the Book of J, volume ten of
the *Child's World View Encyclopedia*. It was my second-to-best
friend, and when Jimmy Krzcynkl was being punished or his
bike was broken, I turned to Jason and the Argonauts, Jesus,
Joan of Arc, and Johnny Appleseed. They had all left their fam-

ilies behind, which inspired me. When I was nine or ten and reading their stories for the two hundredth time, I realized that my heroes in the Book of J were arranged not only alphabetically but chronologically. This seemed meaningful in the extreme, though mysterious; I was years shy of my first brush with structural criticism, and my best guess at the time was that anything heroic I might do would have to fall into line. Jason, Jesus, and Joan were my great-great-grandfathers and my old great-aunt. They begat Johnny Appleseed. He was my father. He walked around the country barefoot, sowing seeds. He wore a tin pot on his head. I spent a few weeks wondering what would happen to me. I tried on the pressure cooker once, and it fit, but it was remarkably heavy. Finally, I asked Ellen what she knew about Johnny or any of the other Appleseeds. She was still teaching junior high history, and none of us knew that it would be her last year in the classroom. She brought me up to her room, where she made me a root beer Fizzy and handed me volume A of the *Britannica*. A for Appleseed versus J for Johnny? It had never occurred to me that my encyclopedia was not authentically alphabetical. I immediately grabbed Ellen's volume J. Jason was just a single line, with a cross-reference back to A for Argos and Argonauts. Joan was stuck with the other saints in volume S. Jesus was the only one who appeared as a J in the adult world. I cut my ties to the *Child's World View Encyclopedia* and to Appleseed, Johnny. I was a free man. My history was ahead of me, and it was printed on see-through thin pages in proper alphabetical order with very few illustrations and no photographs. Ellen mixed me up another Fizzy, and I got acquainted with the Danish maritime scholar Andrew Aagesen.

INDEPENDENCE

Every English sentence must have one independent clause. You can add thirty of your favorite phrases, seventy-seven extraneous modifiers, and dozens of auxiliary verbs, but no amount of verbiage will obviate the need for one independent clause. The elements of the independent clause are two: an actor (say, Celia) and a related action (for instance, sleep). It is not enough to throw together a noun and a verb. "Bus laughed" is not an independent clause. A clause is considered independent when it can stand alone. <u>Celia sleeps.</u> <u>Mark reads.</u> <u>Janice shops.</u> These are perfect English sentences. I know some of your teachers did not seem to think so. They wanted to know where Celia slept, what Mark was reading, how often Janice shopped, and why. As you no doubt knew in the third grade, that was none of the teacher's business. Independent clauses do not depend on more information. Of course, we depend on teachers to help us explore possibilities and express complexity. That's what they were after with their questions. But do not let their interest in the whole story confuse you. Your simple sentences did not raise the questions; your teachers did. Clauses that raise expectations for more information are dependent clauses; they cannot stand alone. Typically, a dependent clause is an independent clause (Celia sleeps) preceded by a word or phrase that refers to time or cause (such as *after, before, while, because, by the time, as soon as*). <u>While Celia sleeps.</u> What? <u>Before Mark reads.</u> What? <u>By the time Janice shops.</u> What? These are dependent clauses.

They are incomplete sentences, or fragments. They raise unanswered questions and conditions. An independent clause is a solid stand-alone sentence, but life is not always so simple. Our stories are complicated. We have to learn to integrate independence and dependence, and this requires coordination. When we do it well, we achieve grace.

the twoness of route 1

THE THIRTY-MILE DRIVE from my house to Boston is a straight shot down Route 1, the old Post Road. For a few miles, you travel under the arbor of tall trees, and you are surrounded by steep, clovered hills and snaggletoothed stone walls. The far-away rural past is nearby and charming. If your car radio works, you can add music, and you remember that space and speed are your inalienable rights, and every pop song is a national anthem. I do not envy my ancestors their extended families stacked up in stone cottages in small villages. I love leaving, especially at night, when the horizon retreats before your headlights and the background is dark but for the glint of someone's high beams in the mirror, another escapee, a fellow traveler, one more immigrant crossing the border into the land of the free. Living alone, I only encountered people in the middle of a round-trip or when someone pulled off the road into my little rest stop for a day or two. And so, as I folded my father's

clothes, woke him for a late lunch of cheese and tomato sandwiches, and helped him to tuck the fresh linens under the mattress of the guest bed, I found myself wondering how long he
intended to stay. He had rearranged the beach towels and my
stock of cleaning supplies and turned the freestanding bathroom shelves into his dresser. While I made lunch, he salvaged
the stem ends of the tomatoes and put them in the refrigerator
in a bag he called "our stockpot," to which he added the butt of
a big celery that I'd jammed into one of the plastic drawers. He
considered the hard rind of the cheese and the morning's coffee grounds an opportunity to begin a compost heap in my
backyard, adding, "The flowers will thank us." It's true that I
treated my plants like prisoners; they got dirt and water, and if
they didn't behave to my liking, I moved them into a patch of
coreopsis or sedum, lifers who'd learned to prosper by my ne-
glect. "And you might want to pick up a few bags of pulverized
lime to save your lawn. You've got grubs." I was more anxious
about the raccoons who'd be stopping by for cheese and coffee.
They were born scavengers and squatters, always shopping for
an empty attic to call home. Because my father hung around
and listened in as I played my accumulated messages, I felt I
owed him an introduction to the cast of characters. I told him
Abel was a historian, but that seemed inadequate, so I said that
Abel and his wife were really Julius and Ethel Rosenberg, and
my father liked them immediately. Opal, the great hostess of
Cambridge, was planning another dinner party, "and I am making rice pudding in your honor, so shave and bring someone
handsome who's likely to be impressed by my tired old performance." It had been a big day for rice: Rachel Reed left a recipe
for risotto and beet juice, which she'd found in the Sunday

paper and wanted to warn me about. "It's pink, which is always disturbing in a food, and smells somehow of yesterday's dishes. I hate to throw it out until you've investigated it. I have a large sample. Call me with suggested uses." My father muttered, "Compost." I told him Rachel only grew ivy and wisteria in her small brick backyard; I didn't mention her salmon and white impatiens, which returned to the planters each year despite my objections. We listened to a few other friends' complaints and questions, several hang-ups, and then I paused before the final message because my father looked confused. Then he said, "You're lucky, Mark. Those people—they're the heart of you." This carried more emotion than was immediately apparent, and it took us both by surprise, like a sudden squall. When I looked at him, I was relieved to see he was staring out the window, jaw set; like me, he had decided to ride it out in silence. After a few unsettled moments, I played the last message. It was Marie Bond inviting me to join her for dinner in Cambridge at seven, "to talk about your job search. You know, don't you, that MCU is going to make you an offer. They have ten thousand illiterate kids, and Derby won't fund any basic skills courses. You're perfect for them. They can sneak you in behind Psycholinguistics or some other facade. I bet it'll be Classical Rhetoric. Am I right? I'll be at the Pacific Rim. The College will pay. Why not, right? I'll make sure they save us a table outside so you can smoke. I should warn you—never mind. Rachel says you hate surprises, so I'll surprise you." My father waited for my summary bio of Marie Bond. She was more than could be simply said. Like the Hindu deity Vishnu, she embodied all contradictions. She was the Juggernaut. Marie Bond was a genuine life force, and that meant she embraced the inevitability of death and destruction. With her appointment as dean of the faculty in the mideighties, McClintock's sleepy professors and docile students had been roused into a frenzy of productivity and polemics that often climaxed in human sacrifice. An admissions counselor who'd routinely called in sick to avoid recruiting trips to urban high schools was tossed into the flames; she landed on top of the charred remains of the entire Special Ed faculty, who'd refused to adopt Marie's agenda for inclusive classrooms and thus became de facto segregationists; and at the same time, some nincompoop in Literature who thought he'd joined the new dean's Multicultural Bandwagon found himself lying in the path of Marie Bond's chariot, where he was wagging copies of his own death notice, a course he'd proposed "for students interested in the oral traditions of pre- and illiterate African societies." Marie Bond's ideas were dangerous because they put the campus in contact with the World, and oxygen started to leak into the traditionally airless environment, where the so-called noble gases had been circulating for years, waiting to explode. Marie Bond herself was considered dangerous, too, because people were drawn to her. They wanted her approval, which was much more pleasant than her disapproval. But it was hard to stay in her good graces because what she liked most was a good argument, a disagreement, a philosophical fistfight. She rarely did her own boxing; she sent her associates into the ring, and anyone who lost more than once was off the team. Her admirers and detractors alike, all of whom knew her better than I did, described her as complicated, contradictory, unpredictable, and inscrutable. I always suspected this meant she had a broken heart. I was not immune to her appeal, but I had the blessing of my friendship with Rachel. No

one below the Third Floor understood the precise balance of
power at McClintock, but everyone knew that Marie, Rachel,
and President Agatha Kroll had discrete dominions. It was only
in rare cases of political unrest that this Gang of Three took a
public stance against one of their loyal serfs. When I flunked
Rashelle Whippet for the last time, I heard the ominous chink
of chains, and from the window in my underground office I
watched as the three drawbridges were raised and Whack!
Whack! Whack! I was cut off from the kingdom. It was some-
what perverse, and therefore predictable, for Marie to develop
an interest in me after I was banished. But then I thought
about that surprise she had mentioned. This gave me indiges-
tion, which would at least save me the trouble of ordering dinner and waiting for the tamarind sauce to kick in. My father
poked around in the refrigerator, and I felt bad about leaving
him alone. Of course, an hour earlier I had been wondering
when he would leave. As a measure of my confusion, I invited
him along. I baited the offer with an alluring portrait of
Boston's skyline as seen from the Tobin Bridge and a description of the audible buzz of prosperity in the Back Bay. I assured
him the city had changed and grown. He said, "Since when? I
took the train from Maine to Boston two days ago." I had been
thinking of him as Rip Van Winkle, but he had not been asleep.
He had been awake all those years. It didn't endear him to me.
"I thought I'd do something with some of these vegetables," he
said. "You bought too much, really. Maybe we should invite
some of your friends up for the weekend." That's it, I thought,
I'm calling Ellen tomorrow. He pulled out a carton of eggs and
decanted them into the little molded-plastic nesting rack on
the refrigerator door, one by maddening one. Then he grabbed

the bag of lemons. He counted them. "A dozen?" I told him they'd been on sale. "So's the house down the street. Did you buy that, too?" He made me laugh, and this didn't eradicate the bad feelings I'd built up against him, but it made them seem puny; he could step over my defenses at will. "You know what I'll do?" He grabbed a few eggs. "I'll make you a lemon pie. Sister Celia's recipe. Watch and learn." It was five o'clock. Marie Bond would be forty-five minutes late. He was my father. I had time. He cut a sample slice of lemon, about half an inch thick. He said, "You see, we don't peel them. We use the whole lemon, rind and all." He set me to work on the rest of the lemons while he made a crust. I asked him if Sister Celia ever saw the Negro Jesus again. He made a funny face and said, "Is that who she'd seen at the window?" I had to leave, but not before the pie was assembled and I learned that Celia did have another encounter with the Man, and someone else had discovered Celia's hidden Gift. The Shakers were with me on the hilly northern stretch of Route 1. But then I lost them at the junction with Highway 95. Just before you pass over this interstate, the road is flanked by two huge so-called service stations, both self-serve, and their fluorescence is a sign of what's to come. The rest of Route 1 is the cultural equivalent of a used-car lot. The mall-like sprawl of parking places and goofy theme-park architecture is fascinating and forlorn. It's our Las Vegas; retailers retreat from Boston to Route 1 like performers who know there is life in them yet, though they can't fill a concert hall or a legitimate theater. Purveyors of Polynesian pu-pu platters, German wursts and kraut, English fish and chips, and other once exotic cuisines that fell out of favor in the city are packing them in. Faded concepts like build-your-own burgers, stuff-your-own omelettes, hook-your-own catfish, and karaoke-while-we-cook seem like bright ideas out here. Isn't it time you owned some deerskin slippers, dinette furniture, or an above-ground pool? And even if you never eat a pizza in the Leaning Tower or dine in one of the crenellated towers of the Chung-King Palace, Route 1 reminds you that it took a lot of bad ideas to make America great.

DICTION TIP
To, two, too much

These are annoyingly common words, and thus our confusion. Two of them have two meanings or more. Ironically, *two* has only one: it is a number, the sum of one plus one. *To* can be a preposition ("<u>to</u> the city"), a verbal noun in infinitives ("<u>to</u> come" and "<u>to</u> go"), or an adverb ("Rip Van Winkle came <u>to.</u>") *Too* is an adverb that intensifies our situations (someone might arrive "<u>too</u> late" or turn out to have "one <u>too</u> many annoying habits"), and it also means "also." Got it? If a single person says, "You can come <u>to</u> my house and live here, <u>too</u>," the <u>two</u> have <u>to</u> learn <u>to</u> live as one or else come <u>to</u> an agreement <u>to</u> satisfy the needs of the <u>two</u> together, and those of each one, <u>too</u>.

blackboard specials

I DISTRUST PEOPLE who hate rain. I suspect they wash their cars. They are often peculiarly well groomed. And as they age, they tend to develop an adversarial relationship to weather in general. As I crossed the Tobin Bridge, the skyline melted beneath the mercury of an overdue summer storm that roiled Charlestown Harbor and bounced and pooled and beaded on all the hot tin and tar. Rain reminds us that it was not always dry land where we live, or at least Walt Whitman remembered that fact and wrote it down for the rest of us to recall in wet weather. I parked in a Residents Only space across the street from the Pacific Rim in Cambridge; I'd lived there once and still had the stickers to prove it. I also had seven McClintock stickers and seven Ipswich Resident beach parking passes plastered to my windows, and this stamp collection usually impressed the meter maids. I listened to the rhythm of the rain for a few minutes, and when I realized it was not about to re-

lent, I prepared myself for a two-hundred-yard dash. I had four
or five collapsible umbrellas in the backseat. These were inadvertent gifts from absentminded passengers, and I only used
them for distance events, or when I had to run a decathlon in
the rain—mail the letters, forget to buy a book of stamps, drop
off the dry cleaning, buy coffee filters and a carton of cigarettes, return Opal's pie plates, wonder if I needed milk, admire
a sofa in the window of Design Details, buy the milk, get cash
from the machine, and leave the umbrella with the automatic
teller. The interior of the Pacific Rim was designed to look like
a Parisian café in an Indonesian rain forest, and there were six
or seven big fat Buddhas overturned to remind diners that they
were the sort of people who'd ransacked Burmese temples.
Scanning the place for Marie, I spotted myself in the mirror
above the bar. I shook my head, and the rain worked like a hair-
care product, keeping things in place. However, the shoulders
of my blue oxford-cloth shirt were droopy and dark, and from a
distance I looked to be sporting some oversized epaulets. I felt
something soft on my neck, and it was Marie's hand. She stood
very close and nudged her side against mine. She whispered,
"You're late." She'd had her hair shaved down to a smooth
brown waterproof mat. The rain beaded up on her face, but her
silky black dress showed no sign of spotting. She pressed her
hand against my back and said, "At least you live in the middle
of nowhere. I'm an hour late and I live around the corner." She
frowned at her reflected self in the mirror, and if she really was
disappointed, she was the only one. Everyone else who saw her,
including a raucous circle of Japanese tourists in the bar and
the muscular man who was supposed to seat us, was silenced.
People smiled when Marie Bond passed, and many of them

sighed as if they wished they'd been waiting for her. She pointed toward the middle of the darkness and led me through the fronds. She stopped suddenly and bent down to embrace someone, and then she swung around and unveiled her promised surprise. We were having dinner with Gillian Cherbourg, the sociopornologist who'd advised Rashelle Whippet to charge me with "prejudgism." Gillian was a short, spherical woman with a fantastic excess of energy that she released by talking, and when she had to be quiet, her head moved incessantly, like the valve on a pressure cooker. She was wearing brown pajamas and a braided length of rope around her neck, which she told us her son had made at camp last summer. I asked if it was a noose, and she mustn't have heard me, because she said, "What news?" But Marie heard me; she grabbed my forearm and squeezed, and she didn't let go until we were seated and she'd snagged a passing waiter and convinced him to bring us a bottle of wine. Gillian said, "It's awfully good to see you, Mark. I hear you've had a number of job offers already." Marie said, "Let's not talk about school yet," and filled everyone's glass to the rim. "Whatchyall gonna eat?" Marie's voice went south suddenly, and she read aloud from the menu, charming us with her drawl. "Yall eat blackened stuff? What a fish wants is a crust ana kick. Am I right? Pea pods in ginger—gotta have summa them. Now everybody pick a noodle dish. Yall likem crispy or wet?" I'd had dinner with Rachel Reed often enough to understand Marie's performance. She wanted to prevent a disaster. While it was possible for a member of the Administration to enjoy a meal with a faculty colleague, things always went bad when two or more professors were present. Academic life affords teachers little opportunity for healthy interaction with other adults. We do tell each other that our classrooms are laboratories, but unlike proper scientists we'd never consider dropping in to see how a colleague's experimental work is progressing. We complain about the precipitous decline in standards, but we don't ask another member of the department to review a set of essays; we put the bad ones at the bottom of the pile, turn up the television, and use the B— to reduce the number of rewrites we'll have to read. Of course, we are all members of ten or twelve ad hoc and standing committees, and theoretically, faculty governance emerges from our meetings. But what do you get when you put six or seven faculty members in a room for an hour? Six or seven lemmings. The tenure system ensures that junior faculty, who are seeking sinecures, will support the status quo; tenured faculty are basically on lifelong disability, teaching two limited-enrollment seminars a semester, and they see no profit in shaking up the very institution they are shaking down. And that leaves research. The good news is that most college professors no longer grind out the arcane, supercilious articles that made the university irrelevant to everyday life while the NEH and NEA were operational. The bad news is that we now grind out articles on gangsta rap and supermodel-induced eating disorders at the same rate—that is, slowly, unlike our students, who work on deadlines. Academics used to be chronically out of touch; now we are simply out of date. Put two or three professors at a table with an administrator, and what do you get? Spoiled brats out to dinner with their working mom. Gillian hogged all the attention, recounting the plots of several gang-rape movies she'd been studying as colonization narratives. I behaved like a bored teenager, scarfing up her and my share of the first bottle of wine and leaving the table without a word to sneak a smoke in the bar. Marie basically ignored us. She studied the menu and ordered food for fifteen. I'd seen Rachel do the same. They worked six or seven days a week and never got home before eight in the evening. They didn't enjoy these nights in crowded restaurants with surly companions, so they did their food shopping for the week, which explained their preference for cold noodles and spicy entrées that would survive a couple of spins in the microwave. We ate as much as we could, and then it seemed evident we would have to talk. Gillian asked to see the dessert blackboard, and Marie Bond snapped, "Just order a fruit plate." She meant something else, but it was hard to know what. Gillian seemed to understand she was being scolded, but to no avail; the waiter came back with the handheld slate and prepared to lecture us on the night's specials. I thought maybe Marie was mad at Gillian because she didn't want to hear about the hand-gathered ingredients in each dessert. "Rice pudding." The tall waiter put a finger to his buzz-cut red hair and said, "This is basically rice made into pudding." He'd obviously been to college and learned to state the obvious, so I wanted to hear his explication of Mango Flan. "That is basically another pudding as far as I know. Flan is French." Gillian said, "Oh, yes. *Flahn.*" I asked if *flahn* was the French word for crème brûlée, and Marie clamped her hand around my wrist and ordered a big plate of fruit. The waiter asked Gillian to hold the blackboard while he recorded our order, and she looked embarrassed and said to Marie, "Oh, I get it. The blackboard. It does sort of stand for Rashelle, doesn't it?" The waiter left without his prop, and Gillian could not figure out what to do with it. It did not fit under the table, and when she balanced

it against the legs of her chair, a waitress tripped and nearly fell.
Marie said, "Now *she* can sue us, too." Too? Gillian was forced
to wear the blackboard like a breastplate until the waiter returned with our fruit and coffee—two decafs and my regular,
which he worked like a shell game, guaranteeing someone a
sleepless night. I asked Marie who else was suing "us." Marie
said, "Rashelle Whippet has been talking to a lawyer." Gillian's
head started to twitch, and she was playing with the rope
around her neck. It was evident she'd got my caffeine. She
stabbed a wedge of melon and spoke a little too loudly. "Let's
face it," she said, "I've created a fucking monster. I'm sorry, but
it doesn't surprise me. This often happens when I work to impact women's lives. I empowered her. Now she's out of control." Marie Bond sat up very straight in her chair; she looked
like a cobra when she said, "*Monster* may be the wrong word."
I mentioned that *impact* was not a verb. Marie tilted her gaze
my way and said, "I didn't buy you dinner because I miss your
wit." Then, as if she really was my annoying sister, Gillian said,
"It's your stupid spelling test that I blame for this whole disaster. The least you could do is help us out now." I understood:
this was not my problem; I was relieved to know I was not part
of the "us" who were being sued. I concentrated on Marie. She
had paid for my dinner (though like all grand administrative be-
quests, my noodles would come out of the students' pockets),
and she looked a little sad. It was obvious I ought to be gracious. I asked Marie how I could help. "Rashelle wants you to
testify against the College," she said. I liked the sound of that:
Mark Sternum, Witness for the Prosecution. I did not smile. I
tried to look sincerely confused, an expression my students had
taught me by their daily example. Gillian was twitching. Marie

said, "Basically, Rashelle flunked her 300-hour practice-teaching experience. We worked out a deal on her behalf with the supervising teacher and salvaged half the credits to count as her 150-hour practicum. But she can't do another 300-hour until the spring semester, which means she can't graduate in December, so she has decided to sue McClintock." Marie paused. She put her elbows on the table and balanced her head in her hands. "I need your help, Mark. Comprenez-vous?" When Marie spoke French, she always meant *"I'm only going to say this once."* Gillian was desperate to speak, but the waiter swooped by to ask if we liked the fruit, and Gillian crazily accepted more coffee from him. She quickly added way too much cream and then dumped her cup in her lap—this seemed purposeful, like self-medication. To her credit, she said, "Now I can sue somebody, too," and she dashed away. I asked Marie how the blackboard figured into the story, but she had her own agenda now that Gillian was gone. "Gillian hasn't said so, but she instigated this legal action. Maybe she isn't even aware of what she's done. Rashelle came to see me in April, when it was clear she was in trouble in the classroom. She casually mentioned that Gillian had told her she ought to sue you. I don't know what Gillian was thinking. She gets worked up about people's civil rights." Now *I* wanted to pour coffee over Gillian. Marie said, "Maybe you already know all this from Rachel. She must have told you." Rachel Reed had never mentioned it. I signaled the waiter; it was clear that I was going to need a lot of coffee. Marie waved the waiter away and said, "So, it was something of a surprise when, last week, the College received a letter from Rashelle and her lawyer retracting her original charge of prejudice against you. Not that anyone on the Third

Floor ever took her charge of racism seriously anyway. It was never made a part of your files." She was rewriting my history as she spoke. Abel Nagen had long ago warned me that my tolerance for revision would come back to haunt me. Marie brushed her hand across her head and then grabbed my forearm, as if she was rubbing something off on me. "Rashelle now proposes to sue every McClintock faculty member who ever gave her a passing grade. Her contention is 'If I am not literate, they were derelict in their duties.' " Gillian returned. She was wearing her tunic backward to hide the stain. In her Social Ethics class, Rashelle had earned a B−; in Body Politics, Rashelle got an A. Marie excused herself to make a telephone call, and I understood: Gillian would have to fight her own battle. Marie's long history of support for Gillian's tenure case was on the ropes. Gillian said, "Did she tell you about the blackboard?" She didn't look at me. She stared after Marie, then flagged the waiter. Intelligently, she ordered a scotch. He said, "On the rocks?" Gillian said, "Fuck the ice. Just get me a drink." And he said, "Oh, I see, a double," which he delivered very quickly. "It happened right after spring vacation, in April." Gillian spoke into her half-full tumbler. "Rashelle had typed notes to the parents to remind them about the art project the class would be starting after vacation and what supplies the kids should bring back to school. She misspelled a few words and, unfortunately, she used the spell check." Gillian had yet to look at me. She put her hands into her lap, and then she stood up and started to dance around her chair. She was trying to reach her tunic pockets, which were behind her. Finally, she snagged a small slip of paper and laid it before me. It was a typed list of Rashelle's mistakes: *food die, white flower, #3 led*

pencils, two empty cans (from frozen jews). "Four of the mothers
got together and charged into the classroom, waving the notes.
One of them said, 'Where's the idiot who can't spell juice?' The
supervising teacher was in the back of the room on the reading
blanket, and Rashelle was doing math with the other kids. Before either of them knew what was happening, one of the
second-grade scholars—a typical Cambridge smart-ass—stood
up and said, 'She has a disability. Look.' Rashelle had put a
word problem on the blackboard." Gillian turned over the little
note on the table. There, on the flip side, I read the problem-
atic problem: *2 appels + 2 limes + 2 cherrys = X total fruits.* I did
the math: X = the number of years Rashelle Whippet spent in
school (16) $\times$ the estimated number of teachers who failed to
teach her (60) $\times$ the number of students in a second-grade
urban classroom (25) $\times$ the average number of years in a
teacher's career (40) $\times$ the probability that Rashelle's education was not singularly bad (100). X = the 96 million assorted
fruits of our labors. Gillian finished her scotch, which made it
possible for her to look at me. She looked discouraged. "I know
you lived in Cambridge for a while, Mark. So you've seen the
problem. You know that the kids here get computers when
they're three. They all have private tutors or nannies with flash
cards. This is all about social class." This was desperate, even
by sociology's standards. Gillian was trying to invoke the Mc-
Clintock Doctrine, a theory of predestination that says our lives
are governed by Race, Class, and Gender, the secular Holy
Trinity. I could see Rashelle Whippet was just a pinball being
flicked from one category to another. I was happy she'd found
a lawyer to yell, *Tilt!* When Marie Bond returned, she didn't
seem to be surprised that Gillian had failed to explain my role

in the defense of the realm. She suggested that Gillian order another scotch, and she might as well have added, "On the rocks, like your tenure case." The telephone call had renewed Marie's spirit, and she was obviously eager to be done with our dinner. I suspected she'd arranged a late-night date. "You know better than anyone how hard you worked to teach Rashelle the basic skills, Mark." Marie had shoved her chair closer to mine, and now her shoulder was pressed against me. "You know McClintock is doing more about basic skills than any college in the country. You know the intimacies—I mean, the intricacies of our historic commitment to teacher preparation." I also knew I was in sole possession of the paper trail that documented Rashelle Whippet's so-called progress on the Competency Achievement Test. Marie put her hand over Rashelle's word problem and dragged it off the table. Gillian nursed her drink. Marie said, "I know it's too late to get you to reconsider your decision to leave the college, what with MCU gunning for you." Before I could ask her to define "decision," she speared a slice of mango for me and popped two cherries into her mouth. She spit the pits into her hand and shook them like dice. "I know Rachel wouldn't say so on her own behalf, but as academic dean, she is the person of record. Her actions are the ones that will be litigated." She tossed the pits into the fruit dish. Snake eyes. "But I'm betting that with your cooperation we can straighten this thing out before it destroys anybody's career. Give it some thought over the weekend. Call me on Monday if you have any ideas." She stood up, but she kept me in my seat with a hand on my shoulder. "I'm running late. You two stay and finish the fruit. I took care of the check." As she left, the muscular man at the front desk handed her two shopping bags. Had she just threatened me? Was she really holding Rachel Reed hostage? The only thing I knew for sure about Marie Bond was what she'd be eating for dinner next week. Gillian was almost drunk, but she knew what had happened. She tossed back the last inch of her scotch and said, "What are the chances I can write an important book about incest or something and get it published before I have to defend my tenure case in December?" This seemed especially unlikely since she'd put her tunic on backward. I offered to drive her home. She stood up and decided she could make it on her own and walked away, but before she left, she came back to the table. I figured she wanted the fruit. But she said, "Isn't it funny you don't hate me? It makes me feel better about the whole mess. Does it make you feel any better?" It *was* funny. Gillian had treated me badly, and I didn't like her for it. She was reckless, but I had to credit her tirelessness, her ever-readiness to hoist a flag for someone who had no place in the parade. It was true that she often poked someone else's eye out in her haste to lead the way, but I didn't like to think of her car crashing into a mailbox. What I missed about McClintock was precisely this ambivalent, awkward, confused moment, or as Rachel would say, the luxury of having colleagues and other problems you do not have to solve. I went to the bar to smoke before I called Rachel to ask for her advice on the lawsuit. The Japanese tourists were still there, and they had somehow convinced the bartender to have a table set up for them so they could eat, drink, and smoke without commuting. The bartender pushed a coffee my way and said, "This is from some American guy sitting with the Chinamen." Everyone at the table had dark hair, a dark suit, and none was noticeably taller than the rest; having expended my private stock of cultural clichés, I decided it must have been Gillian or Marie who'd bought me the coffee and had it sent undercover. I left to call Rachel, and I got her, but she was already talking to her son, who was in France. Call waiting: the electronic version of coitus interruptus. Somehow, Rachel already knew I'd had dinner with Marie, and she correctly guessed the terms I'd been offered. She said she'd be free in half an hour. I thought about my coffee and vainly hoped I would not be. We agreed to talk the next night, Friday evening. Back at the bar, the Asian contingent had disappeared, but my cup was full again. This time I noticed that it kept coming with the right amount of cream, and I didn't think anyone in China or Japan had the secret formula. The bartender said, "It's caffeinated," as if he was thinking about cutting me off. Caffeine is an alkaloid, like cocaine, as a man whom I trust had once told me. According to him, no one quite understood why these distinctive, nitrogen-rich compounds occurred in some plants. One theory was that they repelled grazing animals. I liked to think that Nature, in her chemical wisdom, tried to reserve cocaine and coffee for those of us animals who were saddled with self-consciousness. I also liked to think about that trustworthy man, Paul Pryor, who worked at one of the big teaching hospitals in Boston. His job, insofar as I have ever understood it, was to get doctors from various parts of the world to talk to each other about their ideas of standard practice. I had not spoken to Paul since early May, just before I left McClintock and he left for South Korea—not Japan or China, but close enough. Paul Pryor believed in small favors, like getting your coffee to exactly the right caramel color. In an old hard-candy tin in my glove compartment I kept the key to his Cambridge apartment. I didn't know where he kept the key to my house until that Thursday night. When I let myself into his apartment, the place was dark. I switched on the hall light, and there beside his front door, recently matted and framed, was the key I'd given him years ago. Beneath it, he'd taped a Chinese-cookie fortune, like a caption. It said, "A small house will hold as much happiness as a big one."

SPELLING TIP
Combination platters

English is part German, and the Germans make famously great cars. One of the virtues of this heritage is that our nouns can survive collisions with other nouns unscathed. The Germans love to make new words by smashing dozens of small words together, and while we Americans are not so reckless, we have our share of fender benders. The rule of law is reliable when this happens: treat the first noun (say, *black*) as a prefix that does not change the spelling of the root (say, *board*); thus <u>blackboard</u>, <u>black-out</u>, and <u>blackmail</u>. (Think of <u>knock</u> and <u>brat</u> and all the other <u>wurst</u>-case scenarios.) Even if the results of these accidents look like they need fixing, leave them as they were. <u>Bookkeeper</u>, <u>roommate</u>, and <u>nighttime</u> may strike you as needlessly repetitive, but the two nouns involved ought to be admired for having survived intact.

c o m i n g s   a n d   g o i n g s
— n a m e l y ,   m e n

PAUL PRYOR LIVED at the top of an ugly five-story brick apartment block built in the forties, and like everything associated with him, I thought it was near perfect. Each of his windows faced south. He had sun all day and moon most nights. The building abutted the Cambridge Common, a large oval of grass dotted with patchy-trunked sycamores and bronze men standing on platforms of stone. The pedestrian paths were lit with soft amber light. The park was ringed by Harvard's colonial brick buildings and weather-vane angels atop gleaming white spires. Beyond this postcard from the past, across the banks of the Charles, rose Boston, which in Paul's windows was well represented by the Prudential Building and the all-glass Hancock Tower. When you lay on Paul's extra-extra-firm mattress, you saw treetops and stars and the weather pole on the Hancock, which blinked red for rain and blue for fair skies. His kitchen was shaped like a shoe box with a window at one end.

It sat between his bedroom (a shirt box with two windows) and his living room (a sweater or suit box; three windows). The front hall and bath were pastry boxes, and like all the rooms they had nubbly white walls and plain oak floors. Paul had no rugs, and but for the bookcases and my key, there was nothing nailed to the walls. In the big room he had a plain cherry sofa and chair and a long library table; his kitchen was all counters and cabinets, with a painted white table and chairs by the window; and then there were his simple cherry bed and two bureaus and an old blue wing chair, where he meditated in the morning. His bike was usually parked in the hall. It was hotel living, really, with an elevator ride up, the paper delivered right to your door, and a chute for bagged trash in the back stairwell. It was clean, and impersonal in the right way; you could see that this was a man who would not invest his ego in decorations or gilded things. His six-over-six windows, for instance, suffered no treatment at all. I sat at his little kitchen table, staring out at the ancient earth and the preserved American past, with the modern world looming in the distance, flashing red for rain in our immediate future. Sister Celia had sat at such a window when she woke from her herb-induced sleep. I could see her, in a wooden chair, a little groggy, wondering why she had been put to sleep in a strange bedroom at the top of the Dwelling House, on the children's floor. She pressed her hands against the frosted windowpanes and made the glass weep. The Kentucky dawn was still an hour or so away. The purple night air was bruised with black suggestions of trees and eaves and chimneys. She felt her cloak suspended from a peg near the bed, and she dressed and hung her nightclothes, and then she tipped the chair and hung it, too, upside down, so dust would not settle on the seat. It was a small room, not the infirmary as she had first thought. There was an empty cot beside the bed. What time was it? The morning bell had yet to ring and the halls were dark and quiet as she passed down from the third floor, unlatched the front door, and felt the electrically cold air spark at her cheeks. She hurried away from the Dwelling House. Her breath puffed up in little locomotive clouds, and high above her she heard a few uncertain birds worrying the night sky with their when-will-it-be-when-will-it-be-dawn songs. She was looking for the Man, but she saw a bright light flare up behind the barn and something smelled sweet. Woodsmoke? Every Shaker knew too well the smell of arson. Fire was the tax the World made the Shakers pay for taking in the wives of drunken husbands, for freeing slaves, and for their celibacy and famously delicious food. Celia hurried. But the barn was not burning. There were fires in the orchard, benign and perfect little pyres glowing underneath the peach trees to protect the fruiting limbs from the late-spring frost. A black figure emerged from the branches, and Celia steadied herself while his shadow darted and danced. He grew bright. It was Brother Richard. "Yea, Sister. You were looking for someone else?" He wiped the sweat from his black brow and put on his straw hat. "The fruit has been saved. Another frost defeated." He had brought warmth with him. Then—apologetically or humbly, Celia wasn't sure—Richard said, "Portray to me this Negro Jesus." Even Richard? Even before the break of day, Celia could see what had happened: in the eyes of Richard and the eldress and the other Sisters and Brothers, she had been Gifted with a vision. She was no longer the only unmoved Shaker in Kentucky. In vain protest, she said, "I saw a man,"

but Richard said, "The eldress said you have been opened."
Celia didn't speak. A breeze blew up behind her, and she raised
her arms to catch the cold air; she didn't want to carry anybody's hopes of heaven. Richard's hat was flicked off by the
wind, and he knelt to retrieve it. He did not get up. Celia said,
"Maybe I saw a reflection, Richard. Maybe it was me," and she
almost believed it. She was almost willing to forget the Man at
the window if the rumor of the Negro Jesus went away with
him. So she said, "The work of Jesus is done, Richard. It is
1903, and the American Negro has done his time on the cross."
Celia knew that the World did not understand this, but surely
Richard understood. He had been manumitted by the Pleasant
Hill Family when he was just a boy, a so-called slave. He had
lived free, lived the black and white Shaker Gospel for almost
fifty years. Didn't he understand that the color line had been
swept away by the Shakers? Richard said, "Maybe you are
right." He got up. He stood at her side, but he was not at ease.
He said, "Can you convince the others that there was no one at
the window?" Celia said, "I can say with certainty I did not
meet the Christ." Richard fingered the brim of his hat. He
faced her. He was frowning. "That is not enough, Sister. You
will have to say you saw nothing. Say it was candlelight. Or
else, you must admit it was a Gift. For the others surely will not
believe you saw a man and did not open the window to invite
him in." He was right. No version of her story was credible.
Thinking about her predicament exhausted Celia, and she was
still suffering the effects of Emma's stinky tea. She needed
help. She reached for Richard's hand, but the bell above the
Dwelling House swung—Dawn!—and clanged against its ham-
mer. Sunlight pried at the horizon, opening that oldest of

wounds, dividing the earth and the sky. Richard said, "Must be time." Celia turned and saw little Esther charging out of the Dwelling House, followed by Rebecca and Eleanor—or was that Frederika with the milk tins?—and when she turned back to Richard, he was gone, deep beneath his trees, dusting down the fires with fistfuls of clotted soil. Celia heard Sister Ethel limping along the road behind the barn, taking her time, taking the long way to the brick chicken coop where she fully expected to find Celia completing the morning chores they shared this month—after all, Celia had slept clear through the previous day and left Ethel to stoke the stove and clean the beds. Celia hurried. She lit the stove, spread fresh hay across the wire bunks, and stashed the warm brown eggs in willow baskets, which the Shawnee had taught the Family to weave years ago in exchange for linseed oil pressed from Shawnee flax at the Shaker mill. Then she ran with the baskets to the livestock barn and left the eggs for the children to collect, and she got back to the coop before Sister Ethel arrived and tried to shake something out of the eggless hens. And someone said, "Spare two eggs?" Celia turned to respond. She saw two fat striped hens paddling their blunt wings, tamping down their nests. A black cock strutted by her feet, pecking at the trail of grain that led to the sunny pen. Once outside, he reared up, showing off his comb and proclaiming, "I need food!" She stepped closer, as if the bird might have something else to say for himself, and the cock crowed exultantly, startling Celia and sending her crashing back against the open feed sack, which scared the hens, who hurtled from their roosts, thudding and screeching as they hit the ground. Celia steadied herself. A squall of white down whirled around her, and then the feathers settled on the birds' bent backs as they fed. Celia pitied them. Feathers were the Gift of Flight, but they felt as foreign to those hens as the rain and snow that fell from the sky, and so they shook them off. She knew she had heard a man speak, so she said, "Breakfast will be served soon. You may join us." And someone somewhere said, "I'm naked. I'm a Negro." Celia found it was easy to talk to him; it was like praying. She said, "Do you want to become a Shaker?" And the invisible Man said, "Maybe I better talk to your daddy." Celia said, "He can hear you." She briefly recalled her father: a wavy-haired black-coated man of medium build, always seen from behind, the credible flip side of any painted portrait or bookplate illustration. The Man said, "I don't see your daddy nowheres." Celia saw something move outside in the bright pen. It was Sister Ethel's shadow. Celia said, "The Sisters and the Brothers believe you are a spirit." And the Man said, "I'm near enough dead, that's true and—Dammit! He bit me!" A heap of burlap shot up from the corner, catapulting a confused hen into the doorjamb. Sister Ethel and her shadow retreated, kicking up quite a storm as they limped away on the gravel road. The Man was still hidden when he said, "Je-sus. Anybody sees me, I'm a dead man." Celia stuck her head out the door and watched Ethel carrying the latest news of the Negro Jesus. She said, "Well, you have come to the right place. If you are dead, you can be sure somebody around here will see you." He sat up. He was not heroic as he had been at night; he was shrouded in shredded burlap, and he had seeds in his hair. He was about her size. He said, "I'll need some clothes." Celia handed him her cloak, but he let it drop into a puffy mound, which he compressed with one hand. Most of the air seemed to go out of his body, too, and he said, "A man's clothes. I seen some of your servants wearing nice coats." Celia puffed herself up like a hen and said, "This Family does not believe in servants. We never kept slaves. You are among the Shakers." The Man laughed. "Hope you gonna tell me all about the great deeds you done for me. You and crazy ole Mr. Lincoln." Celia said, "*President* Lincoln," but even to her this sounded pious and fatuous. Whose president had he been? Neither Negroes nor women had the vote, and Shaker Brothers refused to exercise the privilege. Still, Celia had met the Shakers who'd met Lincoln. And it was Lincoln who conferred on the Shakers their status as the nation's first tax-paying community of pacifists. She said, "Abraham Lincoln was crazy?" The Man snorted and said, "You ever seen that hat he had? His crazy excuse for a beard? Yain't never heard stories about his wife?" He grabbed her crumpled cape and swirled it around his shoulders. He stood up. The cape suited his hortatory tone. "Mr. Lincoln means the world to me. But in this world, takes a crazy man to marry a crazy woman. Only a crazy man thinks he can free the slaves by saying so. Stupidest Negro in Mississippi knows they kill you for saying such. You talk freedom, and they put you down. Like they put down Mr. Lincoln." He strode to the door, but the light of day seemed to repel him. "Don't give me Mr. Lincoln. I ain't crazy. I can't live with Mr. Lincoln." And Sister Celia understood: Mr. Lincoln dead meant the World. She said, "You are safe among the Shakers." He wasn't listening. He kicked aside a balled-up white shirt that was stiffened with blood. His brown trousers were hanging from a wooden brace; one pant leg had been shorn. She said, "We make clothing." But the second bell— Breakfast!—bonged, and barn doors slammed, rakes clanged as they were hung beside shovels and spades, and the cistern pump sucked water to the washrooms. The Man slumped down on his side. Was he asleep? The black cape slipped off his shoulder. Celia could not see his back when she bent toward him, but she grabbed his clotted shirt. He grabbed her wrist. "I'm tired. I trust you." She dropped the shirt. Tiny delicate scabs stuck to her hand. He said, "Nobody else saw me, right?" He closed his eyes, and nearing sleep he recalled a handsome man, his serene and optimistic self. He must have heard her getting up to go, because he said, "Don't tell them you saw me." And Celia said, "I saw him again," almost as soon as she sat down at the eldress's long dining table. At the other end, the eldress sat with her fork and knife pitched greedily above a steaming plate of coddled eggs and brown bread. "When I sent for you, Sister Celia, I expected you would bring your breakfast from the Family dining room. We must eat." The eldress looked a little desperate. "The rye bread was made by the Swedes." She yelled, "Sister Constance!" When the young Sister backed in from the pantry with a loaf of bread in her hands, the eldress said, "Bring Sister Celia's plate from the dining room. And is that a fresh loaf? Sister's will be cold by now." The eldress received the hot bread as if it were a child. Constance returned with Celia's place setting and scooted away. The eldress stabbed a sharp knife into the loaf and slid one half toward Celia. "Speak freely, Sister." She spooned out two heaps of butter and shot the crock down Celia's way. Celia was tempted by the food, but she was chastened by her memory of the hungry Man. "He wants clothing. And he is hungry," she said. The eldress had slathered some egg onto a hot slice of bread, added a dollop of butter, and folded the whole thing into her mouth. Celia was appalled. Urgently, she said, "The Man I saw at the window is in the coop." The eldress craned her neck, and like a bird with a fish, she muscled the mouthful down her throat. "They make terrible Shakers, those Swedes, but their bread is unassailable." She cut a second slice, and she did not look at Celia as she said, "I know my appetite appalls you, Sister. You are afraid to admit that you are hungry. You are even hungry in the presence of the Negro Jesus. Our bodies need food." Celia said, "But I spoke to him." The eldress said, "Yours is a remarkable Gift, such as we have not seen since the last revival. It brings hope to the Family, which is much in need of members. Now eat, Sister." She waved her hand impatiently. Celia said, "You do not understand." The eldress said, "It is you who misunderstand, Sister." She was still waving. "Send back the butter to me." Celia wondered if the eldress had finally gone dotty; there was no time for seconds. "Sister Celia," said the eldress, as she got up and grabbed the butter, "it is breakfast time. We are Shakers. The Gift is yours, and it will come to me and to the others as you pray and sow and bake and dance among us. Now, eat." Celia obeyed. The eggs were smooth and sweet as custard, and twice the eldress had to call on Constance to replenish their supply. But Celia would not eat the bread baked by the Swedes; she resented their tenancy in the dilapidated Dwelling where the West Family had once resided. The eldress ate Celia's share, and she repeated what Ethel had told the Family—that she had stood outside the coop and heard Celia speaking to the Negro Jesus in Sanskrit. When Celia said the words they'd used were English, the Eldress nodded and said, "Sister Ethel was deeply impressed by that bald Hindoo Swami Ravidranathan who stayed with us last summer.

She has been eager for a Tantric Gift. And at Ethel's age—oh, our age, really—one's hearing is not perfect." The eldress untied her bonnet, and Celia saw her rosy scalp beneath a fragile web of white hair. It was time. Celia remembered that she had walked with the eldress the night after her mother left her at the village, when she was afraid the Shakers might make her leave. She had asked if she could wear the eldress's bonnet. It fit her like a frying pan. But before she gave it back, she asked to touch the eldress's hair. She was relieved to know that it was real—that is, it reminded Celia of her mother's hair. And now Celia thought again of her mother and wondered if she was still alive and whether time had spared her beautiful hair. Breakfast was done, and the eldress finally let Celia lead her to the coop. As they passed the swaggering cows in the barnyard, Celia worried that the man might have run. Would his impression remain in the hay where he had slept? But the eldress suddenly stopped. She took Celia's hand and whispered, "Is it he, Sister?" Celia saw the caped figure in the distant pen. As they approached, he retreated inside. The eldress made Celia wait at the gate, and she went in alone. It was quiet, and then the eldress emerged, smiling and shaking her head. "The Negro Jesus will reveal himself as he will. Presently, it is only Brother Richard and the hens inside. After his work all night in the orchard, Richard rinsed the dirt from his clothes while he bathed, and now he is waiting for them to dry. Come, Celia, we have our work to do. There is a Canadian man who is interested in purchasing some of our land. His name is Mr. Goodrich. You must take pains to instruct him in its value. He is wealthy, and his initial offer was far less than we require." Celia watched Richard step into the sunlight. He pulled the cape around him, but it was too meager to cover his chest, and it did not even reach his knees. It was Celia's cape, which she had left with the Man. She recognized the shirt, too, as Richard draped it over the fence. It belonged to the Man. She wished the eldress would wait and watch Richard try to stuff himself into the wet rag, which was about half as much shirt as he needed, but the eldress had started up the road, and she was urging Celia on to the sad business of selling more land. For the rest of the day, Celia spoke to no one of the Negro Jesus. She tried and failed to understand why Richard had not confided his full knowledge of the Man when they met in the orchard. He had said, *You will have to say you saw nothing or else admit it is a Gift.* Celia understood now: this is what the Man had told her, too. *Don't tell anyone you saw me.* Why? Richard had warned her that no one would believe she'd seen a man at the window. And the eldress and Sister Ethel had proved him correct. Maybe Sister Ethel was right; it was all Hindu. The only simple truth was that the truth was simply a riddle. Celia led Mr. Goodrich across the fallow West Family fields. He asked about the acreage, but he wasn't interested in the hybrid Shaker clover underfoot. It was incense to Celia, bitter and sweet, like crushed hopes. Finally, Mr. Goodrich planted himself in the shade of the mulberry grove, and Celia told him it had been the center of the Shaker silk industry. "It was trying work, and not economical. Our cloth was too fine." Mr. Goodrich fished his shirttails from his trousers and wiped his pink face, exposing the generous white drapery of his belly. He was panting, and his tall, sad daughter appeared from under a tree and fanned him with his broad-brimmed leather hat until he grabbed her skinny forearm and said, "Leave off now." Celia did not like him, but she reminded herself that he was a Canadian, and perhaps this explained his vastness, his gray ponytail, and his habit of referring to "the Sursters" as Catholic nuns. His daughter, Rhea, wore clothes made of hemp and unbleached cotton stitched with string. When Mr. Goodrich introduced her, he called her his child bride and giggled, and Rhea stood on her toes and pointed her face to the sky and looked like a just-sheared sheep rearing up in confused humiliation. "Need yer land fer reasons of my own. Aim not ta fool yers. Ain't no silk trader. Ya can have all yer worms. Trees'll be mine, though, less ya root em up soon." He turned around slowly. "I wonder bout the buildins, though. If instead of a rentin arrangement, we could work out a price." As much as Celia resented his proprietary stare, his way of extending his fat arms as if he owned the very breeze, she was pleased to think Mr. Goodrich might displace the Swedes. "Guess I oughta have a tetter-tet with Muther Surperior bout the chance of buyin the buildins." Celia said, "You will find her in the deacon's office after dinner this evening." But Celia found her first, at the deacon's desk, which was the eldress's desk now that the Family was not so numerous. The first official acknowledgment of the decline of Pleasant Hill had come after Elder Frederick died on the second day of his ninety-third year. A new elder was not appointed; instead, the eldress assumed the spiritual duties of the elder. The Godhead's male and female principles, the twoness of Jesus and Mother Ann Lee, were thereafter represented by a single Shaker. Later, the Order of Deacons, the man and woman who tended to the community's temporal needs, was likewise unsexed and halved, and then it, too, was folded into the role of Eldress Anna. The Pleasant Hill Shakers were fewer than fifty strong. Celia could see they were not sufficient to their tasks. They had more buildings than Believers. When she'd arrived at age eight, the limestone Dwelling was reserved for the Church Family, and the West Family buildings were full of Shakers, not Swedes, and Celia shared a bedroom with the Bulgarian girls in the spare white wooden home of the East Family, where all the recently gathered Believers learned the Shaker way. The East Family had represented the dawn of the Shaker day to come. But for thirty years, that dawn had stalled, and now the sun seemed to be receding, and the Bulgarian girls had married two miners when they were fourteen, and the East Family properties were empty and dark. Finally, the eldress looked up from her ledger and said, "The Canadian child will sleep with you tonight." Celia was pleased; this was a logical explanation for her move to a strange bedroom. But the eldress added, "I do not mean to burden you, Sister. I know you are carrying the hopes of the whole Family today." Celia knew exactly what this meant. She had understood it at dinner when Sister Louise pressed her thigh confidentially, acknowledging Celia's overdue Gift, and Emma stared from another table, as if Celia had been transfigured and might levitate at any moment. Brother Joseph had said Grace right over her head, and the others sent cryptic, congratulatory signals Celia's way: there were half-salutes and reverential nods; glasses were tipped and napkins were waved; and shy Sister Mary Irene winked and blinked madly until Celia finally left the room to spare them both a bout of dizziness, which certainly would have looked like another Gift. The eldress put away her pen, and she led Celia out through the Visitors' Store with a lantern until they reached the doorway, where they were moonlit, and the eldress hung the lamp on a peg and led Celia toward the old West Family land that was soon to be sold. As was their habit, the Swedes had left every window open even while the powerful Shaker stoves spewed forth sweet hardwood heat into rooms—occupied and un— that were bright with both electric light and lanterns. When they were under the cover of the mulberries, the eldress leaned against a tree, and Celia marveled at the ease with which she lowered herself to the lawn. Was time kinder to the Shakers? It stole and silvered their hair, but it did not seize their joints or stupefy them. They lived longer than the World's people. Was it the work they had to do? Or was it the vinegar and verbena tea? Rather too late, Celia said, "The grass will be wet." The eldress said, "As it is every spring night. But it is warm. No frost tonight." Celia understood: the future is available to us. The eldress asked if Celia remembered a time at Pleasant Hill before the Swedes. But they had come before she had. The eldress said, "Yea. It was just after the war. Our means were meager. The soldiers were all dead—the soldiers we had nursed and fed, as well as those who stole our horses, tore down our fences for their fires, tramped down several years of harvests, and broke almost every window more than once to protest the Brothers' nonparticipation. We needed help with the rebuilding, the restoring, and the rejuvenation of our lives. We had been corresponding with a small band of Believers in Sweden for several years, and what little money we could send them was not enough to get them settled into new homes where they might be spared the persecution they suffered daily from their Christian neighbors. It was evident to us, and to the Central Ministry up north in Lebanon, that those hardy, fledgling Shakers in the hinterlands of Scandinavia were a spiritual and temporal Gift waiting to be received here, at Pleasant Hill, where they could live and work among the Family. I was the only obstacle to their arrival. I took my time. I had another hope. I hoped the freedmen from the South would come to join us in Kentucky, where their brothers and their children had always had a home. I expected we would have to build new Dwellings to accommodate the thousands of Negroes who had heard something of the Shaker Gospel and our practice of equality. I waited, but in time, the Negroes went north, past Pleasant Hill, and I knew then that we Shakers had not impressed them. We were a hundred years ahead of abolition. Do you suppose that made us seem old-fashioned? We had telephones before Philadelphians, and our streets were lit with electricity while Chicago still relied on gas, so why did no one see a future with the Shakers?" Celia said, "No one but the Swedes." The eldress stared intently at Celia, and then she giggled. "You know what I am thinking, don't you, Sister?" Celia said, "Yes. Were it not for their bread . . ." The eldress was delighted. "You understand, then. Your Gift is overdue. The Shakers need the Negro Jesus. We cannot leave the World as it is." Celia might have disavowed any connection to the Negro Jesus, but just then she saw the Man. He was standing fifty yards away on the stoop of the Swedes' kitchen door. In the prodigal yellow lamplight, he looked like a statue of himself, and he was robed in Richard's capacious shirt and trousers. He saw Celia. Her body registered his gaze like a touch, and she drew in her legs, readying herself to run. The eldress stiffened. "Is He here, Sister?" The Man lifted his arms. He was holding a big loaf of Swedish rye in either hand. The stolen bread looked like men's heads. Celia whispered, "He is near, Mother," and she realized that the fig-

ure framed in light, with arms outstretched, was a folk painting
of the crucified Christ, with a criminal hanging at his right and
his left. The eldress raised herself to her knees and leaned in
close to Celia when she said, "Will he speak?" Then she tipped
right over into Celia's lap, and though she stood up quickly and
smoothed her cape before Celia could help her, the Man was
gone. The eldress seemed to blame his disappearance on her
own clumsiness, and she walked away. Celia wanted to know
why the Man had not left the village. What did he want from
her? What was Richard's role in his appearance? She did not
press herself for answers; for now, her questions were hawks
circling in the sky above her, circling even as she draped a
nightgown over her naked body in the dark bedroom on the
third floor of the Dwelling, and Rhea said, "Howsit everthins so
purty here?" The child was almost invisible in her cot. Celia
walked to the stove and lit a candle, and she said, "This way we
can see each other." And Celia could see that the room was
purty because it was definite, and from the floorboards to the
ladder-back chairs that were hung on pegs near Rhea's dress
and underthings to the chair rail, which ran the length of every
wall and traced the outline of the door and window frames, the
room's geometry was emphatic. And geometry is the language
of reliable space. Celia carried the candle toward the center of
the room, and Rhea scooted beneath her blanket, trying to hide
herself, because she knew Celia had seen what she was wearing. Celia had seen her mother's green organdy gown, evidence
of a material mother, the one who went away. Celia managed
to say, "You are very, very pretty." Rhea stayed low, but the fullness of the dress puffed up the blanket like a popover. "Jes
makin bulieve. Din't tend on stealin em. They wuz upstars. I

wuz alone and went war I oughtn've. They yer dresses?" Celia
could not remember the song her mother sang in the green
dress, so she said, "Will you stand up, Rhea, and let us have a
good look at you?" Rhea obliged. She tried to make some sense
of the abundant old gown, twisting the sleeves and fussing with
a thirty-year-old fold that stuck out like a fin from one side. "It
don't always fit jes so." Celia tried to be of some help until she
realized that Rhea's modesty—or maybe it was just desperation—had caused her to put the dress on backward. She turned
away, to hide her laughter, and she carried the candle to the
window. "Thuthers is under the bed." Rhea ducked down to get
the case. Celia composed herself and turned around. Standing
beside the huge old suitcase, fixed in the pale light, Rhea
looked like an illustration in a children's book, like a runaway
princess. Celia asked Rhea what the dresses made her believe.
Rhea was embarrassed. She said, "Jes nuthin," and slapped her
fin. Celia said, "It might spoil it if you tell. Keep it to yourself.
And you keep those dresses, Rhea." *The dresses are a Gift.* Rhea
sprinted to Celia and grabbed her waist, weeping with relief
and gratitude. Celia picked her up, and Rhea bent her knees
and folded her arms obligingly, like a baby, and she closed her
eyes as Celia laid her down on the cot. She waited a few minutes, and then she said, "Yer a Shaker, ain't ya, Surster?" Celia
said she was. "Yer lucky." Celia smiled, but she wanted Rhea to
explain her good luck. Rhea was flabbergasted. She said, "Yer
here, ain't ya? It's so purty and there's hot food and pies. Poppa
sez it's zactly like heaven cept ain't none of yuz dead." And my
father, who also wasn't exactly dead, had told me no more of
Celia's story before I left him alone in my house. I missed him,
and I liked the feeling, because I knew it could be remedied,

like a hunger roused by the aroma of a turkey in the oven. I missed Paul Pryor, too, but the only man in sight had taken up a dark seat on a bench in the Cambridge Common about an hour earlier and stayed while I told myself the story of the Kentucky Shakers, the southern branch of my twisted Family tree. I turned on the kitchen light, and I was surprised to see the hands of Paul's clock approaching the midnight mark. I turned out the light, but before I left, I looked down at my polite friend on the bench. He was gone. End of that story. As the elevator slammed me down on the first floor, I regretted my failure to leave a note establishing my presence in Paul's place, which he would certainly doubt. The door cranked open, and there stood Paul. We were both surprised, but his reflexes were better. He said, "Visiting a friend?" His dark eyes were ringed with too little sleep, and I must have looked terrible, too, because he said something about the grim fluorescence in the entry hall, and he walked me out to the dark street, where we could remember each other's faces fondly. We walked around the park and veered off into Harvard Yard, and it wasn't until we'd walked half a mile north, past my car, that we got around to figuring out that it had been Paul on the bench in the Cambridge Common, wishing I was in his dark apartment, where I was, wondering where he was. We didn't say so, but we both knew it was typical of us, and it made us sad. We weren't young anymore, and Paul was a little older than that, and whatever we were waiting for was awfully late. We'd known each other for ten years, and when I first saw him I knew . . . well, I knew then everything I knew and did not say as we wandered back toward my car. Paul said, "So pick up your phone next time I call." I said he'd have to leave a message, like everyone else. I optimistically attributed one-third of my hang-ups to him. We both leaned on the car. We were the same height, and we tended not to say most of the things that occurred to us, so there were long silences, all of which made moments like this seem romantic. But Paul sounded sad when he said, "If your phone policy isn't negotiable, maybe we should say good-bye now. I got that job at the NIH. I'm moving to D.C. in August." I got into my car and grabbed the steering wheel. It wasn't petulance. I felt queasy, and I knew I'd sober up if I could make myself envision the long drive home. He squatted beside me and put his hand on my head. I knew his face so well that I'd come to believe it belonged to me, as if I'd let him have it as a loaner with the understanding that it was mine when I needed it. He said, "I think it would be a lot easier to leave you if we'd ever figured out how to live together." I responded by telling him that my father was not dead. This probably *was* petulance; I wanted us to be even, shock for shock. He said, "How do you know he's not dead?" I told him to drop by on Saturday. Then I pulled away. And all the way to Ipswich, I worried that my father would be gone when I got home.

SPELLING TIP
The only rule we remember

For reasons unrelated to logic, our introduction to spelling comes in the form of a memorable rhyme about the middle of words: *i* before *e* (bel**ie**ve), except after *c* (de**ce**ive), or when sounding like "ay," as in n**ei**ghbor and w**ei**gh. This is what most people mean when they exhort students to learn the fundamentals of spelling. What they don't mention, and perhaps do not know, is that this rule, like all so-called fundamental truths, is riddled with exceptions. If you were lucky, you might have run into a politically insensitive teacher who taught you a sentence that identifies some of the words that do not conform to the rule. It goes like this: The weird foreigner neither seizes leisure nor forfeits height. These are exceptions because they neither involve a c nor sound like "ay," and yet the e comes before i. All forms of these words are exceptional, such as either, seizure, and forfeiture. The sentence has the xenophobic problem of that "weird foreigner," but we can console ourselves by supposing that the "foreigner is weird" because he does not conform to the stereotype; he is not lazy (he does not "seize leisure") and "neither" is he short (he does not "forfeit height"). Still, the problem with exceptions is that we often forget why they are exceptional. So, yet another trick is needed. Remember that we are weird, and you might remember that in all exceptions, the e precedes the i. So much for simple truths and basic skills and other forms of fundamentalism, right? And there is yet another basic problem with the "i before e" rule we memorized. As surely as science fouls up Creationism, it also offends the "except after c" business; we spell science with an i before the e even though it does come after c. In fact, none of the sci (knowledge) roots are covered by the rhyming rule; therefore, our so-called basic skills must be extended to include conscientiousness and prescience.

the other side

THERE ARE NO mirrors in my dreams. When I appear as a character, I am faceless. In some dreams, I am present only as a camera, and sometimes, I am not a presence of any kind but a viewer, an audience of one. I believe in my dreams. I don't think they are foretellings of my future, because I am chronically unprepared for the events of my life. I know it is popular to treat dreams as reiterations of the past; dream analysis is based on an idea of dreamers as short-order cooks who work the night shift, scrambling all the eggs they laid during the day and trying to digest them. But my nighttime menu is assembled from exotic ingredients I never encounter in real time. The only real similarity between my life and my dreams is that they are typically forgettable, and even when I remember a sequence or an image, it never quite makes sense to anyone else. I think I am dead when I dream, or living in a fullness of time that does not respect my limited, linear ideas about the past, present, and future. That's why I am not reflected in my dreams; I am only present in the impressions of other people who anticipate and recall me. The great solace of a dream life is the experience it offers of the world without us, which is the only way to believe in a world without end. Before I fell asleep on Thursday night in Ipswich, I sneaked downstairs and stared at my father. He was not snoring, so my joy at having him in my house was unmitigated until I went up and listened to the one message left in my absence. It was a word picture from Ellen, and it made me sad to know he had heard it, heard his daughter's voice describing his dying wife's eyes, which had not opened for two days. It was easy to imagine him sitting on one of my kitchen stools, trying to get comfortable while Ellen spoke these words: "She is dreaming of Dad. I can see him on her face, which relaxed once she closed her eyes for good, as if she is no longer straining to bring things into focus. Her hands are tucked under her thighs today, too; she won't be needing them. The cello suites are not bringing tears. Wherever she is, she is beyond even Bach now, in a perfectly composed place whose harmonies need no rearranging. Greylock is green. Summer is here ahead of time. The maple leaves are already bigger than my hands." I'd also received an e-mail from my anonymous adviser. Because I'd just left Paul, it occurred to me that the jumble of buildings on Brookline Avenue that contained his office had recently sprouted a food-and-beverage mall, including Bits and Chips, a computer café with terminals built into the tables. Of course, this maze of hospitals and hospitalities was only a few blocks from McClintock, so this was hardly evidence of authorship. The message had been typed in the early afternoon. It went like this: "The law cannot teach a child to spell. If

Rashelle Whippet wins in court, how will schools respond? Teachers cannot be frightened into greatness. But administrators can be scared silly. Their schools are staffed by college graduates who don't know a fragment from a run-on, who cannot remember if the apostrophe goes before or after the *s*. The immediate effect of all litigation is compensatory. Rashelle will get a cash award; she will not receive the overdue gift of an education. And in the long run, we will expect less of our students and less of ourselves. That's how the law works; it establishes a standard for the least we can do. Most of America would fail your Competency Achievement Test. So, why should a little college in Boston squander its resources on no-tuition workshops in spelling and grammar while the rest of the country votes to cut tax payments to public schools so it can pay its cable TV bills? No, your test will have to go. It forces students to look at what they don't know. It reflects badly on them, and this adversely affects their self-esteem—that is, their self-regard. Our students are just young citizens, and they don't want to be chided with self-improvement. They want to watch TV. Our classrooms are now equipped with cable and CD-ROM and VCRs; it's the least we can do for them. Today, I feel sorry for you. You're broken. Like that fabled Mirror, Mirror, on the wall, you alerted students to the Sleeping Beauty in them all." The previous notes from my adviser had not prepared me for the melancholy tone of this one. I was not above accepting a little sympathy for my fate, but I didn't like to think I was broken. Although I still could not guess the identity of my secret adviser, I now knew that she or he was subject to dramatic mood swings. This was not much of a clue. I had come to believe bipolar illness affected everyone with a beating heart;

manic-depressed, awake-asleep, here-there, this-that, then-now, to be or not to be—human beings run on alternating current. Finally, I read an e-mail from Abel Nagen. He had checked his meticulous records and discovered that Rashelle Whippet had twice enrolled in his History of the Civil War and twice dropped out during the second week of classes, "which will infuriate Agatha and Marie, who would like nothing better than to see me in court." He was not among the faculty who would be sued for passing Rashelle. He figured, probably correctly, that Rashelle had dropped out of his class because of his syllabus test. Abel knew that students would not read the twelve- to fifteen-page tomes he handed out on the first day of every semester, so he gave them a multiple-choice test at the second class meeting that required memorization of his policies about late papers, class participation, and grading. This did seem to spare him midsemester questions like "Are you gonna count our grades on this test?" It also kept several community colleges in business; about half of all McClintock students fulfilled their American history requirement with summer school courses like the American Experience: Hollywood Presents the Past, or Cowgirls: The Unkept Journals of Working Women. When I finally went to bed, I intended to make myself miserable by dwelling on Paul's job news, but I fell asleep. No matter how old I get, I do not get insomnia, that noble disease that plagues most of my smart friends. It's embarrassing that my life isn't worth losing any sleep over. My father must've known I'd got in late, because Friday morning's porch breakfast was nonperishable. He gave me a bowl of something he called "wheat berry crunch," a granola he'd made. It tasted of honey and fruit, and except for a few big jawbreakers at the bottom, it had the consistency of perfect toast. He was in a good mood, and he credited my house, which he liked because it "represented a challenge." For thirty-five years, he'd made his home at Sabbathday Lake, down the road from the Shaker Village. He refused to admit he was a Shaker. According to him, the Shakers closed their Covenant in 1965, about the time hippies started to stream into Maine and New Hampshire from points west. The Family's decision to admit no new members to the Covenant caused bad feelings between the Sisters at Canterbury in New Hampshire, who'd devised the strategy as a way of protecting the assets in the considerable Shaker Trust, and the Sisters in Maine, who saw some cause for hope among the junkies and draft dodgers drifting their way. After many years of ill will, the last of the Covenanted Sisters left Maine to die in Canterbury. On any given day, Sabbathday Lake was now home to as few as six and as many as thirty "fake Shakers" (my father's words), who served as tour guides, dressed in clothes no Shakers had worn for a hundred years, and worked alongside tenant farmers and a few local weavers and canners who labeled their goods "Shaker Quality" or "Still Made in the Shaker Way." And even though Sabbathday Lake had always been the least prosperous Shaker Village, with the rockiest fields and the worst winters, the challenge of laying out gardens and deciding what ought to be grown where had been accomplished long before my father got there. In Ipswich, he saw much room for improvement. He had ordered tomato plants from a local nursery, and despite their warnings about the dangers of starting so late in the season, he wanted me to help him dig up half my lawn and prepare a "proper garden, or the start of something more useful than a few poppies and some crabgrass." I directed his attention to a healthy stand of crocosmia, whose leaves were flat blades that would reach five feet before the red and yellow trumpet flowers appeared and attracted hummingbirds to the perimeter of my porch. I was proud of these flowers, which looked like freesia and required a thick winter mulch. My father said, "You want to eat those with your spaghetti in November?" He had already cordoned off a patch of sunny grass for our labors, and we dug, side by side. He did not mention Ellen's word picture, but after a while he asked me if I knew why my mother had staged his death in 1982. I started to explain the letter she'd sent with the details, and it wasn't until I'd finished that he remembered he had received a copy of that letter with a note from my mother that said, "F.Y.I." He did remember what had prompted her murder-by-mail scheme, and he began to explain their odd habit of reciting the Rosary on the telephone, but I interrupted to let him know I'd heard all about it from Ellen, who'd got it from Tommy. In a few curt sentences he explained the rest. Sister Ruth died in 1982 at Canterbury, and on the night after her body was buried, he called my mother, as was still his nightly habit. Before they began their prayers, he said, "After more than forty years of two calls a night, one to the Shakers and one to the stucco house, now it is only you, Nora." Of course, since 1942, my mother had believed their phone affair was monogamous. He said he got halfway through the first decade of the Rosary before he realized the line was dead. When he called the next night, he got Tommy, who didn't recognize his voice but said, "My mother won't be able to speak to you. She found out last night that her husband, my father, is dead." He said Tommy started to cry at that point, and he heard my mother saying something to com-

fort her son, and it was the last he heard from her. In the letter
she composed for her children and the few friends who still
asked after my father, my mother blamed his death on an
aneurysm, and she mentioned that his head had exploded "like
a water balloon apparently, God help him." And it seemed for a
while that my father and I might not have anything else to say
to each other; maybe our summary knowledge of the stories of
our lives was sufficient to the brief future we could foresee.
But when he needed a respite from digging, he leaned on his
shovel and asked me if Ellen still taught history. I told him
she'd retired from the classroom in 1969. He smiled knowingly,
and he said, "To protest the war, I suppose. Didn't want to be
passing on a lot of lies about the glorious American past." This
pompous and absurdly inaccurate assessment revealed so many
unpleasant facts about both of us that I just went on digging his
damned hole. I was indignant that he would presume to understand anything about his children, least of all Ellen, whose
birth he hadn't bothered to attend. I was amused, in my snide
way, by his groovy political sentiments; even while the rest of
his joints were seizing up, his reflexive, knee-jerk liberalism
was operating like a well-primed pump. And most of all, I was
appalled by his detachment from it all. He spoke of the First
Family as he spoke of the Shakers in Sabbathday Lake, as if he
understood them better than they understood themselves. In
his estimation, everything was ersatz, inauthentic—my garden,
American history, his marriage, the Shaker museums, the
Catholic church, boxed cereal, and even his own best book of
photographs. I believed more than ever in the utter truth of his
death in 1982. I did not doubt that the force of my mother's
will had been enough to keep him alive, if only just, for forty-

odd years. I know my mother had loved him, even after he left the second time. But she made her children love him, too, and I was not grateful for this gift. She had whittled away at her own heart until there was nothing left of it but a string of ebony beads that were no bigger than grape seeds. She could put her rosary away when she'd had enough of him. But my brother and sisters and I had regular human hearts, which did not come with zippered carrying cases that could be stuck in a dresser drawer. The news of his death was not real news for any of us; it was just a refresher course, a review of what we'd lost. And as I dug into the earth beneath us, I wished he wasn't with me. I wished he was not there to watch over me with his tender, affectionate, proud gaze. I wished my heart had not survived so many disappointments. It made me susceptible to him. It made me happy to know he was not dead. It made me make a mess of my backyard on his behalf. My brain was of no practical use in the matter. It did nothing but manufacture complaints about my sore shoulders, the heat, and how unfair the World was, that even Thomas Sternum, bad father extraordinaire, should still have the power to cast a spell, a natural enchantment, and thereby bind himself to his otherwise unfettered son. When the forty tomato plants were in the ground, my father cut them to within an inch of their lives, which he claimed was what they wanted. For dinner, we had green beans he'd pickled in soy sauce and lemon, and a vat of scalloped potatoes with a thick cheesy crust. "Sister Louise's recipe," he said, tipping a bottle of Jim Beam toward a glass. He opened a fresh bottle of wine for me, and we went down to the porch, where I could smoke without killing him, and despite myself, I admired the new vegetable patch. My father said, "Given your habits, it might have been more economical to plant tobacco. Of course Shakers, even we latter-day, make-believe Shakers, don't indulge." I lit a second cigarette. He said, "Of course, we have a history of tolerance." Then he told me that Mr. Goodrich, the Canadian, had finally paid ten thousand 1903 dollars for the old West Family farm, which was less than the eldress wanted but more than she'd expected, so everyone was marginally satisfied. He intended to grow tobacco, and Celia was surprised the eldress would tolerate the cultivation of the prohibited weed on Shaker soil. "Yea, Sister," the eldress said. "But rest assured. The Pleasant Hill Shakers will suffer no temptation from his crop. He has agreed to hire the Swedes as farmhands, who cannot grow a lily in a pond, so I suspect Mr. Goodrich's harvest will be too meager to fill a gentleman's pipe." This worried Celia, especially on Rhea's behalf, and she asked the eldress if it wouldn't be right to warn him about the Swedes. But the eldress was more philosophically—and economically— minded. "This is tilled land without rock, cleared and leveled by the Brothers. The price is fair. This very month," the eldress said, "I committed twelve thousand dollars to growers throughout the county that we might have fruit enough to fulfill standing orders for Shaker jellies and jams. Our profit is small on fruit we do not grow, but we have not the hands. After a few failures with his tobacco, Mr. Goodrich will grow oats and hay, crops we Shakers need for our animals, and his proximity will serve us then, as his price will not be inflated with transport costs. But that he is so enslaved to his chew—Sister Louise saw him spit into his own hand while he was waiting to be served his lunch—we would all be spared the folly of tobacco from the start." And so Celia was silent as she watched the two

Canadians board the train that stopped just across the Kentucky River. Rhea said she was "some kinda sad" to leave, and Celia kept an eye on them until the train was no bigger than a bird. Then Sister Colleen swooped by and landed at Celia's side. She bowed and whispered, "I must confess, Sister." Celia spun around. Colleen's tiny face was pink, and her pug nose was puffy. "I know you moved from our bedroom because I tried to touch you too often." It was true that Colleen was unduly solicitous, always offering to comb Celia's hair or pin the hem of a new cape, but Celia would not have made an accusation of it all. Had she underestimated Colleen's affection? Celia said, "It is nothing, Sister." But this made Colleen furious, and she slapped her thighs. "I must confess. You must intercede on my behalf with the Negro Jesus." Celia didn't say he was too busy stealing from the Swedes to offer any consolation, but she noticed that Colleen's neck was changing colors. "Be careful," she said. "Be calm, Colleen. Your hives are coming, and quickly." Colleen pressed the skin above her collar and released a scarlet tide. She scratched behind one ear. She rubbed her chin. Each touch raised an island of tiny purple welts. Her neck was swelling. Colleen said, "I will make a better confession at Meeting this week." Celia hoped not, but she said, "Go, Sister, with haste," and she watched Colleen sprint up the road. The Dwelling House was better than any destination you could reach by train. Colleen would find water boiling in the kitchen and a prepared poultice in the infirmary. The Sisters would warn her off dairy for a while, and they would serve her oats sweetened with cherry preserves instead of eggs. The eldress would urge her to lie down for the afternoon. Sister Frederika would replace her bedsheets with iced linens. Sister

Emma would arrive with mint tea and a steaming bowl of aromatics. The community was compensatory, especially when its individuals were not. Sister Louise must have watched the whole episode, because when Celia finally saw her up the road, Louise looked a little exasperated and hollered, "Walk with me, Sister." She was a big solid block of a woman, and she set out with speed. Louise said her energy was "God-given gusto," and she exhorted other Shakers to seek it instead of the fancier Gifts like Tongues. She was undiminished by her age, which was the same as the eldress's, and she fueled herself constantly. Today, she had raisins, and then she pulled a potato from her pocket, which she offered to Celia after taking a first snap at it. "Fresh as the day we dug it." When Celia declined, Louise said, "Yet you will eat meat when it is offered." Louise had been inspired by Sylvester Graham, who had come to Pleasant Hill when she was a child. Her dietary law was "Never consume a food you would not eat as your breakfast." This ruled out cooked meats, complicated stews, and salted items. Her amazing appetite made her an innovative preserver of fruits and vegetables, and thanks to her experimentation, the Kentucky Shakers enjoyed mushrooms, tomatoes, apples, cherries, and other seasonal treats throughout the year. She had a profound devotion to the sweet Vidalia onion and all varieties of the potato. In March and April, she traveled to the other villages to help the other Families select the best potato slips for planting. Celia said, "Sister Colleen accosted me to confess her affections." She stopped, hoping this would slow Louise down, but it did not. Louise yelled back, "Colleen misses you. She is unsettled by what happened to you. As we all are." She paused to let Celia catch up. "Even I dreamed of you last night. Don't you see, Celia? If you have gone ecstatic, where does that leave the rest of us? You were moved. The last Shaker in Kentucky has seen—" Celia said, "It was not the Negro Jesus. I saw a man. I have spoken to him since. I can offer no proof. But I know Brother Richard has spoken to him, as well." Louise finished her potato and she said, "A man has a soul. A man is a spiritual event. It has meaning. Why did no one else see this man, Sister? You of all of us, who have always been unmoved, marooned between the Shakers and the World. Now you are ahead of us. You turned and saw something. Don't you see? It is time. We Shakers are not able to sustain our separate lives. We cannot grow the food we need. We must learn to approach the World." Celia said, "It was prophesied long ago that our numbers would dwindle to two or three before the next revival swept the World." Louise laughed. "I suspect that prophecy will be of comfort to all but the last of us." Then she picked up a chip of white rock and tossed it up the road. "There is nothing to fear. We know what is ahead. When we reach the stone, we will die or we will not. We know this." Louise set off with renewed energy. Celia was tired, and she sounded pouty when she said, "I prefer to believe we will survive the rock in the road." Louise stopped and put her hands on her hips. "You *prefer* to believe? Your preferences are immaterial." Then she stepped on the stone and kicked it Celia's way. "I will die first. Or you will die first. Or we will go together. It has always been so." Celia stuck her hands on her own hips, mocking Louise. "Well, if given the vote, I will elect to go together." Louise bent over and yelled, "Ha! Such a vote would be truly universal suffrage. But we are forgetting our stone." Celia looked to the road. It was dense with indifferent gray and white chips impacted in the powdery soil. Louise walked directly to a ladder that was pitched against the roof of the East Family front porch, and she climbed it. At the top, she crawled out to the edge and sat with her long legs and skirts dangling like an old leafy vine. Celia was impressed. And a little nervous. She climbed the ladder reluctantly, one more ordeal in an annoying week. She sat beside Louise, and inevitably, Celia found herself looking in vaguely the same direction because looking, that still and silent task, is the lifework of each of us, our labor of love, and we do not want our companions to labor alone. From somewhere in the east, beyond the clovered field, from deep within the yellow pine wood, arrived the echo of excited animals. Hounds? Suddenly a slice of sky went black, and a vast arrowhead of birds shot out from the treetops and skimmed along the forest heights. Celia said, "Canada." Louise said, "Geese." But their words blew off in the breeze with the geese as a tiny child burst out of the dark stand of trees and ran into the bright green field, arms wagging and dark hair flopping, trailed by the black path she made as she sped toward the Sisters and—Crack! The child stopped, screeched, tipped forward, fell. The report of the gun boomed behind her. The shock jolted Celia backward and, without a word, Louise tumbled off the roof. Celia tried to hurry down the ladder, but it shuddered, and she slowed down until she was on the ground, and then she saw Louise on her side. She was colossal, and her bonnet had slipped back on her head, and the woven rim stuck up like a tiara. Stupefied, Celia yelled, "Are you dead?" And Louise said, "Is the child alive?" Celia tried to right Louise, but every time she touched her she elicited a yelp of agony, so she ran around the porch and out into the field. She heard a scream, but it was above her. She stopped. A single goose sped across the empty sky, crying. She spotted a darkness in the field, a slight depression, and when she reached it, she saw that the clover was matted with soil, but the child was gone. The nest had been plundered. She stared down the solitary trail into the woods, and she saw a man holding something on his shoulder. He threaded his way through the trunks until a shaft of light fell in from high above him, and in that bright moment he was gone. The gunfire had drawn Sisters from the Drying House and Brothers from their rows of tender seedlings. Soon the clover was teeming with Shakers. Brother Joseph conscripted the coats of the curious and tied them around the ladder to make a stretcher on which Louise was lifted and carried like Cleopatra to the infirmary. Celia threaded her fingers through the clover, searching for blood evidence, but her hands came up black. Her progress to the infirmary was slowed by questions: Was it a boy or a girl child? Black or white? Dead or alive? The eldress met her in the hallway and hugged her. "Oh, Celia, I am so pleased you were not hurt. Come with me. Louise is in no danger." Celia wept. Since she had seen the Man at the window, her every action, her very presence caused calamity. The eldress hooked her foot around the door of the infirmary and slammed it shut. From her bed, Louise bragged. "What a fall! Should've killed me. Where's the child, Celia?" Sister Frederika, who had ascertained that nothing was broken, backed away and looked to Celia for the answer. Celia said, "The child." The eldress stared at her, wanting more. Everything was unpleasantly still until Sister Emma arrived. She was carrying a tray of steaming vessels that stunk up the room. Frederika accepted her demotion from physician to laboratory assistant, and she performed her duties with grace, stirring and straining according to Emma's split-second prescriptions, procuring materials for the preparation of several large poultices, tucking and tying little packets and swatches of herbal cures all about Louise's pliable body and administering the potable doses with huge gobs of honey, a bait Louise could not resist, no matter how acrid the accompanying broth. Emma worked her magic furiously, madly sniffing and dashing from patient to tray, occasionally poking Louise and then prying the cork from another amber vial of pungent oil, as if the cure depended on a calibration of minute changes in the temperature and odor of the victim. Celia stood with the eldress by the window and said, "It is revolting." The eldress said, "It works. But if the county doctors witnessed this, Emma would be arrested. I am certain of that." Celia said, "Were she not a Shaker, Emma would be a witch." The eldress squeezed Celia's hand and whispered, "Nay, Sister. She is a witch. Were she not a Shaker, she would have spent her life brewing tea for her husband." Louise belched. Emma dropped her pestle and stared proudly at her patient. Frederika drew a large sheet over Louise's patched and bandaged body. Sister Louise had passed out, and she took the day down with her. Louise's long rest was a reprieve for the Family. Everyone sensed that the mystery of the child was related to the Negro Jesus. Some of them wandered through the woods, looking for answers. Several spent their social hour speculating on the next revelation. Many dreamed. Sister Celia sat on her strange bed and watched the clouds collect outside her window. And then my father's snoring started to bug me, so I led him to his bed, and I was sorry I'd missed my chance to tell him the real reason Ellen had quit teaching, but it was too late. It was too late even for me to know for sure why I felt so lonely as I climbed the stairs, shut off the lights in the kitchen, and then climbed up another set of stairs to my bedroom, where I was happy, if only for a moment, to see moonlight. I remembered soon enough: it was the spill of the streetlight. It was too late to call Rachel. I sat on my bed, like Sister Celia? I closed my eyes, like my mother? I hoped I didn't snore like my father. I had some other concerns, I'm sure, but none was nearer than sleep.

MECHANICS
Garden-variety clauses

The simple English sentence is just an independent clause. The complex English sentence is actually rather simple, too. It is either a combination of independent and dependent clauses or a series of two or more independents. That's the all of it. When mixing independents and dependents, follow a simple punctuation rule. If you start with a dependent clause, you use a comma. You need no comma when the dependent clause follows the independent. When you want to use two independent clauses, you cannot simply slap them together. For example, Thomas cut the tomatoes his son dug the hole is a run-on sentence. This does not mean you are running on too long; it means you lack coordination. Putting a comma between the two independent clauses is not much help. Thomas cut the tomatoes, his son dug the hole is a comma splice; you have tried and failed to splice together two independent things with a comma, which is not strong enough to bind them to each other. Most students' sentences fall apart because they can't make independent clauses work together. Don't be a klutz. It is easy to develop coordination. After you insert the comma, add a conjunction, (, and his son or , but his son). Of course, you could also make the son a dependent: Thomas cut the tomatoes after his patient son dug the hole. The father, too, might become dependent: Before Thomas cut the tomatoes, his son had to dig the whole hole. Finally, if you still don't like the way they're working together, separate them. They can survive on their own: Thomas mowed down the tomatoes. His son dug the damned hole. See? It didn't kill them.

m o d i f i c a t i o n s

THE FIRST NIGHT I slept in my house, I learned a lesson that I try to apply to all new situations. I was tired. I had lugged boxes all day. I was proud. The place was a wreck—its sills were rotten, the roof was a tar-paper sieve, the floors sloped away from the center beam at steep angles, and the so-called walls were really just bent studs and plaster dust wrapped in wallpaper bandages—but it was appealingly old, it cost less than a studio in Harvard Square, and it came with trees and a number of other scraggly things in the yard. As soon as I shut my eyes, something in the neighborhood banged. I waited, listened—nothing. I closed my eyes. Bang. The sequence was established. It was tiresome the second time, and it only got worse. I'd get up, look out the window, get back into bed. Bang. It was a door, swinging in the wind, and I'd noticed that all of my neighbors had doors, and some of them had three or four. I tried to listen carefully: Bang. Across the street? Bang. No, two doors down. Bang. It was impossible to establish the direction because the wind was unstable. Bang. Bang. I'd paid too much for the house. Bang. The neighbors were bums. Bang. I could hear my real-estate agent bragging to her friends about how she'd unloaded that little dump near the river on some dope from the city. Bang. I pulled on my jeans and went out to investigate. Nothing. I noticed a light in a bedroom across the street. Bang. Another light next door. Obviously, I was the butt of a practical joke. Bang. A light at the corner. They wanted to drive me out of the neighborhood. Bang. I walked right out into the middle of the road, made brazen by my sense of injustice. Bang. I saw the source. Bang. It was a wooden gate swinging on one hinge, just barely attached to a tumble-down fence I had recently purchased. Bang. It was my gate in my yard, and while I was trying to make the rusty latch work, I cracked the rotten wood and sprung the last hinge. I tossed the splintered mess to the ground. The neighbors applauded. Somebody yelled, "Don't worry. Our windows used to fall out." Then the other houses went dark, and I stared up at my bright bedroom. I could see it more clearly now, and it was surrounded by problems. Still, it looked promising. I had always known it would take a lot of work to make a home in the world, but that night I really bought it. Since then, I'd always slept well in my house. But on Saturday morning, the eighth of June, 1996, I realized I had outdone myself. I did not get out of bed when I awoke. It was ten o'clock, and I felt I had to invent an explanation for sleeping so long. My father wasn't exactly above reproach on any number of moral issues, but he was my father, and I didn't want him to think his youngest son was a slug. The house smelled of corn bread and something greasy, like bacon or sausage, and I hoped he was in a mood to fry up some eggs. I never cook for myself, but I am very fond of food. If she promised to make eggs over easy and English muffins, I'd invite Oprah Winfrey to spend the night. She'd like my father. She's a collector of Shaker things, one of those antique pilgrims who know there is something irreplaceable and irreproducible about their spare tables and chairs. Shaker-made things are material evidence of perfectibility. This is not only an aesthetic ideal. We're made of material, too. We have to figure out how to make our lives. Isn't it odd that no one teaches us the Shaker way? They were Americans. They did not deconstruct their individual identities. They made themselves into communities. They did not respect race and ethnicity; they left all that behind, in the World, where it had been invented. They made Families of people whose pigmentation varied, like the infinite shades of the wood they worked. I am not pumping for a revival, but I am curious about our willful ignorance. I mean, children are taught Irish step dancing, origami, steel drumming, and the piccolo. Is there no time in the school year to mention that Americans lived in peaceful, prosperous, well-fed, architecturally ideal, egalitarian harmony for more than two hundred years? Wouldn't it be nice if instead of molded-plaster statuary and pinto-bean necklaces, the kids came home from school with a durable little stool or a decent loaf of bread? The Shakers are the inadmissible evidence of American history because they serve neither the prosecution nor the defense in any of the great partisan battles. They were Christians who sought the wisdom of the East. They were celibates who knew the earth was rife with natural contraceptives and abortifacients like squirting cucumber and birthwort. They became wealthy by cultivating trade routes along which they sold the first-ever packaged seeds, yet they did not patent their mechanical inventions because they believed progress was a Gift of time and, therefore, the rightful inheritance of all people. They refused to accept the tax-exempt status offered to them because they enjoyed the benefits of paved roads and reliable delivery of the mail, and they believed in rendering unto Caesar. They did not take up arms; in their hearts, like all people, they knew killing was wrong. It was expedient, but it was not the Shaker way. They practiced Family values; no woman was demeaned, no man disrespected, and no child was left in the care of strangers. If they are gone, and if we are tempted to think of their disappearance as the judgment of history, we should review the evidence. We have the chairs. We know what they left behind. Imagine what they took with them. I finally got out of bed. It was almost eleven, and I had no excuse, which may be the best reason of all to have someone living in your house who loves you. Unlike the scolding parent I'd imagined and unlike my own recriminatory conscience, my father was tickled by my lassitude. When I passed him in the kitchen on the way to the shower, he told me he'd slept until eight, and he congratulated me on my greater achievement. "I'll fry you up some eggs when you're ready to eat," he said. He was cooling the corn bread. "I'll be on the porch." As I shaved, I heard a radio announcer's voice, and my father responded occasionally, as if the news of the day was so interesting he just had to talk about it. My only telephone message was from Rachel, who said she might have to deliver something to a friend in Gloucester and would drop by if she did. I knew I was unprepared for guests. I had not formulated a plausible means of introducing my father into my life. But I

wanted people to meet him, to see him. I thought he might
clarify me, or at least fill in a few of the gaps in my character. I
thought of Ellen, and before I thought about the conse-
quences, I dialed the stucco house in Pittsfield. I got the machine. This was a slight disappointment, but I was in no
position to indulge that reaction. I was certain Tommy had told
Ellen every detail of his visit to Ipswich, but I repeated what
he'd said when I first saw his shadow in the doorway, about our
father being many years dead. I paused, and then I said I was
taking bets. I drank some juice and wondered who else I could
call. I wanted people around because I was happy, and the significance of this was not lost on me. I lived too much alone. I
was as far away from the First Family and the so-called Mc-
Clintock Family as I was from the Shaker Family. My friends
were arranged around me at various distances, and I looked to
them as I looked to the stars, hopefully, trying to see a coherent portrait, a constellation, but they were not the Pleiades or
the Ursas, major or minor. My friends and I were far-flung, unstable in our attachments to each other, and our movements
were not governed by the celestial laws. We looked like any
other American family. This momentary review of my solitary
existence probably should have depressed me, but the air was
still thick with the smell of breakfast, which is helium to the
spirit. I joined my father on the porch. He was in a wicker
rocker. He smiled, but he did not want to be interrupted just
yet. He was still tuned in to that radio show I'd heard from upstairs. I was a great fan of this particular show, too, though I
had forgotten it was scheduled for this Saturday morning. It
was Paul Pryor, Live from Ipswich. Paul said, "Which is the
only time I've ever seen him lose his temper." Then he saw me

and said, "Mark," and he stood up. And I hesitated, not noticeably, not for long, just enough time to choose a side in my lifelong debate about demonstrations of affection. In that hesitant instant, I considered my options—kiss/hug/pat on the shoulder/nod of the head/ironic smile/handshake/feign surprise and back away/Hi—and communicated my uncertainty to Paul, my assigned target. He didn't flinch. He shook my hand, and then he put his left hand on the back of my head and pulled me in for a kiss. It seemed unwise, just when my father and I had achieved some peace about all of his comings and goings, to complicate matters with a coming out. But the gesture was made; another volume of the Hidden History of the Sternum Family had been published. My father regarded us with true solemnity. After a while, he said, "I promised you eggs. And you'll get them. Over easy?" I said yes, and so did Paul. My father started to rock. He said, "I just wanted to sit here, though, the three of us, ya know?" He started to cry, and he rocked a little more, and said, "Just for a minute, just sit here with you." His cheeks were shiny with tears, and then he heaved out a big, sad breath and wiped his face with the back of his hands. He smiled at me, but there was something urgent about his gaze that I did not understand. He stood up and walked to the door. He leaned there, with his back to us, and then he turned around. He was crying again. Very quietly, he said, "I've been to D.C. a few times, Paul. The museums are quite good. But trust me—" His voice broke, but he managed to say, "Trust me, Paul. You will miss my son." He was exhorting us to love, to live as he had not. He looked miserable, and he groaned, and then he whispered, "Oh, God, you fools. Look at me," and my father, my father held out his old hands, begging me to embrace him.

And I didn't hesitate, and I haven't ever since because I saw
that like my father, I was never going to exceed my limits. He
could not reconstitute the past. I could not guarantee the future. We could grab each other, hold on to a moment, and live
in the fullness of time. If what we seek is eternity, immortality,
there is no use in waiting for the end of our lives. The end is
with us. You can see it—the grooved pads of your fingers, the
calloused skin at your heel, the end of you. Beyond our selves,
out there, we are something better. On the other side of the
corporeal border, outside the painted lines and surfaces that
compose our Worldly portraits, we are known and loved forever
by those whom we have touched. I did not know this until it
was impressed upon me by my father when he held me in the
doorway, on the threshold to my home. Paul lightly touched my
shoulder, then stood behind me, at attention. My father said,
"The eggs," and went upstairs. Paul relaxed enough to pour me
coffee. He looked around the room nervously. I understood.
Where did that leave us? I was unemployed, and unless I was
mistaken, his solo flight to D.C. had just been canceled. He
said, "There are some colleges in Washington. And Virginia." I
thought we should add Maryland to the list, but my knowledge
of mid-Atlantic geography was a little shaky, so I just nodded.
Then I remembered that I had an interview with Fred Hogworthy on Monday, about a job at Massachusetts Commonwealth University. Paul said, "I can't imagine you at MCU. I
mean, imagine having to admit you work for Nervy Derby." Apparently, I had a generous imagination. I could see it. But I said
it was just one of several places that had called after I'd been
lynched. Paul stared out through the screen. I could see he was
confused by the tomato patch, but he didn't ask about it. He

said, "Looks like your father's been busy." Paul looked good. His thinning dark hair curled up slightly at the collar of his shirt. His canvas hiking shorts were grayed from years of wear; another of his commendable personal habits—hanging onto clothing until the number or the size of the holes was immodest. Hiking and biking and other activities not enjoyed by anaerobes like me had made his legs thick and strong. I'd often seen him stand his ground in a violent storm tide while I was somersaulted back to shore. He had a slight paunch, too, an inestimable virtue in a well-made man, and a rare one in the last years of this century. He kept it up despite his balanced breakfasts, so-called lunches of yogurt and fruit, and those frozen dinners people buy based on what they do not contain. Because when Paul ate a cookie, he normally finished the box. And sometimes, in the middle of the night, he'd get up and have three ice cream sandwiches. He smelled so good when he did this that I'd think I wanted one, but I usually just smoked a few cigarettes while I rooted around in his cabinets and freezer, reading the awesomely detailed labels on his prepared foods. In culinary terms, we were a uniquely unpromising domestic partnership. I asked him if he could keep his job in Boston. He said, "Of course," but he immediately realized that this sounded like a boast, given my recent experience, so he added, "I'm sure the hospital would be happy to have me stay. Nobody wants to conduct a candidate search and spoil their summer. In fact, I could make a strong case against my going to the NIH. Fortunately, I don't have to bother. I'm having lunch with Peter Castle on Monday, the doctor who started this whole initiative to explore global standards of practice. He"—Beep!—"hired"—Beep!—"me"—Beep! Rachel had arrived.

Paul turned to me. "Castle thinks my going to the NIH is a step right off the cliff." We heard a car door slam. Rachel had found a place to park, and I could only hope it was not in a neighbor's daylilies. We heard her footsteps in the kitchen above us. Paul said, "We should go up." But we stayed on the porch. I left my father to fend for himself. He and Rachel would have to figure out how to insert him into my life. I asked Paul to tell me what he thought would happen to us. He sat down beside me, poured us both more coffee, and stirred in the right amount of milk. Because we both knew we were not really talking about jobs, we talked strictly about jobs. It was perfectly obvious that he would either keep his job or go to the NIH; I would work at MCU or some smaller version of it in Boston, or I would try to find a job within commuting distance of the Capitol. But we discussed the various options as if we were dealing with re-combinant DNA. Just when it seemed we had arrived at the end of the spiraling possibilities and would have to articulate the reasons we had spent ten years not living together, one of us had the wit to mention New York, and this led us on a tour of the world's greatest cities. We decided we did not want to live in Bangkok. Then Paul smiled slyly and said, "What about Pleasant Hill?" I asked Paul what time he'd arrived this morn-ing. "About eight-thirty. It was weird for a while with your fa-ther, because neither of us wanted to mention you. He talked about Kentucky." Most fathers carry pictures of their kids in their wallet; my father walked around with the Shakers on his sleeve. I wanted to know how much Paul knew and if he un-derstood what it all meant. For instance, was I Celia? Was I Brother Richard? Was Rachel Celia? Was Rashelle Whippet Celia? Was she the Negro Jesus? Paul said, "I don't think so," meaning "None of the above." He added, "I think Celia is Celia. Richard is Richard. The slave Master is the Master. And so on." The Master? The Master? I didn't think that title had persisted into our century. I suspected maybe Paul had heard a different story. I told him my story couldn't involve a Master because it happened in 1903. Paul looked honestly confused when he said, "Isn't that the point? I mean, isn't that what Celia didn't see?" Then breakfast arrived. Rachel and my father had made a feast: omelettes stuffed with soft cheese and roasted red peppers, and a platter of ripe tomatoes and basil. The corn bread was arranged like cake—two slabs sandwiched with strawberry jam. They had fresh coffee, too, and Rachel had stuck a bottle of water under her arm before she left the kitchen. She was wearing a broad-brimmed blue hat and several silk things the color of pearls. After she'd kissed me and hugged Paul, she laughed, and we all waited for her to explain. She never missed a cue with people; she knew when it was up to her to make things work. "I was just thinking how much we all have to say to each other. Paul. Paul?" Her voice rose for the question. "I haven't talked to you since you went to Thailand." He said, "Or Korea." Rachel laughed again. "Korea? Then we'll have even more to say. And then there's the matter of—." She tapped me on the head, and she meant "You owe Marie Bond a telephone call." And she also meant "Where the hell did you dig up a father?" But she said, "All that has to wait. I am going to impose on this kind man here. I have to unload a chair on some old friends who think they want it. You know, Mark, the recliner that often deposits you on your head? They say it's worth something for some reason. I say they can have it. We'll be back in . . ." She looked at her watch, which usually stopped yesterday. It was a windup, an early gift from her Mark. She glanced at me, just barely, to let me know she had arranged the heist of my father because she knew Paul and I had a lot to talk about. I said it wouldn't take much more than two hours, even if they drove up to Rockport to look at the wooden boats in the harbor. Rachel, my friend, said, "It's one of my favorite places on the whole East Coast." I could see from her quick grimace that she would be counting on her friends in Gloucester for directions to Rockport. I asked if she would stay for dinner. She told me to get a lot of wine. Then she left, with my father looking like he knew he was the luckiest man in New England. Paul said, "She is the most remarkable woman I have ever met." I seconded the motion. Then he said, "I can't believe you gave up a job where you got to work with her." This was reminiscent of Marie Bond's referring to my decision to leave McClintock. There seemed to be a consensus forming around the idea that I, and not Rachel Reed acting on the orders of Agatha Kroll, had fired me. Paul started to say something more, which would surely have reopened the Spelling Case, but he thought the better of it. And I thought the better of him for that. After all, we had only two hours alone, and we had our entire history of not living together not to discuss.

MORE MECHANICS
Misplaced parts

Every individual word and phrase we use to refine or alter the meaning of a noun or a verb in a sentence can be considered a *modifier*. These words modify, or change, the meaning. But sometimes our modifiers get lost in our sentences. And then our meaning is lost. This happens because we write faster than we think. In fact, we do most things faster than we think. That's what makes us human, right? We're errers. When it happens in a sentence, it is easy to repair. Consider the following: <u>We put the leftover food in plastic bags, which Rachel and my father ate later.</u> Surely, the bags went uneaten, even after that long ride to Rockport. The modifier was misplaced; it was <u>the leftover food which Rachel and my father ate.</u> You might say that <u>Paul told me the story of the Master in his old gray shorts.</u> Paul certainly knew the Master more intimately than did I but not so well that he would have swapped clothes with him. In truth, <u>In his old gray shorts, Paul</u> told me the story. We must be mindful of our arrangements. The meaning of our lives is not fixed; it is modified by the people to whom we are closest. You see, I might have asked Paul about the Shakers over eggs and corn bread, but I'm sure he would have refused to serve them up as a condiment.

h a t s   o f f

WAS IT CONFUCIUS who said there are as many versions of an event as there are witnesses, or was that P.T. Barnum? I know that Paul Pryor's way of understanding the Pleasant Hill story was not my way. He did not see it as Celia's struggle to understand the Man at the window. For Paul, that was just Celia's problem, which he considered one element in a story about a Family and its capacity to accommodate one balky Sister. For instance, Paul was impressed by the Family's expectation that the Gift Celia had received would not interfere with her assigned chores. And he liked old Sister Ethel, who fully believed Celia was in contact with the Negro Jesus but still considered her a pest in the chicken coop. Ethel had a method of scaring the birds into delivering enough eggs for breakfast, and when Celia met her in the coop the morning after Louise's fall from the porch roof, Ethel was choking one of the "nervy birds." The frightened hen did produce an egg to save its neck, but Celia objected to the violence, so Ethel left, and it was up to Celia to tell the cook that there were only eleven eggs for fifty Shakers. Celia and most of the others ate porridge, which was nourishing, Paul admitted, "but not in the same league as, say, this." He ate a big chunk of his omelette to prove his point. It was Sunday in Kentucky, which meant Meeting at five o'clock, which meant Celia was supposed to make lemon pies for the Family's late lunch. But with Louise laid up, someone had to see to the potatoes, and Celia understood that this responsibility also fell to her. She liked it out there among Louise's root vegetables, near the edge of the Shaker land. It was an unusual mess of a garden, because Louise protected her potatoes by planting a hodgepodge of good grazing material, like sweet peppers, wax beans, and zucchini. These vegetables grew fast and often, and Louise expected they would be pilfered by "raccoons and other vagrants who'd otherwise make themselves sick on a dinner of my unripe potatoes, leaving us all disappointed." The path to the potatoes led past the old East Family Dwelling, the site of Louise's big tumble, and Celia was pleased to see the ladder back in its place against the porch; it stood for everything being set to rights. Except it didn't. Why had that ladder been there in the first place? Who needed to climb on or off the porch roof? These were the questions on Celia's mind, and Paul figured I could anticipate the answers. He said, "Of course, you're guessing that the Man was inside that abandoned Dwelling House, that Richard had arranged the ladder for his nightly forays to get food. That way, the door would always be latched and no one could enter unseen by the Man, neither the Master nor a curious Shaker. That's what Celia was thinking as she stood on the front steps. So she tried the door, but it was latched. She peeked inside through one of the lancet windows, but she only saw herself." Paul paused to mop his plate with a piece of toast. Then he said, "Her reflection," as he chewed. And I understood the story at last and said so. I knew she would never see him again, that somehow Celia herself was the Negro Jesus. Paul said, "You have amazingly bad instincts. In fact, the door opened, and the Man grabbed Celia's wrist, dragged her inside, and waved a piece of paper in her face." He offered me more coffee, which I refused, because I felt he had set me up. (Petulance.) Paul must have known I was annoyed; he shrugged and asked me if I'd rather hear the rest of the story from my father. I didn't care who told me the story; I just wanted to know what the hell it meant. I poured myself some coffee, which Paul correctly interpreted as my apology for poor sportsmanship. He said, "The Man was wearing Brother Richard's trousers—you remember, they'd switched clothes in the coop, right?—and they were bunched up around his waist, tied with a piece of rope. He was sweating, and Celia could see the tendons in his forearms and the blood-swelled veins bulging up in his neck." Paul waited while I stacked our empty plates and set the corn bread down between us. Then he told me that the Man had latched the door, handed Celia the hand-written note, and yelled, "Read the damn thing." Celia scanned the page, but this infuriated him. He hollered. "Louder! Read it out loud!" And Celia read the letter fast, in a nervous voice: *I am here. I am here for you. I can kill the child whenever I damn please. Yesterday, in the field, I did not kill the child. That was just to warn you. I know where you sleep these nights. Trust me. I can kill the child and I can kill you. And Brother Richard? No reason I can't save a bullet for his black hide.* Celia lowered the letter and met his gaze. She tried to reach the door, but he grabbed her wrist, and the letter slipped out of her hand. She said, "Why do you want to harm me? I saw you at the window. I know nothing else. Please leave here, and leave Richard alone. Do not harm the child." She heard a rumbling above her, and she and the Man both stared up at the ceiling as Whack! something was slammed shut. They regarded each other suspiciously. The footfalls above them moved through the upstairs rooms. A voice called out, "Yea, Thomas? Yea, it is Richard. You need not hide." The Man dragged Celia with him to the bottom of the stairs, but before he could speak, Celia yelled, "Leave the house, Brother. He has a gun. He will kill you, too." Richard clomped down the stairs, taking them two at a time. The Man walked to the door and peered out the window. Richard spoke to him first, reassuringly. He said, "No one saw me enter the window." Then he turned to Celia. "Why are you here, Sister? How did you enter?" She pointed to the Man as he stooped to pick up the letter. She started up the stairs, hoping to find the child, but Richard stopped her. The Man said, "I found it this morning. Under the front door. This woman was standing on the porch." Then he handed the letter to Richard. Celia felt she was being accused of something. She said, "He made me read the letter." Richard was reading. The Man looked at his feet, which were housed in a pair of clownishly oversized boots. He said, "Sorry, missus. I can't read." Richard said, "Sister, did you deliver this letter? Or did you see who left it?" The Man looked defeated when he said, "He knows where I am now. He won't kill me. Wouldn't serve him. But yall ain't safe." He climbed halfway up the stairs and sat there, shaking his head. Celia looked at the locked door. It stood for the Man and the letter and all she did not understand. She said, "Who is he, Brother?" Richard put the letter in his pocket. He said, "His name is Thomas. He is being hunted by his Master, tracked like an animal from Mississippi." Celia said, "He is a free man." And Richard snorted and said, "You know nothing of the World." Paul interrupted himself here to scarf down a big slab of corn bread. I was annoyed. The story superseded my limited knowledge of American history. I had never doubted that life was hard for a man with dark skin, but I had not understood that Masters literally survived—and profited by—the Emancipation Proclamation. My grandparents were alive in 1903. Did they live with this knowledge? Paul smiled and said, "A proclamation? That's just a matter of principle, which is immaterial." Then he sliced off some more corn bread. "Thomas was participating in an innovative Mississippi state government program. Convict leasing. It was much more economical than the old plantation policy had been. The Master still paid slave wages, but he paid it to white men, to the wardens for the state." I was beginning to understand, or so I thought. I asked—I did ask—what kind of crime the Man, now called Thomas, had committed. Paul didn't look at me. He said, "You sound like Celia. Don't you see? He was a black man in the World. And he was a gifted farmer, much needed in the fields of the Master. So he'd spent most of his life under arrest for one thing and another, because the Master had worked out a long-term lease with the state." He ate the corn bread he'd cut, and he was eyeing the rest of the loaf. And I said, as Celia had said, that I understood: the child was his, and the Master had staged her death in the field to frighten him. But Brother Richard said to Celia, "He has no family. That is why he is willing to risk this escape. I am going to take him to the coast. On Tuesday, I will have our best team of horses. I am expected at orchards all around the county to inspect the fruit the eldress commissioned. It was to be a three-day journey. That is time enough to gain an insurmountable lead on the Master. Thomas can sail from Baltimore." Celia said, "Where will he go?" Richard said, "Where the Family historically sent slaves to their freedom. To Africa, where there is a country called Freedom." Celia said, "Liberia?" And Thomas said, "Africa," as if it was all of a piece, an undivided continent, a land of unmitigated freedom. Richard said, "I trust you, Sister," and he put his hands in his pockets, as if there was nothing else he could do. But Celia heard the crinkle of the letter, and she thought of the child, and she turned to Thomas. She said, "Before you leave, you must think of the child. Who is the child? Surely the Master would not taunt you with his own child." Richard said, "The Master hanged his wife and made him watch." The Man just stared at his big boots. Celia said, "But what of the child?" Richard yelled, "Sister!" But the Man said, "Her name is Ruth." Richard swung around and faced Thomas. Thomas did not look at him. He said, "She ain't mine." Celia said, "Then why is she here? Why did he bring her to you?" Thomas didn't move. He slumped down, and with his head in his hands he said, "You gotta believe me, Richard. Dint tell ya cause it only makes it harder to help me." Richard leaned on the newel post to steady himself. Celia said, "Why is the child here?" Thomas smiled and said, "Cause she can pass. Magine the Master trying to travel with Lester. Lester's dirt black and big. Lester woulda known where they was headed and put an end to it. Likely as not woulda killed the Master soon as they left Mississippi." He glanced at Richard when he said, "Lester's my boy. Had him when me and Zimma was still counting on finding a way to buy us our freedom. Then came Ruth. Came from nights when I was in prison and the Master had his way with Zimma." He tried to assess the effect of all this on Richard. Then he said her name again, "Zimma," and then again, "Zimma." Celia could see that the name was an herb for him, his bittersweet. "Reckon that's why I said she was dead." Thomas stood up, as if he was done, but he had nowhere to go, not yet. He said, "Yaint breaking up no family, Richard. No fool's gonna take Zimma to prison with two kids. Ventually, she'll be let alone, which is near enough to freedom. Can't that happen till I'm gone, though. Master won't hurt Ruth. Gainst the damn law, even in Mississippi. He wants me, and he wants me alive. Negro ain't worth nothing to him dead." Thomas sat down on a step below Richard and Celia. He said, "Still on my side?" Richard slid his hand along the smooth banister, and then he said, "The Shakers saved me. I left a lot of people behind myself. And all I've ever done for them was this. Here. Tried to live right, the Shaker way. But the World doesn't seem to be getting the message. Guess it's time. Time I paid my debt. Time I saved a man. First thing is to keep you safe for a couple of nights. We leave Tuesday." Thomas went upstairs. Richard said, "It was simpler when I believed his wife was dead." He shook his head. "Guess it takes time to know someone, though. I remember when you came to us, Ceily. You and your silly dresses. I thought you would not stay. You were as white as the painted gate, and you were free to go. I did not understand that you were free to stay, as well. I did not see that you were my Sister. I am sorry, but I was still a very young man." Celia smiled and said, "You were mostly a boy, and skinnier than anyone I'd ever seen. Whenever I baked with the Sisters, I had you in mind." Richard said, "Thus, I became your Brother. How shall we bear Thomas in our minds? How shall he be seen? The Man you saw at the window, Sister—." And Celia said, "Thomas." Richard said, "You must not tell the others. The Master might be anywhere, watching us and asking questions. He may be among us tonight, at our public Meeting." Celia hated to think of the Meeting. She walked to the door and looked out the window. "I will be expected to witness to my Gift, Brother." Richard said, "Say you have seen the Negro Jesus. Think of the agony he has endured. Surely he is the Negro Jesus." Celia said, "You can trust me, Brother, though the Family cannot. What does it mean, Richard, that we are taking this matter into our own hands? It is not the Shaker way." Richard said, "*We* are Shakers." Celia said, "But what does that mean now? Look," and then she tapped the window glass. Richard walked to her side. There was not a Shaker in sight. Consolingly and not without some wonder in his voice, Richard said, "Yea, Sister. I see it now. The World is near at hand." Then he unlatched the door, and Celia headed down the path to the potatoes. It was already too late to make the lemon pies, which would be sorely missed. The least she could do was see to Louise's work. She stopped at the Drying House to gather some hand tools, and when she came out, the eldress was waiting for her. "Walk with me, Sister." The eldress charged off in the wrong direction. When Celia caught up with her, the eldress said, "I am much in need of company, Sister." She kept up a brisk pace, and Celia understood she was not to ask questions. It was a silent tour of the village, and Celia had taken it many times before. It

was the eldress's way of reassuring herself about the Family's
future and fortunes, as if the beauty of the place was enough
to sustain them. They paused to admire Emma's physics garden. The gray and humid afternoon air was like plaster holding
everything in stolid, stark relief: strict rows of spindly stalks;
raised beds of silver-green, pea-green, and striated foliage;
stands of tiny topiary trees and miniature formal hedges; and
vast beds of sweet cedar mulch dotted with little volcanic
cones of black soil out of which sprung tender shoots and
seedlings. After an unusually long arc around the grazing fields,
Celia saw the gleaming white limestone of the Dwelling House
rising up ahead like the bow of an enormous boat, promising
safe passage. Was the eldress reassured? Celia veered off toward the east, eager to get to the potatoes, but the eldress said,
"And now to the Swedes," and she set off toward the west.
When Celia caught up with her, the eldress said, "I was told
the Swedes were breaking ground today on their tobacco fields.
I went out with a basket of our best syrups, as a gift. After all,
they are good about their bread. Now, I want you to see what I
saw." They stopped in the shade of the mulberries. The eldress
said, "This is even stupider than tobacco." She waved disparagingly, as if she could not bring herself to point directly at
the crowd of Swedes gathered in the lot recently deeded to Mr.
Goodrich. Twenty or more men were leaning on their shovels
along the perimeter of a big white loop that had been painted
on the grass. Two men were working to widen the outline with
lime dust, which they scooped from a huge supply at the center. It was an intriguing convocation of elements, and Celia
guessed that the lime was a substitute for snow and that the
entire operation was a Scandinavian ritual, a pagan sacrament.

The eldress said, "It is a racing track for horses." Celia was relieved she had not spoken. The eldress was disgusted. She said,
"I suppose they are not satisfied with the rate at which they are
able to waste their wages on ornamental figurines and whiskey.
They have chosen well. This enterprise will impoverish them.
They have always made bad Shakers. Look at them, in their
Sunday suits, contemplating the foolish task they have invented for themselves. What a quaint trick. The Swedes have
turned themselves into southern gentlemen. Come, Sister, we
are late to lunch." Lunch was grand, no thanks to Celia. The
morning porridge was reconstituted as dumplings studded with
raisins and bacon. Slices of crusty rye were baked with cheese
and herbs and floated on a chicken soup strewn with spring
onions. In lieu of lemon pie, cinnamon biscuits glazed with
pecans and honey were slathered with preserved green
peaches. When tea was served, so was the last of Sister Mary
Irene's mint syrup, which the eldress had almost wasted on the
Swedes. It was a preparatory meal. For the first time in years,
the Pleasant Hill Shakers expected a full house of visitors at
Meeting. News of Celia and the Negro Jesus had spread, as
Richard had implied. Tonight, the World's People would see
the Shakers at work. The Family looked forward to the
evening's labor, and in no time, they were bathed and dressed
and lining up in the hallway of the Dwelling. Celia closed her
eyes; she wanted to feel connected to the others. She had not
been in the Meeting House since she'd seen the Man at the
window. Her dread weighed on her, but she was buoyed by the
deep waters that ran beneath this moment, the solace of accumulated years. She balked before she walked into the Meeting
House, but Sister Mary Irene urged her on through the Sisters'

door, whispering, "Are you afraid of the crowd? Nay, Sister, no fear. When the World's people are among us, they are as scared as schoolchildren." Celia went in, and the visitors did look terrified. Dark-suited men ranged around the outside of the room, stiff as timber. Beneath them sat their bedizened wives and daughters, who seemed especially nervous about their hats—they were headdresses really, and Celia saw that the Shaker bonnet had been designed in response. There was something else strange about the room. She noticed the solemn Swedes standing in a corner by themselves, but they were not it. She peered around the room, but Brother Joseph stood, and the crowd congealed. Joseph recited a brief summary of recent Family business. Collectively, the World's people hmmmed—the Shakers *were* wealthy. Celia closed her eyes until Joseph sat. Then she watched the eldress move to the center of the room, beside the chandelier. The eldress said, "I confess that I have coveted the company and consolation of one of the Sisters. I pray you will forgive me." Celia stiffened. The eldress continued in a strangely high voice. "I have burdened her to lighten my own load. I have kept her from full communion with the Family. I have coveted her Gift." Celia slunk down as far as she could, and she heard a deeper voice behind her call out, "I confess." It was Richard. Colleen cut him off by jumping up and squealing, "I have been incontinent in my desires. I have held her in my gaze too long and—." Sister Bertha dropped from the bench to her knees and said, "I dream about our Sister," and then Frederika raised her hands and said, "I, too. I, too, have desired—" and Sister Ethel was muttering and Brother Joseph shook his head and gurgled and Celia was the only Shaker seated when the eldress cried out, "Abna habba

habba cro jodian vool," and her head tipped back and she turned until she was spinning beneath the chandelier and Celia stood as Sister Mary Irene floated down to the floor, slain in the Spirit, and the children were stomping and calling out, "Jesus!" and "Mother!" and the eldress was suddenly still as a stanchion beneath the hanging crown of candles and she began to pulse and shake as capes swirled around her and bodies twisted and the Shakers shouted rhyming words and howled until they were not voices but a vortex sucking in the energy that sustained the spinning so that bodies finally toppled over to rest on the floor and someone yelled, "Aramantha, Shawnee Spirit of the Dead, sing to me!" and the eerie mourner wailed, "We are a homeward people! We are a homeless people!" and she sang as the Shakers stood and swayed and raised their hands and hummed and laughed and the eldress seemed to be welded into her impossible position, bent backward, until she groaned and slowly came upright. Sister Rebecca hummed softly, and it was rain on their upturned faces. And the Shakers came to rest. They sat. Celia was standing. She had become a matter for confession. What did she stand for now? She stood for someone who could not exceed her limits. She stood because she suspected that those who received Gifts were themselves the givers. And she stood among the Shakers because she loved their generosity, their desire to make Gifts and to share them, their humble belief that the self was not the best they had to offer. She loved them right up to the bumpy hives on Colleen's red neck. She stood to receive the Gift of them. And she stood to see the World's people. There were more of them than there were Shakers. The laws of Nature favored the World. Gravity drew and held a body. Standing on the surface of the bent Earth, lit by a sun so bright it seems to have no choice but to shine on us, and entranced by the pale possibilities of that magnetic moon, a body feels perfect, balanced, timeless. And so it is, thought Celia. The body has no place in time. Time does not wait on us. It is the nature of our bodies to dissipate and disappear. We are not even momentary. We are gone before we know it. A crocus will come back, and we will not be here. Celia was still standing. Something blue alerted her. Rhea raised her hand and waved. Celia clapped her hand to her heart. Delighted, Rhea stood up, and she tipped right over and clunked her head on the floor. From the floor, Rhea hollered, "Jes visitin, Surster." Then she stood up, shook off her tumble, and took her seat. The spectators were still as the storm suspended above them in the sky. Maybe they were afraid they might start toppling over like Shakers. Or maybe they were simply astonished by Rhea's fancy dress, which fit her like a flood. The eldress stood and said, "Shall we labor?" The Brothers and Sisters pushed back the benches. They faced each other. Brother Joseph started to clop his boots against the floorboards until the rhythm was roomwide and true, and Celia walked to the chandelier rope at the window and—Crack! Thunder. And then a storm-splitting shock of lightning. And rain pounded down on the roof and slapped at the windows. Everyone turned with relief, welcoming the rain, but Celia saw it coming again, someone on the other side. It was a man. He stopped outside the window and held something up to her. She did not hesitate. She flung the window open, scattering those near her. The eldress cried, "Sister!" Celia held out her arms and bent into the night. The man's hair was pasted to his head. She could not see his body below the limp ribbon tied at his white collar. He offered her a sleeping child, and Celia pulled the little girl to her breast and backed into the center of the room, where she clearly saw the abundant curly hair, and she realized that the child was Ruth. The man burst in through the Sisters' door and yelled, "She is hurt. Her hand. I didn't know where else to go." The burden of attention pivoted back to Celia. Her blouse was red with the child's blood, and when she tipped Ruth's shoulder, she saw that four of the child's fingers and most of her palm had been torn away. Ruth's eyelids flicked open and revealed nothing but a marble whiteness filigreed with veins. Sister Emma steered Celia out of the room with a hand at her back and drove her through the rain into the Dwelling until Ruth was on her back in a bed opposite Lousie, who slept. Sister Frederika organized several Sisters into a corps of attending nurses. They set to work under Emma's instruction. Emma's voice was soothing, and her cadences were steady until the eldress entered the room with the gentleman who had delivered Ruth, and Emma screamed, "Give me the fingers. At once!" He said, "Her fingers? I didn't chop them off!" And Celia thought, Someone did; someone purposefully maimed this child. Emma said, "We might have saved her hand." The Sisters stood straight for a moment, and breathed out their hope, and then bent back to work. Emma said, "How long has she bled?" Every question unsettled the gentleman. He said, "She was near one of the shacks across the river. I didn't look for her hand." He seemed to be asking for forgiveness when he said, "I just wanted to save her life." Emma said, "The wound is brutal." It was revolting, and Celia was afraid it would soon be just another facet of the mystery she had made. She was desperate to exonerate herself. She was determined to see through the innocence that masked this stranger. Celia said, "Where were you headed on our road?" He said, "Here." The eldress posted Sister Colleen outside the door to ward off the curious. Then she pulled three chairs from the wall and invited Celia to join her and the gentleman. He wiped the wetness from his forehead back through his hair, and his handsomeness evaporated for a few seconds. His skin was cadaverous. His skull was too prominent, simian, and his eyes were unlit. His lips were thin and gray. He said, "I've come from Raleigh. Raleigh," he said again, emphatically. "In Carolina." Celia said, "Oh, South Carolina," as she pulled a towel from a drawer in the wall. He said, "Yes," and wiped his face dry. "I mean, No. North Carolina." He stood and bent his head into the corner, drying his hair until it was the color of chestnuts. When he sat, he was handsome again, all smooth rectangular planes, like a beautiful bay horse. He peeled back his coat and draped it over the chair, and Celia saw a bullet belt sewn into the lining. His holstered pistol drooped by his thigh. The gun convinced Celia that this was the man who called himself Master. He said, "I was in Lexington, selling. I grow tobacco. I was told in town there's to be a new farm here. I came to offer them some of the finest rootstock in the South." The arrival of several trays of medicine forced them from their seats. The gentleman never looked at Ruth. The eldress led the way out of the infirmary. He said, "I have a room only a few miles from here. May I return tomorrow? I feel responsible." He was peeking into open rooms. The eldress said, "You are welcome. But tell me. The child was entirely alone?" He said, "I will ask after her parents tomorrow. I yelled for help but failed to rouse a soul." Celia and the eldress watched him mount his horse from the doorway of the Dwelling. The eldress said, "The rain has not relented." Celia said, "Perhaps it will wash the blood from his coat." The eldress said, "He will have a hard ride home tonight, but the spring wheat will profit by his inconvenience. Now leave me, Sister. I want to go and sit a while with Louise." Celia wandered up to her new bedroom. Rhea was wearing a white nightgown and sitting on the windowsill. The rain was silver behind her. "Yer friend Richard brang me up here, even hauled my case. He sure smells good. An he tole me bout the kid's thumb. Ain't it awful? Worsen no hand at all, jes a thumb." Rhea held up her hand and made a fist, then she stuck out her thumb and examined it from all sides. She shook her head. "She ain't that ole, but she ain't so young, neither. Don't spose she's able ta make anya them fingers grow back." Celia hugged Rhea and turned her around so they could watch the rain together. She said, "Are you here to stay, Rhea?" Rhea snuggled into Celia and said, "Jes a day or two, tops. Poppa sez Tuesdee if we's lucky, Wensdee if we ain't." Celia said, "Is your father here?" Rhea snorted. "Sez he gotta see some people and I's too sweet for the likes a them." Celia knew the story of orphans too well; so it begins, she thought. She said, "You know, I would like you to stay for a long time, Rhea." Rhea weighed this offer and said, "Les say Tuesdee." Celia said, "Or Wednesday. Or longer." And Rhea reconsidered. "Maybe. But likely jes till Tuesdee, Surster. Me an Poppa's purty lucky." While the storm exhausted itself, Rhea fell asleep in Celia's arms. Celia laid her on the cot and headed out into the night. A few of the World's people lingered by their carriages, still speculating on the meaning of the evening's events. As Celia climbed the stairs to the bright Meeting House, a man yelled, "Yall startin up agin,

Sister?" She stopped and hollered back, "You will find pie is being served in the store. You are welcome next Sunday." Someone else shouted, "Had our fill already." To herself, Celia said, "Of pie or prayer?" As she entered the room, the eldress was dousing the candles in the chandelier. She left two lit. Richard stood from one of the Brothers' benches. Celia drifted toward the window. The eldress said, "We are all wet. Unlike our land, we don't wear the rain very well." She sat opposite Richard. "Sister Louise woke for a while. She recognized the child Ruth. And Brother Richard has confessed to me the story of the Negro Jesus whose name is Thomas." Celia looked around the room. "Is he here?" Richard said, "He is safe." Celia said, "Mother, I confess I was too eager to—" but the eldress said, "Sit by me, Celia. It is I who was wrong. You tried to tell me you had seen a man. And, of course, Jesus is a man." Celia sat beside the eldress and looked right past Richard, out the window. The eldress said, "I ask you this only once, Brother. Must we help him escape even at the expense of his natural family?" Richard blew out a long breath and said, "We can secure him his rightful freedom in the World, Mother. His exercise of freedom, well, I believe that is his burden to bear." The eldress said, "I will honor your promise to him until the end of this week. Then the Family must be told the truth. You leave Tuesday?" Richard said, "Tuesday morning." The eldress walked to the window and said, "If he desired to join the Family, he and his wife and his children would be safe and free." Richard said, "The World's people have adopted our circular saw and our automatic washing machines. They have time. Perhaps they will learn the Shaker way." The eldress opened the window and let in the cool night. She said, "The Creation was a week of work,

Brother. I am sure not even the Shakers will change the World overnight." Richard smiled and said, "We have this night and another, Mother." The eldress turned to him. She smiled, too. "Yea, Brother," she said, "work as if you had a thousand years to live, and as you would knowing you must die tomorrow." She bowed and walked to the door. Then she turned to Celia. "I watched the gentleman who delivered Ruth to the window. I watched him while he dried his beautiful hair in the infirmary. Did you notice, Sister, his casual manners in the room where the injured child lay? He impressed me as a man capable of great cruelty. And yet the Swedes say they know him as Caleb Kroll, a tobacco grower from the Carolinas." Celia said, "He carries a gun." The eldress said, "As did the Union soldiers. As does the sheriff. Oh, the World. They turn their plows into swords. No wonder their food is so bad." The eldress left without another word. Richard closed the window, doused the last two candles, and said, "Walk with me, Sister." He led Celia to the riverbank, where he sat on the wet grass. Celia sat beside him. They could not see the train depot, but they knew it was there. Richard said, "We are free to leave, too, Ceily." Celia said, "Africa?" It sounded impossible. But then Richard said, "Africa," and it sounded massive and clean. Celia said, "I think we have been there before, Richard." Richard said, "Nay, Sister. I would remember Africa." And Celia said, "You remember, Richard. Africa. It is just another name for the World." Richard smiled and placed his hat on Celia's head. It fit easily over her thin bonnet. "Today, after lunch, I missed the lemon pies, Ceily. Maybe I love them too well." Languaged love; longing love; linear love; one-to-one, one-on-one, one is always waiting—Do you love me?—waiting for word of love; Celia knew what came of love like this. Bruised brides came to Pleasant Hill. Middle-aged widowers incapable of cooking an egg came. Frightened children came. Celia came of love like this. She unlaced her bonnet, pulled it off, and looped the strings over Richard's hat. She tied a bow. Richard said, "Our hats fit each other." Celia looked at them, and then she flung the hats toward the river. The contraption bobbed in the grassy still-water slough, hesitating beside the current. "Where will they end up, Brother? Will they stay together?" Richard said, "We don't know." Celia stood. "Two bodies buoyed by a current they cannot control. It is an intriguing mystery." She offered Richard her hand and helped him to his feet. Richard smiled at the river. Celia knelt and reached her hands out over the water. She said, "We are more than just a couple of hats." As she spoke, she snagged the string of her bonnet, but the waterlogged bow was limp, and Richard's hat slipped away. It skidded toward the center of the river, upside down, and then it sank. Richard did not move. Celia could not repair the inadvertent omen. Finally Richard said, "I don't have the heart to leave alone." And then Paul said, "Neither do I, Mark. I really don't," and he went right to work on the last of the corn bread. I stacked up our dishes, wondering if we were just a couple of hats. Paul looked good in a baseball cap. Of course, Paul would have looked good in a shower cap. I, on the other hand, had tried everything from bowlers to beanies, and the net effect was always the same: I looked dumb. I don't mean foolish; I mean, people who saw me pegged my IQ at 12 and held open doors or asked me if I needed directions. As a matter of pride, I did not like to think of myself in a hat, never mind as a hat. I decided to change the subject. I said, "Caleb Kroll? As in Agatha Kroll?" Paul smiled.

"I hadn't thought of that," he said, and then he stood to help me carry the dishes upstairs. He said, "Do you mean it's a little suspicious that the Master's name is Kroll?" Now I did; previously, I had been tickled by the seeming coincidence. I said, "Do you suppose my father renamed him to suit me?" Paul thought about this in silence. When he dumped the dishes in the sink, he said, "What about Thomas, the Negro Jesus? That's the one that made me wonder." I didn't like to think my father would cast himself in the plum role, but it certainly improved his chances for redemption if you considered that he'd left the First Family in a sound stucco house, whereas Thomas the Negro Jesus had left a wife and son in slavery and the White Jesus had abandoned the Holy Family in the desert.

DICTION TIP
People and their possessions

Whose or who's? Its or it's? Their or They're? We have a simple means of choosing between *pronouns* that are working as actors in our sentences (such as You are; it is; they are) and those that are *modifiers*—that is, *possessive pronouns*—such as whose, its, and their. Spell out all contractions. Remember, the apostrophe tells you that something was lost: who's lost an *i* (who is) or a *ha* (who has); the same is true for it's; and they're lost an *a* (they are). Subject pronouns are actors; I, he, she, it, we, you, they, and who can all do things. A subject pronoun (Who?) and the action can be smashed together: Who's (Who has) been sleeping in my bed? The possessive pronouns (his, her, hers, its, our, ours, your, yours, their, theirs, and whose) are not contractions. Nothing was lost, and thus they do not need an apostrophe. Again: possessive pronouns are not subjects or verbs; they are modifiers that tell us a bit more about nouns in our sentences: <u>Whose</u> hats are those? The hats are <u>theirs</u>. Did <u>her</u> hat lose <u>its</u> partner? Where is <u>his</u> hat? All accomplished without an apostrophe, because <u>whose</u>, <u>theirs</u>, <u>her</u>, <u>its</u>, and <u>his</u> are not the subjects, and the verbs lost no letters (<u>is</u>, <u>are</u>, and <u>did lose</u>). If you are still confused, use the rule of fashion. If the apostrophe is a hat, then whenever <u>I</u> wear a hat, something is lost. <u>I'm</u> telling you the truth (I am); <u>I've</u> no reason to lie (I have); <u>I'd</u> tell you if there were any exceptions (I would). The same is true for <u>you</u>, <u>she</u>, <u>he</u>, <u>it</u>, <u>we</u>, <u>they</u>, and <u>who</u>. Of course, <u>you</u> can do whatever <u>you</u> like with <u>your</u> head. It is <u>yours</u>. Wear a hat. But if you're wondering whether you're looking a little lost in it, as I do, you <u>are</u>.

left dangling

EVERY FACT IS like a snowflake, pointed and particular and cool. And fragile, too—by themselves, facts are unstable. They do not survive contact with our curiously warm bodies. Still, there is nothing so charming as snow, fresh facts. They arrive in admirably ponderous pieces, too many to count, but they add up to something bright and coherent that temporarily obscures the worn-out world. Snow doesn't go away; it seeps into the sleeping earth and feeds the deep-down dreams of spring. Of course, if you grow up in the Berkshires, you're bound to run into more than a few blinding blizzards, not to mention the occasional snow job. I was nine. It was the winter my sister Ellen quit her job at the junior high and went to work at the Circulation Desk of the local paper. I wanted to quit school, too, because Sister Mary Magdalene was making us read aloud from Chapter Six in our *Health & Hygiene* textbooks, "The Miraculous Egg," but that did not explain Ellen's decision; nor,

as my father had guessed, was Ellen's decision political. I
think all Ellen had intended to say about her career change
was "I really don't like kids asking me questions all day. It
would save a lot of time if they would just shut up and listen."
But then my mother suggested Ellen should apply to one of
the Catholic schools. Ellen said, "That would be worse. Today,
a ninth grader asked me if it snows in Bethlehem. I told him
Bethlehem was not in Switzerland. Then he wanted to know
why every Nativity crèche he'd ever seen had snow in them."
My mother said, "It. *Every* is singular. Every crèche has snow
in it." Meanwhile, I had been thinking of the painted people
and cows arranged around a manger in our hallway. They were
all knee-deep in cotton. My mother did not want Ellen to quit
her job. She was already spending half her time job hunting for
Tommy, who had just got himself fired again, this time from a
restaurant whose neon sign mysteriously turned up in the
trunk of Tommy's car a week after he'd started waiting tables.
My mother said, "Couldn't you explain that the snow was symbolic?" Ellen said, "Of what?" My mother looked defeated.
She was stirring spaghetti in a vat of boiling water. She peered
into the vapors, and for a moment I thought she might stick
her head into the pot. Ellen asked again, like a kid in her class,
"Symbolic of what?" My mother's glasses were foggy when she
turned around to the table. She didn't bother to wipe them off.
She said, "Symbolic of snow, Ellen." She was holding her
wooden spoon in the air, so she looked like a blind crossing
guard. Ellen was persistent, and she was sneering, all of which
made me think she might've made the right decision about
teaching. She said, "How can snow be symbolic of snow?" My
mother removed her eyeglasses and looked over her shoulder

at the boiling water. Did she want to stick Ellen's head into the pot? She said, "But it is not snow in the crèches, Ellen. It is cotton. Cotton is used to represent snow." Of course, Ellen knew this, but just thinking about kids in a classroom had turned her into a dolt. I'd never seen any of her report cards, but I think she might have had a tough time as a student. I mean, I bet the other kids loved her, but the teachers couldn't have found this sort of thing endearing. Meanwhile, I was putting together the snow facts for the first time. I did know about the deserts of the Middle East, where the Jews spent most of history wandering from one plague to another. I knew the White Jesus was a Jew. But I'd been lulled into complacency by all that symbolic cotton batting. Until that night, just a few weeks shy of Christmas Day, I had believed in snow in Bethlehem. It was humiliating, reminiscent of the unmasking of Santa Claus, and I spent the next few days trying to identify other so-called facts that might be mere symbols. I questioned the Miraculous Egg of Life, of course, and the Vietnam War, which adults liked to say was not "an official war." A friend of the family had recently given us two huge rugs that he called "Orientals," though the tag on the back said they'd been made in Pennsylvania, and I wondered about them. My new skepticism made me reluctant to address the nuns as "Sisters," too, because they weren't, and I refused to call the parish priest "Father." My vigilance must have been wearisome, and as she always did, my mother gracefully bore the brunt of it. She began to take me to plays at the local high schools, and we'd go out for ice cream afterward to discuss what it all meant. For Christmas, she gave me a huge book called *The Odyssey,* and she warned me that it was filled with all kinds of truths, symbolic and factual. On Christmas night, she offered to read me the first chapter. It was the best present I've ever received. She had not sat with a book in the wing chair by my bed since I'd started school. I was worn out, and so was she. For a while, she just hugged the book and stared at me. My eyes soon closed, but she was watching, as she always was. I could feel her. I can today. She was never too tired to look after her children. Since that Christmas night, my mother and I have often disappointed each other. I have tested her limits when I might have let something pass. But I have never forgotten that I was beheld, seen, watched over, and made safe all along the way. I don't know if she thought I was asleep. She spoke from her wing chair in a whisper, as if she might be talking to herself. She said, "We are handed the facts of our lives. We're artists, son, and it is up to us to turn those sad facts into something we can live with, to make them mean something good." She didn't leave until I was sound asleep, engaged in my own dreams. It was midafternoon when Rachel returned with my father, a jug of wine, and some halibut steaks. Paul was halfway down the block, setting out for a walk along the river, and my father was happy to join him. Rachel and I sat on the deck above the porch and tested the wine, which tasted like tart springwater but cost considerably less. She let me know that I was expected at a meeting on the Third Floor, which she'd scheduled for Tuesday. As she said, "by then you'll have traded your soul for a job at MCU, and you'll have nothing to lose but a few hours, during which we can stave off Rashelle Whippet's lawsuit." She dismissed my characterization of Marie Bond's threats. She was certain Marie had the college's best interests at heart. But Rachel was not a cardiologist, and she often misread the vital signs. Regular exercise had made Rachel's heart reliable and strong, but some of her closest associates had hyperactive spleens and giant gallbladders, and their hearts were weak and small, which made them good candidates for cardiac failure. I agreed to attend the meeting; it saved me a telephone call to Rashelle. Then Rachel asked me my other sister's name. I never talked about Bridget; I thought she'd want it that way. Bridget had cut herself off from all blood relations with the help of a licensed social worker she'd hired to figure out her unhappiness. The social worker had initially found fault with Bridget's husband, who made piles of money and traveled too much, but I don't think my sister wanted to break up her immediate family or surrender her Land Rover, so she paid the social worker to prove that her husband and the trouble he caused were symbolic of distant relatives who had traveled to our house and made her miserable when she was a kid, all of whom had the added appeal of being dead. I've noticed that social workers and other licensed therapists do some of their best work on the dead. For live consultations, they charge a lot of money, though I guess it's cheaper than paying a dentist. Unlike therapists, dentists are forced to go to medical school before they're allowed to root around looking for cavities and hidden disease. And dentists blame the victims; they scold you for not flossing, and they show you photographic evidence of the disaster you could have prevented. Therapists never produce any proof, so they are not allowed to handle drills, which is good news for all parents of adult children. Still, I think therapists are guilty of malpractice. They are not cardiologists. And unlike the rest of us who handle each other's hearts without any formal training, therapists do not rely on the healing power of love. Indeed, the so-called ethics of their so-called profession strictly forbid love, which therapists like to call "transference," and they teach themselves to "counter" it. I think if you're going to accept money from sad and lonely people and invite them into your well-appointed room, you ought to be honorable about it; in other professions that eschew love, the practitioners have enough respect for their clients to fake it. But all Rachel wanted to know was whether Bridget's nickname was Bambi. I assured her it wasn't. She gulped down some wine and said, "I didn't think so, but your father seems to think so." She filled her glass. "He also seems confused about a few other details. Maybe he's tired." The irony of my father developing Alzheimer's was sickeningly apt, and I decided then and there to stop using aluminum foil. After another dose of wine, Rachel said, "How tall is your brother Tommy?" This was a matter of my mood; Tommy ranged from an inch to several stories high, though he generally stabilized right around six feet. Rachel said, "That's what I thought. Taller than you." She usually nursed her third glass of wine, but apparently she was off duty. She was holding the jug by the neck when she said, "Because I thought you'd told me Tommy and your father were the same size, that Tommy had worn your father's tuxedo at his wedding." Rachel was an archivist when it came to people's pasts, and she was always sorting through her records, updating her files and cross-referencing new entries with the historical data. She wandered around the deck, staring off into my would-be sea, and when she landed back in her chair, she said, "What do you make of Caleb Kroll?" She'd heard the story. For a moment, I felt like the stupidest kid in the class. The teacher was spending time with everyone but me. Hoping to redeem myself, I said it was a pointed name for a slave Master. She said, "Kroll? To say the least. Of course, we can't prove *that*," as if there was something else we could prove. Then she smiled and said, "I bet you haven't heard about Celia and the blue dress. I'm sure I'm supposed to tell you. That's why he went off with Paul." I did not understand. (Petulance.) Rachel was surprised. (Generosity.) "Don't you see? If we all tell it, it becomes our Family story. It's awfully sweet of him to give me the dress and the golden apples." Rachel said that Celia woke on Monday before Rhea, and she saw the gowns, the only gift she'd ever been given by her mother, the gift she gave to Rhea. Celia tried on the blue gown. She swished around the room in the shiny old thing, hoping to inflate it with feeling. It didn't work, and Celia didn't want Rhea to see her in the dress when the first bell bonged. It was tight, and her breasts puffed up above the scooped neckline. She unhooked it at the back and pulled it halfway over her head. Then she breathed deeply, and the air reached her belly, which had been flattened by the bodice. Something snagged somewhere, but Celia couldn't reach the problem, so she tugged blindly and "thpt." That's what Rachel said: "Thpt. Celia felt a shock deep in her left breast, and she instinctively ripped the dress off." Rachel rubbed her own breast. "Celia traced the tear in her skin. It was tender—as you cannot imagine, Mark, but I can—but it was not bloody, and pretty soon Celia realized it was a flap, a hatch door the size of her thumb, and so she lifted it a bit and saw the translucent chunk of fat severed from the rest of her breast. She pressed it back into place, and she felt her frightened heart—." Rachel clapped her hand against her heart and shivered. "But when she tried to pry it open again, the wound was sealed. Inside the blue dress, she found the problem. The corset blades stuck out at both ends of their sheaths. This made sense of Rhea always wearing the damn thing backward." Rachel was not as enthusiastic about Sister Ethel as Paul was, but she did mention that Celia later caught Ethel in the coop with a cleaver poised above the neck of one of the Family's fattest hens. "Like Abraham and Isaac," Rachel said, "and Celia played the part of the intervening angel, though Ethel said they'd never eat another custard unless something was done about the chariness of the birds." It wasn't until after lunch that Celia had time to visit with Louise, and Caleb Kroll had posted himself in the infirmary like a sentinel, so they could hardly speak. Ruth's hand was bandaged, and her splinted arm stuck up like a mast pole. Louise whispered that Emma had resorted to a concoction of deadly nightshade to dull the child's pain, and she forced Celia to stand beside Kroll and check Ruth's respiration, to be sure Emma had not overdone it. The child's breathing was shallow but steady. Caleb Kroll said that he had heard about Celia's "congress with the Negro Jesus." Celia stiffened. She could see the lump of his gun. Kroll said, "What does he look like, Sister? Describe him to me." Celia hoped Richard had hidden him well. As a safeguard, she said, "The man I saw is much taller than you, sir, and he didn't speak. He read to me. From a book. And when he turned, when he turned, his back was broad and smooth, as if no human hand had ever touched his skin." She moved away. She'd come as close to accusing him of beating the Negro Jesus as she dared. She didn't leave him alone with Ruth and Louise. She waited for Sister Frederika to arrive with her knitting needles, which would be weapon enough if one was needed. Celia went directly to the Laundry, where Louise would have been if she were not in her bed with her bruises. But Sister Bertha prevented Celia from entering the steamy building and walked with her into a spot of shade. Bertha was dripping. She said, "I can see to this, Sister, if you will go to the orchard. Brother Richard needs help with the grafting." Celia had heard nothing about this project, and Bertha said maybe she'd slept through it, referring to the day after her first encounter with the Negro Jesus. "Blame the Brothers and their beautiful chairs," Bertha explained, "because as I was told it, the governor of West Virginia was so mightily impressed by the sixteen straight-backs the Brothers made for his new mansion that he sent us forty seedlings of the new Golden Delicious apple tree, which was recently invented by a farmer in his home state. Of course, Richard has heard tell of the wonders of the new fruit, but the trees themselves do not survive their first bearing season. No one can keep them alive. Richard is prepared to try. He's expecting me in the orchard, but your hands will do as much good as mine." When Celia found him, Richard was bent over the soil. He smiled and said, "The new fruit is a hybrid, and it has resisted general cultivation." The West Virginia saplings looked weak— thin, forked twigs stuck in a big red pot. He pointed to some taller, thicker little trees planted in a wooden crate. "Those are sturdy Baldwins. They will serve as understock." He brushed his hands across the delicate nettle of their branches. "The Baldwins are a mainstay of every Shaker orchard. We know the quality of fruit they would bear." He eyed the scrawny West Virginia scions. He seemed to doubt their promise. "We will sacrifice our own to make the others strong." They carried the stock to the neatly furrowed row Richard had prepared, and there they knelt. Richard plucked one tree of each variety from the dirt and set the roots in a bucket of water. They bubbled. He drew a knife from his leather satchel and tipped its point into the bark of one tree and then the other. He used his thumb to pry away a bit of the bark, and he saved some filament from the wound. He placed one square of bark and some fiber in his palm, and he held this out for Celia to study. He said, "We are grafting by approach, Sister. We do not penetrate the tree itself. The bark—the colorful apparent skin—is broken to reveal the cambium, which is hidden. The cambium is the living skin." He tied a quick little knot around the two trees, and their exposed skins met. From his satchel, he pulled a paintbrush and a bottle filled with something inky, which smelled like tar. He painted the area around the wounds and planted the twinned trees. He looked a little sad when he was done, so Celia said, "They look healthy now." Richard hmmmed before he spoke. "If the juncture heals, in a few years the Shaker stock will be cut away," he said, shaking his head, "but there is no other way. Now, if you are confident in this work, Sister, I will leave you and make ready for the morning and my departure." Tuesdee, as Rhea had said. It was time. Celia performed her first approach while Richard watched. She was surprised by the depth of cut required to penetrate the apparent skin, and she made several passes with the blade before the bark fell away. She thought of her wounded breast, the ease with which she had pierced her own flesh, the depth she had achieved, and the wound throbbed, and her progress on the second delicate trunk was even more tedious. Richard finally said, "I hope to get to my packing before the sun sets, Sister," and when Celia turned to him, he laughed. "I am sorry to hasten you in this work, Celia. Your careful method poses no risk to the West Virginia trees, but being Shaker stock, the Baldwins may well die of boredom." Before he left, Richard promised her that the Man, the Negro Jesus—Thomas— would be safe for the night. He told her he would need her help in the morning. She was to let Ethel carry the eggs to the kitchen, and then Richard would join Celia in the coop. It would fall to Celia to distract Caleb Kroll while the escape was made. Celia wondered if once he was beyond the fence, Richard would decide to sail with Thomas to Africa or New York, or somewhere she was not. But for the time being, she let him go with a nod, knowing she would see him at least once again. Then Rachel offered me a refill from the jug of wine and said, "I guess we'll hear the rest of the Shaker story tonight." And then a number of things happened all at once, or else we'd had enough wine to blur the sequence into si- multaneity. The front door squeaked and someone walked in. The telephone rang, and a message was recorded. I kicked over the jug but quickly righted it, and the loss was minimal because it was by no means full. Paul appeared on the lawn, waved, and joined us on the deck. He said, "Your father is going to shower before dinner." Right then we heard my father starting down the stairs to his room. And finally, after a few blissfully calm minutes, Paul said, "Is he alright? Something about the way he talks to me when he talks about you makes me think he's not well. He wanted assurances, or promises about how I'll feel about you after he's gone." Rachel said, "After he's gone?" Paul said, "Not in so many words, but that was the idea." Rachel tucked the jug in under a table. She was leaning forward, which obviously meant "Anything else?" Paul said, "He is talking a lot. As if he doesn't think he has much time left to . . ." Paul and Rachel both sat back in their chairs. Was my father sick? Neither of them spoke. Apparently, it was up to me to force Paul to deliver the sad facts. And because I'd made a virtue of my bluntness, because I'd been willing to make the tough call about Rashelle Whippet's future, I looked right at Paul and said, "Should we cook the halibut on the grill?" Paul shrugged. Rachel raised her empty glass, but then she turned down Paul's offer of more wine. Paul held up the half-empty jug and studied it, as if it was an hourglass, a measure of something. He put the jug on the floor and said, "I guess you had plenty of time to tell Mark about the dress." Rachel said, "And the apples." They both had figured out more about my father and his story than I had. Paul said, "I know what happened that night." Rachel said, "Monday night?" Paul said, "Yes." Rachel said, "Is it the end?" And Paul said, "No. I think he's saving that for dessert. Here's what happened: Celia was asleep and then—Whack! Something woke her. Whack! Whack! Whack! The noise was below her, but it was moving. Whack! Whack!" Paul banged out the whacks on the arm of his chair, and we felt the force of them. Celia got out of bed and flung open her bedroom window to see what was happening, and the window flew to the top of the sill with the loudest Whack! yet. She leaned out and saw a line of heads below her. All the Sisters had flung open their windows. Celia pressed her body farther out into the night, and she hovered there, like the lead goose above a flock of birds itching to set sail. One of the Sisters on the second floor pointed at something in the distance. Celia saw a brightness well down the road, and it took her a few seconds to see that they were torches, at least two of them, moving toward the Shakers. Or were they moving toward the Negro Jesus? The flames grew taller, brighter by the second, and their tails stretched out like banners in the breeze. It was a long time before the lead torch was near enough to illuminate the figure beneath it. A fat man riding a spotted horse was leading a long line of riderless horses on a tether that stretched back to a taller man on a white horse, the other torchbearer. One of the Sisters below shouted, "The racing horses, for the Swedes," and then the parade looped away from the Dwelling and stamped around toward the unfinished racetrack. Celia sat by the open window. Her breast hurt a bit. She worried that dawn was in the offing when she heard some birds, but they turned out to be crickets, night callers. Rhea snorted occasionally, but she did not wake. Celia fell asleep in her chair. One, two, three. Celia was awakened by three shots fired from a large gun. It was still dark, and Rhea was asleep. Celia stuck her head out the window. Nothing. A horse brayed, and then several cried out together, and then lamplight spilled from the first floor of the Dwelling. After a few minutes, she heard a door slam shut. Soon, she saw Brother Richard and Brother Joseph below, trotting toward the racetrack, their dark coats flying behind them. Celia stole out of her room and made her slow way down the dark stairs. The eldress was standing on the second-story landing. She nodded. "Yea, Sister. We expect it is only the Swedes. A shot of gin and a stable full of horses, and they are all cowboys." She put her hand on the newel post, to steady herself and to halt Celia's progress. "Keep company with me, Sister."

Celia sat on a stair and leaned against the railing. She must have dozed off, because the eldress was hissing at her when she opened her eyes. The eldress said, "The Brothers are back." Brother Joseph stood opposite the eldress, on the Brothers' stairs. Richard stayed well below him. Joseph assured the eldress that the shots they'd heard were harmless. The Swedes had been working all night and were weary of their labors, and they'd begun to shoot at each other's hats. Richard kindly added, "It was only a handful of them, those who were drunk." The eldress sighed and said, "Had they been sober, they would now have holes in their heads. Yea, Brothers. Perhaps we will be granted some rest." That was it. Paul smiled. He pointed to the kitchen door. My father bowed from behind the screen. Paul said, "Take it away." My father joined us on the deck. I stood up and said, "Let's eat fast. I want to know how it ends." My father said, "Shall we grill the halibut?" Rachel hmmmed and said, "Mark's very words." She stood up, too, but she backed away, as if she wanted to take a picture of the three of us and needed distance to fit us all into the frame. She smiled, but you could see it wasn't just joy she was feeling; it was complicated, bittersweet, wistful, and a little unnerving. Paul finally asked, "What is it, Rachel?" She said, "I was wondering if it was the wine, or maybe just the light, but I think it's something else." She didn't move and neither did we. "You can't see it, but you're all even, I mean equal, I mean, it's very Shaker, I suppose. The three of you are exactly the same height." Except we weren't. Paul and I really were the same height. But my real father was as tall as my brother, Tommy of the tuxedo, and as Rachel had reminded me, "taller than you." Rachel could see there was something wrong with the picture. It was too democratic to be true. Like Nervy Derby, who'd lost his bid to become a senator by only an inch or two, the Man from Sabbathday Lake, Maine, didn't quite measure up. It wasn't the wine, and it wasn't the light. It was politics as usual.

MECHANICS
Always ask, Who is the actor?

Participles are *-ing* verbs (cooking, eating) that emphasize the participating. If we add some words to a participle, we get a *participial phrase:* for example, cooking the fish on the grill; eating dessert on the screened porch. But it may be simpler to treat all participial phrases as modifiers; they give meaning to actors (subjects) in our sentences. For instance: Cooking the fish on the grill, my father . . . ; eating dessert on the screened porch, we . . . This is fairly simple, right? But there is a problem dangling just out of view. The dreaded dangling modifier (your third-grade teacher probably used its more formal name, the dangling participle) is a participial phrase (cooking the fish on the grill) that is not attached to the actor (the person or thing—the who) responsible for performing the participle: cooking fish on the grill, the mosquitoes swarmed around my father. This implies that the mosquitoes prepared dinner; the participle (cooking) is dangling far away from the actor (my father). It is tempting to solve the problem by throwing words at it, as if the dangling modifier is a spider we can scare off. Watch: after eating fish on the deck, the lemon pie we ate for dessert tasted a little weird. <u>Who</u> was <u>eating</u>? We didn't get rid of the dangling modifier by throwing <u>after</u> at it. We still have a <u>lemon pie</u> that has been <u>eating fish</u> (after eating fish . . . the lemon pie), which is one way of explaining why it tasted weird, but not the truth. So, when you use a participle (any *-ing* verb), do not let it dangle. Ask, <u>Who</u> is do<u>ing</u> that? Dangl<u>ing</u> around with a bunch of unemployed actors in your sentences, <u>you</u> can expect nothing but trouble.

my father

AFTER EATING FISH on the deck, we did eat lemon pie on the screened porch. And it tasted weird, neither bitter nor sweet. It was yellow mush. Paul poked at the seeds he found in his slice, and Rachel ate a bit of the crust. My father said, "This was a mistake." Unfortunately, it was not the first time he'd come up short. I had taken off my sneakers, but it had not helped. It certainly didn't make Paul any shorter, and I knew Paul and I were the same height, and Paul was still as tall as Thomas S., or Brother Thomas—whoever he was, he missed being my father by a few inches. Had we been alone, I would have put him on a rack and stretched him. I had been fooled, and I had invited my friends to meet the man who'd fooled me, and I wanted revenge—but I also wanted him to be tall enough. Paul now knew the old Man from Maine was not who I'd said he was. I could see it in his stiffness. Right after Rachel raised the height issue, Paul put on an elaborate truss of manners that prevented

informal contact with me and everyone else; it also restricted
his appetite. It was a distracting performance, and I wondered
if he was rehearsing for his own father's funeral. Paul had a
real, live father. Perhaps this explained his quiet indignation; he
knew the fullness of my loss. Rachel looked glum. Having
thrown a bucket of water on my hopes of having a father, she'd
had the grace to dump one over her own head and dampen her
spirits. She and I applied a lot of wine to the problem, but it
didn't help. I was wondering, Who's the elderly actor? Whose
father is he? I skipped dessert; I wasn't ready for the end. Paul
poured coffee. The Man who wasn't my father said, "We still
have the Shakers." He knew. He avoided everyone's gaze. He
did not say anything for several minutes. I pitied us, all of us.
We knew how to behave. We'd had plenty of experience at dinner tables. We knew how to act like an unhappy family. He was
the father in our little drama, and he had the last big speech. It
was my house, but I was not prepared to kick him out. He must
have known my father quite well; they must have been friends.
He was as near as I was ever going to get. And he had done his
homework; he had passed. Paul poured more wine for Rachel
and me. He offered some to the Man, but I said I'd get him his
bourbon. Paul asked if I had any scotch. Of course I did. Paul
had brought it with him this morning. I told him I'd get him a
glass. He asked me to bring the bottle, though Paul didn't drink
much. Just as my father never drank, according to my mother,
even after she saw him with Tommy and an empty bottle of single malt on Easter morning. Scotch, not bourbon—another
miss. Scotch was what my father never drank, like Paul. Still, I
had to give the Man a few points for choosing bourbon. It was
a good guess; Jim Beam was distilled in Kentucky. After I doled

out the various medicines, the family aged. The old Man took his bottle to the wicker rocking chair. The rest of us put our elbows or our feet on the table. We were ready. It was Tuesdee in Kentucky. Rhea was awake before Celia. After the first bell rang, she said, "Time fer me to get up to somethin." Celia wanted Rhea to feel at home. She said, "The other children will be happy you came back, Rhea. They love having you here." Rhea squirmed, trying to shake off the compliment, then she darted to the door. Before she left, she turned and said, "Thanks, Surster. Yer nice. But them kids, theys all orfins. They love everbody." Celia let her go and then headed out to the coop. Ethel was ahead of her. From the porch, Celia saw her limping down the road. Then someone yelled, "Sister Celia!" It was Caleb Kroll. "Where are you headed? May I join you?" He had slept on Village grounds at the insistence of the eldress. He was not invited into the Dwelling; he'd slept among the day laborers, but the eldress had overcome his initial resistance with a lavish dinner at her private table. She'd thought it best to keep him close, where he could be watched. Bunking down with the hired hands hadn't suited Kroll. "You'll have to forgive my appearance," he said, fussing with his hair, "but I wasn't prepared to stand in line to shave." Celia noticed he'd taken the time to put on his gun. She knew it was up to her to distract him, but she had to get to the coop. She hoped Richard wouldn't arrive until after Ethel was gone, as he had promised. Kroll said, "Reckon you're getting accustomed to people trailing you. Everyone hoping to lay eyes on the Negro Jesus." He lagged just behind her, and he spoke over her shoulder, as if he had his gun pressed into her back. As they passed the barn, Celia saw Ethel emerge from the dark coop with a bird in one hand and a cleaver in the other. When Ethel spotted Celia, she bounded back inside. Celia quickened her pace, and someone hollered, "Yea! Master Kroll." Celia turned, and so did Kroll. It was Richard, running toward them. It was happening too fast, and Ethel would be in the way, so Celia ran through the pen and into the coop. She yelled, "Sister Ethel?" This startled the elderly Sister, who was kneeling just below her in the darkness. Ethel stood up and jammed a bird into Celia's breast, where Celia held it, pressing on the wings to calm it, and then she realized that it had no head. The bird shook and chugged warm blood from its neck, soaking Celia. When she turned again, Ethel was gone. The other hens were bobbing and flapping, but they stifled their cries, choking on their fear. Celia smelled her bloody hand; it smelled old, like turned meat. Kroll appeared in the doorway. Richard appeared behind him and shoved him inside. It was happening too fast. Kroll pointed his thumb at Richard and said, "Who is this fool? Tell him to leave off." Richard grabbed Kroll's shoulders and shoved him back to the wall. Celia yelled, "Brother!" Richard stood between Celia and Kroll. His voice was thick and threatening when he said, "Nay, Sister. You do not understand. Thomas is not where I left him. He is gone. The East House door was open when I got there." He turned to Kroll and hollered, "Where is he?" Kroll was sweating, and he whimpered when he said, "I have business," and then he lurched toward the door, but Richard slammed him back against the wall. Celia said, "It will come to nothing if he is harmed, Brother." Richard snorted. Celia's words restored Kroll's swagger. He put his hands on his hips, displaying his gun. He said, "I am a man of business. You pious fool. All I did was save the life of some octoroon's child. What's my reward? A bunk bed with a houseful of dirty niggers, and now this ape trailing me while I try to have a civil conversa—." Richard groaned and swung. His fist cracked Kroll's jaw and flung him up in the air a few inches, and then Kroll crashed into the wall and slid to the floor. Richard moved in above him, and he looked deadly big. Celia said, "His gun." Richard pressed his boot into Kroll's thigh. Nothing. Celia stooped and drew the gun, and then she held her hand to his beating heart. She smiled up at Richard and said, "Just resting." Richard was not consoled by the news. "Thomas put his life in our hands, Sister. We did not protect him. Give me the gun." Celia said, "Let him live." Richard put the gun in his pocket. Once the weapon was out of sight, it was possible to think clearly, hopefully. Celia said, "Hadn't you removed the ladder from the porch roof?" Richard snorted; he meant "Of course." "And the door was open?" As she said these words, Celia understood all was not lost, but Richard did not. She said, "It was not battered? No window was broken?" Her questions made Richard indignant, and he shouted, "No, Sister! He was safe when I left him in the attic. He pulled the ladder up with him through the trapdoor. I had taken precautions. The house was empty this morning, and the door open. Someone got to him." Celia said, "Nay, Brother. The door was locked from within. Surely, Thomas let himself out. Surely he is alive." Richard waved away her words, and he closed his eyes to let her know he would entertain no hope. Celia whispered, "Don't you see?" Richard smiled. His eyes flicked open. And then he laughed. He understood. Thomas must have escaped. He said, "The door was locked from within." Celia said, "Yea, Brother. Does Thomas know the roads to Baltimore?" Richard said, "Perhaps he can find his way. But he will need time. We have to do something more to delay the Master." Kroll dragged the heels of his boots through the dirt, raising his knees. Richard touched the handle of the gun, but Kroll's legs went slack and he fell back into his stupor. Relieved, Celia pressed her hand to her heart. Her hand came away bloodier. She stared at her brown palm. She said, "Yea, Brother. See. See what has happened here. What an amazing story." Richard said, "What is it?" Celia pointed to the carcass of Ethel's sacrificial hen. Richard looked confused. Celia said, "If this so-called Master shot and wounded me, Brother, he would be detained in our county jail for many months. In Kentucky, it is a crime to kill a Shaker, or even just to try." Richard looked at the gun. He was impressed. He nodded. "You are bleeding profusely, Sister. I must get you to bed." Richard unhooked his belt and bent down. Soon, Kroll's hands were bound, and he was slung up, tethered to a wooden brace beneath the lowest roost. Richard touched the yellowing bruise on Kroll's face, and then he opened his hand to shield Kroll and fired the gun at the ground. The hens screamed, and in their panic, they forgot they could not fly. Even after they crashed, they flapped their blunt wings furiously and bounded out of the coop. Richard slung Celia over his shoulder and said, "The gunfire has drawn the others. Your body must be limp." It was a bumpy ride as Richard rushed down the road, yelling to passing Shakers, "In the coop. Bring the man. He shot Sister Celia! He shot Sister Celia!" Celia's belly banged against Richard's shoulder as he ran up the Dwelling House stairs, and then he flung her backward and she bounced down on a bed, and Emma ripped away her blouse. Richard left the room, and several Sisters sped into the infirmary. Emma said, "She smells like a hen." Celia could not distinguish among the clattering voices. Suddenly, the Sisters scattered and streamed out into the hall, and the door slammed, and then the eldress yelled, "Sister Celia!" Celia kept her eyes closed until Richard spoke from nearby. He said, "It is safe to speak, Sister." Celia opened her eyes. The eldress backed off a bit. She looked terrified, as if someone was holding her off the ground by her hair. Emma was scowling. She joined Richard, who was whispering to Louise. The eldress said, "Brother Richard told me what you have done, how you plan to accuse Kroll. But surely Kroll will deny the charge, Sister Celia." Celia said, "But Brother Richard is my witness. He disarmed my attacker." The eldress let some time pass. She wanted to see if this story had wings. Emma reappeared with a knife and cut a ragged hole in the bloody blouse. "Where the bullet entered," she said. She raised the blade. "You will need a wound, Sister." Emma was eager to proceed. Celia sat up. She dragged her underclothes away from her breast and displayed her puffy, scarred skin. The eldress was impressed. She moved in close to Celia and extended her arms, to obstruct Richard's view. Emma frowned. "Is the wound fresh?" The eldress grabbed Emma's wrist and spoke firmly. She said, "It will have to do, Sister." Emma pulled herself free and said, "Nay, Mother." Her insistence impressed Celia; Emma's thoroughness was reassuring. Emma pushed Celia back on the bed and leaned over her breast. She tapped the flap of skin. Celia winced. Emma was very close when she said, "This is not good, Sister. The animal's blood has seeped into the wound. The danger of infection is great." She backed away and dragged the eldress with her. "It will pass as a bullet wound, but you must give me time to remove the rot." Celia sat up and said, "Rot?" She tapped the flap a few times, trying to prove it was not as bad as it looked. The eldress said, "Do not be afraid, Sister. It serves your story. It will appear to the World that Emma put you down to extract the bullet." At the calm center of the mad activity that ensued, Celia wondered what it might mean if, after all, she and Richard had unwittingly conspired to end her life. She was pleased to think she would be a Shaker in the end. Emma cradled her head and fed her a warm drink. It numbed her tongue and made her teeth too big. Sister Frederika held her hand until she could see

My so-called father was snoring. It had all come to a disappointing end. In the story, Thomas, the Negro Jesus, had set himself free. Caleb Kroll, symbol of the Master class, had been taken out of the picture by the Shakers. It didn't ring true. In the World I'd inherited, freedom still cost people their lives, and not just in Selma or Soweto or Tiananmen Square but on the heating grates of Harvard Square, in Boston's so-called Projects, and maybe even at McClintock. Maybe Brother Richard's grafts didn't take. The Shaker stock had been cut away, but what fruit did the next generation bear? Paul yawned. I offered to split the last of the cold coffee with him, but he waved away the pot. Rachel looked at her watch. It was almost twelve, but that was this morning, when Rachel's watch stopped and we all had time. Then my so-called father, Brother Thomas, stood up and cleared our water glasses. He emptied them by tossing the remains through the screen, into the stand of crocosmia. He said, "The tomatoes will want watering every day." The rest of us watched him in stunned silence, as if he was a ghost, maybe Hamlet's father coming back onto the stage for a final bow. He put the glasses on the table and poured out four shots of Jim Beam. He raised his glass and said, "To Thomas Sternum." We all sipped the sour mash tentatively. It wasn't so bad. Even Rachel found it rewarding enough for a second sip. "Your father moved to Maine a few years after Sister Ruth. He had a duplex down the road from the Village. I rented the other half. He spent most of his days doing God knows what with the Shakers at Sabbathday Lake, and he spent his nights talking about his stucco house in Pittsfield, down the road from Hancock as he told it. Sister Ruth moved to Canterbury in the seventies with the last of the Convenanted Shakers, and your father gave up going to the Village after that. He had no family, and he knew it." I was unable to listen for a while. He had no reason to lie anymore, but I had no reason to want a summary version of the father who had summarily dismissed me from his life. Rachel and Paul would have to fill me in on the details of my family history. I was only drawn back in when he said, "Your father was a terrible land-lord, and he complained bitterly about the way I kept the property. Not that he ever so much as cut a blade of grass. He was attractive, though—magnetic. And he made you feel he had a better way of doing things, though he rarely did do anything but take pictures." Brother Thomas poured himself another shot and pushed the bottle toward Paul. "Your father was a perfec-tionist, theoretically speaking. He wasn't proud of the mess he'd left your mother in, but he just didn't know how to fix it. Fact is, he didn't know how to fix a leaky faucet, if that's any consolation." Rachel closed her eyes tight and swallowed the rest of her bourbon. She made a terrible face, and she squealed when she said, "Consolation? Consolation?" She cooled herself off with a little wine and said, "Is that why you came here?" Brother Thomas retreated to his rocker. Paul snapped a bit of pie crust and crushed it into the table. Brother Thomas said, "When I read in the newspapers about what was happening to you, well . . . I don't know. I was going to say I thought coming here is what your father would've wished he'd do, but who am I to say?" Rachel whispered, "Well, you just said it." I asked him when my father had died. "It was 1982. Same year as Sister Ruth. She was buried at Canterbury. We took your father's body out to sea, as he'd asked. He never felt at home in the World, God rest his soul. And maybe the truth is, he was dead when he left the Berkshires after you were born." Paul shook his head and said to Brother Thomas, "I don't think you've got the knack of this consolation thing." Rachel tipped her glass and said, "Hear, hear." It was weird; maybe it was being with Paul and Rachel; maybe it was the sour-mash bourbon, which made even the bitter, cold coffee taste sweet; it might even have been the simple gift of a New England summer night— but I *was* consoled. I wanted to go back to the beginning, to Hancock, to the night I was born, when my father had seen Sister Celia leave the Meeting House for the last time. On the first day I met him, Brother Thomas had told me that Celia had heard something coming up the road. She'd turned around. I wanted to know what she saw then, at the moment she was leaving the World and I was arriving. Brother Thomas rocked. "It was Sister Ruth walking up the road, but Sister Celia didn't recognize her. Celia turned until she saw a man standing by the gate. She saw your father. She didn't know him, though. He was just a darker darkness, so she went on turning. It was time. The paint was slipping from the familiar landscape. The portraits dripped in their frames. It was time. She turned to the Meeting House window, and the last light flickered from the chandelier as a few more flames sunk into pools of what was once wax. She turned around again, and the gate was gone, and everything was dim, as if Emma had herbed her but good, and nothing was clear until . . ." Thomas rocked a while in silence. And then he said, "Until she could see it all clearly, because she remembered that the end had always been with her. And she woke from her stupor, and she saw Caleb Kroll seated beside her bed. Can you see her, Mark? Can you see that we have to stick with the story? Can you see that the ending is not perfect?" I could see Celia waking in the Pleasant Hill infirmary after Emma had operated on her breast. She was face to face with Caleb Kroll. He was still a little fuzzy, and he seemed to be wearing a hat, but then Celia blinked a few times, and she saw Kroll clearly. His head was wrapped in gauze. And the eldress was standing beside Kroll, and Emma and Richard were there, too, and then Celia heard Rhea yell, "Surster? Lookee here." On the other side of her bed, near Louise, Rhea was standing beside a fat man with a ponytail. It was Rhea's father; he had come back. Celia said, "Is it Tuesdee, Rhea?" And Rhea giggled and said, "Ain't so lucky as I sposed. It's Wensdee. But who's countin?" Rhea leaned in and put her hand on Celia's forehead, as she must have seen Emma do. "Stop sweatin, Surster. You's here again. An I ain't no orfin neither." Mr. Goodrich reeled Rhea into his soft side. Then there was a moment of intolerable confusion as everyone started to speak at once, but Louise yelled, "Ha!" and seized the lead. "It turns out that our Mr. Kroll is none other than Mr. Caleb Kroll, a tobacco grower from Raleigh. What do you make of that? His family moved from Ohio to Carolina after the war, when land was cheap. Never been to Mississippi. Never held a slave. Union people. Almost got himself hung here among the Shakers. It was only Mr. Goodrich saved him being tied up to a hitching post by the Brothers. Ha! Not that he doesn't deserve a whipping for all his years growing tobacco when he might've been putting in more potatoes." Celia rolled over and faced Caleb Kroll. She was humiliated; now that Kroll had a few bruises, she could plainly see that he was an innocent man. Celia looked up at Richard, and he understood. "Thomas? I suppose he's made it to Mississippi by now." Celia was confused again. Wasn't Baltimore his destination? And again, everyone in the room began to talk, and one version crashed against another, like waves on the ocean she would never see. When Celia turned to her other side, she saw that Mr. Goodrich had his hat on. It was time. He and Rhea would leave. They would recede into that distance that we only know as a horizon, the dark line we draw between land and sky to remind ourselves that there is more to the World than we will ever see, more than can be fit into one frame. They would all go away. In the full frame of Celia's life, Rhea and Kroll and the Negro Jesus would be small dark dots in the distance, not as prominent as the Brothers and Sisters, or the hens in the coop, or even the fingers on her hand. From among the many voices, Celia pulled together the basic elements of the story. And these survived every telling, which numbered in the thousands before the Shakers locked the doors and left Pleasant Hill. It turned out that Celia had seen it from her bedroom window, but not clearly. It had all happened Monday night. The second torch in the parade of horses was carried by a tall thin man, and he was the so-called Master, not Caleb Kroll. The so-called Master had come from Mississippi to reclaim his rightful property, whose name was Thomas. And he had wounded Ruth on Sunday and left her bleeding, as a warning, at the edge of the Shaker land. Then he'd roamed around the nearby towns, hoping he might meet a Shaker selling seeds or dairy, someone who could show him around the abandoned buildings of Pleasant Hill. Mr. Goodrich was in town trying to hire a man to ride with him and his newly acquired horses, and he liked the looks of the tall, skinny gentleman, who was plainly not a rustler or a thief. And that was how the so-called Master came to ride into the Village, carrying a torch, while the Shaker Sisters watched from their open windows. The Swedes greeted Mr. Goodrich and his friend and offered them some whiskey. And far above, from an attic window, Thomas saw his so-called Master, Ruth's cruel father, and maybe Thomas could see that there was nothing else standing between him and his freedom. He made his way down to the ground floor, and he unlatched the door, from within, and he crept up from behind, and no one saw him until he jumped the so-called Master and looped a rope around his neck. At that moment, Mr. Goodrich rather calmly reached over with one of his big hands and hauled Thomas to the ground. He could not imagine what the hell was wrong with the little man; what was he thinking, a little guy like that trying to choke a southern gentleman who was tall as an oak? The gentleman showed his good nature by brushing Thomas off as a joke. He turned around, and he pointed at Thomas, whose trousers—Richard's trousers—had slipped down around his ankles. The gentleman laughed as he pulled the rope over his head and twirled it like a lariat. He said, "Lose your belt, boy?" And Mr. Goodrich had to laugh. The Swedes who'd circled around had to laugh. And it was funny until the gentleman drew his gun and brought the so-called Negro to his knees. None of them knew what to do. Thomas knew. He took off his shirt—Richard's shirt—and turned around, turned his back, so the Master would not have to suffer the indignity of seeing the face of a man as he beat him. Mr. Goodrich had never seen anything like it. He'd never seen the backside of America. Thomas bent his head to the earth. The Master raised his whip. But it was Mr. Goodrich who shot-shot-shot and woke the Shakers as he killed the so-called gentleman. And though the eldress always hated to admit it, it was the Swedes who suggested the ingenious burial site. They dug a hole in the earth at the center of the racetrack. They shoveled lime with the soil when they filled in the grave, to hasten the body's inevitable decay. Mr. Goodrich gave Thomas a horse—not one of the nervous thoroughbreds but his own horse, a trustworthy animal accustomed to long rides. He accepted no thanks from Thomas. But Mr. Goodrich carried this message from the Negro Jesus to Brother Richard: *It is late, Brother. Too late for Africa. I want to go home.* And that was the end of the story. Celia had slept through it. She sat up a bit in her bed as Mr. Goodrich led Caleb Kroll to the door, but turned to the Shakers before he left. Rhea was almost invisible under his big arm. "Been a helluva time. Got me the best land in Kentucky. Rhea here's got dresses purty nuff fer a weddin, God willin. An this man? Mr. Kroll'll be gettin twice his askin price fer the first shipment of tabacca. I reckon it this way. If ya gotta ask a man ta keep his mouth shut, ta say nuthin bout what he's seen, ya give him somethin sweet to chew on—when he's able ta chew." Caleb Kroll pursed his lips again, which was as near as he'd get for a while to a smile. Then they were gone. Celia closed her eyes. "The truth is—." Celia did not have to open her eyes; she recognized the voice of the eldress. "The truth is, no Shaker ever saw the so-called. As far as the law is concerned, he was never here, not as far as we could see. Lime is powerful on a body, almost as powerful as it is in the blocks of this house." Celia was throbbing with pain, and throbbing with something else, something sweet, something warm, and it was liquid. Emma was bent over her with a foamy beaker and everything melted away, and Celia was spinning in the bluegrass of Kentucky and she was spinning beneath the weather vane on the round barn at Hancock and it was time. It was time. It was time as she turned to the white fence that ran right up against the World,

turned to the dark visitor at the gate,

turned to her Sisters and Brothers ahead,

turned to the henhouse and pastures and barns,

turned faster than ever a body could,

turned to the dark Meeting House,

turned in time to see the window glass weeping like wax,

turned until her wound and every man's back was immaterial,

turned into living skin, and she could smell the harvest being born in budding orchards all across America, where the last of the Shaker stock would soon be cut away and a new breed of apple would thrive in the World, golden and sweet.

a g r e e m e n t   a m o n g   f r i e n d s

THE SHAKERS NEVER lived by the sea. They were inland people. This explains their ability to keep romance at bay. In Ipswich, we are swayed by an ocean breeze. On a hot night, when
the tide is out and the river recedes, the air is rife with what we
like to call salt air. It's intoxicating. You know the ocean is as far
away as it gets, somewhere out there, and yet it is still here, in
your home, in the air. It is swamp gas, really, the complaints of
an exposed band of soft earth that has learned to like it better
underwater, and it stinks. But so do sour mash, and cheap
wine, and egg salad sandwiches. We like it. We like salt air,
which rusts our cars and peels the paint off our clapboards. We
love it. That salt air is a promise. We can smell it. We know the
Atlantic will come back for us again, and again, taking a little
more land every day, approaching the porous stone foundations
of our homes, eager to marry us to its ways, and vowing to make
sailors of us all. On Saturday night, however, there was nothing

much in the air except the sound of my so-called father snoring. Rachel and Paul and I were smiling, and why not? There
we were. We cleared the table, and we tried to do it quietly. But
I splattered a handful of flatware on the floor, and Paul
knocked over some glasses. We woke a dog who lived up the
street, and he yapped about us for a while. The snoring
stopped, but Thomas S. did not open his eyes. He was awake,
but it was too late. Whatever he'd done, he couldn't take it
back. I suppose it had started out as his idea of a Gift. And now
it was mine to live with. Paul finished loading the dishwasher
while I walked Rachel to her van, which she'd nosed in next to
my house, where it looked like a sizable addition. Why Rachel
Reed drove a van as big as my living room was her business,
and she understood that the stranger sleeping in the guest bed
was mine. She didn't ask me how I was going to get rid of him.
She didn't offer any advice for the morning-after conversations.
She put on her hat. She kissed me twice, once on each side of
my face, a habit more Americans ought to take up. And then
Rachel smiled up at my bedroom. It was lit, from within. Paul
was there. She laughed, and then she said, "If you can't figure
out how to make room for that man, please tell him I have a
very big house." The downstairs was dark, and the snoring had
resumed. I listened to my one message. It was Ellen. "I was
reading the back of a bag of cheese popcorn. It was lunchtime,
and we'd finished the Cheever stories. I heard something. Her
eyes flicked open, and she was as surprised as I was. Foolishly,
I said, 'Mom?' Who else would it be in her bed, not to mention
her body? Her lips moved, and she was saying something. Her
first words in more than a year, and I couldn't hear them. Did
she want water? Was she in pain? She said it several times, but

I couldn't make it out. I called the doctor, and then we waited for him to come. Her eyes were open, but I don't think she was seeing much, so I told her to hang on. She dragged her hands out from under her legs and wiggled her fingers. The day was starting to go gray, as it does in cheap romance novels, to warn you that the sexually active heroine is about to be taught a lesson. When the doctor got here, he bent over her bed, and then she said it again. He stood up and put his hand on my arm. I braced myself. He said, 'Your mother wants to know if you have any clam chowder.' He took her blood pressure and checked her other vitals. She was back to normal, normal for her. He said I should be prepared for the worst, because people often have a remission before the end, as if they'd saved something for that rainy day. After the doctor left, she drank a few spoonfuls of soup. She's resting now. I think we'll read something summery next, something she might read at the beach. I hope you didn't make that bet about Dad with anyone else. You'll lose your shirt. I stopped by my office this morning, and I found a photocopy of his obituary and scanned it onto your e-mail. It ran in the Poland Spring weekly in 1982. He is dead, Mark. I still occasionally see him at a diner when I'm in upstate New York, or at the airport, in line for a flight I'm not taking. So let's just say, All bets are off. Rain coming our way, from the west, so you'll have it after the weekend. And I hear there's a turnpike in Massachusetts now. It runs from Boston to the Berkshires. You might want to take a spin one of these sunny days."

Anything was possible. I went upstairs quietly. Paul was asleep. Before I got to the noisy part, where I drop a hanger or knock over the alarm clock, he was awake. Paul is a parentally light sleeper, which works out as a deficit for him and a bonus for me.

He said, "You okay?" I told him I was, oddly enough, that . . . He'd closed his eyes, as if to say, "We can talk about it in the morning. It was just a simple question." I followed him to sleep. At some point in my dream, which was set in a snowy place, everything started to shake and tremble. It took me a while to realize it was Paul. He was shaking my shoulder, and he said my name several times. Soon, despite my best efforts to resist him, I was awake. It was bright in the bedroom. Paul dragged me to the window, and I hoped he wasn't going to make me admire the sunrise. I'd seen it once or twice. Paul said, "He's leaving. I heard the car idling." My car? I was really awake. I looked down. There was a white station wagon in front of the house. It looked familiar. It was Dolly. Dolly's was the only cab company in Ipswich, and Dolly was the only driver. She had seven kids, and she said none of her neighbors had ever wanted her in their car pool. So she ran her old wagon through the car wash one day and started Dolly's Taxi Company. She and her kids had recently moved into a big house with a tennis court; she told me she had a long list of people who weren't invited. I watched the white wagon until it turned out of sight. Dolly was the only way out of Ipswich on a Sunday. The local train didn't run, but you could catch the 7:13 in West Gloucester and be in Boston by 8:00. I didn't know the run from Boston to Maine. I didn't even know if that was his destination. Paul went out for the Sunday papers and came back with cinnamon rolls as well. We sat on the deck and didn't say much for the longest time. Then, somewhere in the middle of the Week in Review, Paul dropped the paper and said, "It's not as if everyone we know hasn't tried to get us to live together. And it's not as if I actually wanted to move to D.C. Who wants

to spend summers in the humidity capital of the world? I love
Boston. It's just absurd that we haven't managed to say any of
this to each other." He was obviously reading as carefully as I
was; I'd finished the front section and the magazine without
learning the date. And I knew what he meant. He meant it as
a question: *Of all people, how did Thomas S. manage to move us
together?* Unfortunately, the answer was another question entirely. I suggested the beach, where not knowing the answers is
part of the routine, and you're also encouraged to take off your
shirts and slather oil on each other's backs. Tide had been out
and was coming in. Paul and I sat on a thin spit of sand, trad-
ing sections of the newspaper we weren't reading, until the
water pushed us back. It must have been all of that rearranging
of chairs and hats and paper that made me mindful of the practical tasks that lay ahead. It was daunting; if we wanted to live
together, someone was going to have to do a lot of packing.
Whenever I moved, I flirted with the crime of book burning.
But even before the lugging commenced, we would have to
agree on a destination. Where would we live? My house was
less than an hour from town, but not if you were Paul, who had
to be at work every day before nine, along with a million other
drivers. Paul's apartment was perfect for Paul and the occasional guest, but I had my research to think about; living in a
one-bedroom in Harvard Square, I would find it hard to get to
my gardening, and though Paul's front hall was fine for his bike,
it was not the ideal place to keep the boat I'd need once I had
tenure. It occurred to me that the reason Paul and I had never
lived together was our desire to avoid this moment of hope-
lessness, of homelessness. I looked at the Sunday paper. It was
the first edition in weeks that did not feature someone's reflec-

tions on me and the McClintock mess. Having escaped from the headlines, I hated to think I would have to start all over again, at the back, looking for a place to live in the Real Estate pages. I suggested we discuss it over dinner. Paul was digging around in his knapsack. He said, "I can't stay tonight. I don't have a suit or a pair of shoes. And the morning commute is . . ." Why say it? He offered me a plum, which was sweet. I reminded him that he had two bureaus. Couldn't he haul one of them to Ipswich so he'd be prepared for an occasional overnight? Paul said, "That's perfect. It doesn't solve the commuting problem, and it will leave you with no place to put a pair of socks in Cambridge, but otherwise . . ." I stood up. He said, "Or were you thinking I could move the bureau every day? Like a briefcase." On the one hand there was Paul, and on the other there was the Atlantic, which had warmed up to about fifty-seven degrees, a perfect temperature for chilling a bottle of wine. I was stuck. Paul said, "I know you hate to acquire anything, but we really have to get a place for me to keep some clothes up here. And a desk for you in Cambridge. I'll be here and there all summer, but nine months a year we'll be spending weeknights in town, right? You'll need a place to correct papers." He was right, of course. Neither of us had to leave home. I'd be teaching two or three days a week, and sleeping in Cambridge would save me time. He wanted nothing more from his weekends than open roads and smelly marshes and something for dinner that was grilled, not boiled in a bag. We could live in both places at once. It was obvious once he said it. That's the pleasure of a twice-told tale; someone else sees it differently. We weren't homeless. We had two homes, and they were both familiar. I could buy a bureau. I didn't need a desk. I liked to sit at one of the tables Paul had next to his windows, where I could look up from the fragments and dangling modifiers and watch people thread their way through the Cambridge Common on one of several well-lit paths. Paul closed his eyes and lowered the brim of his cap. I walked down to the water and sloshed onward until the waves splashed my belly, and then I dove in. It's not true, what we're told about heart attacks being caused by cold water. Our hearts know how to handle a shock. As soon as you start to do something stupid, like swimming in Ipswich before the solstice, your heart stops sending blood to your fingers and toes. It doesn't panic. It slows down. It can't stop you from putting your extremities at risk, but it can save itself, the heart of you. There are people who live for years after they've lost a finger or two. No one doesn't have a heart. That's just who we are. Not surprisingly, the water cleared my head; I was courting brain death, but I knew my skin would thank me for the dunking. I swam out against the incoming tide, and then I turned around and just kept my head above the waves and drifted to shore. Our bodies are buoyant but not perfectly so, and I am always grateful to my mother and my sister Ellen, who taught me to swim. It's one of the skills I picked up quickly. Swimming was easy for me. I had ribbons and tin cups in my bedroom and a place on the high school team because people had taken the time to teach me the basic skills needed by kids. I always knew I wouldn't be good at everything. From the start, even Ellen had to admit I had terrible aim, and if you hit a grounder while I was playing shortstop, you could walk to second base. I didn't make the cut for Little League, but I kept playing baseball, after school, in backyards, and occasionally I'd catch a break; somebody would pop one up for an easy out.

And there was always the swimming season to look forward to. The truth is, if I could overcome one of my limits, I would not worry over baseball, and I would ignore the flaws in my character; I would choose to be amphibious. I've always envied newts; probably I always will, thanks to Thomas S. He told me where my father was. He was somewhere in the Atlantic, coming in with the tide. I could not survive for long in that cold water. I could not wait for him. But I could live with the loss now, because the ocean wasn't really going anywhere. The swimming season was upon us. And I can swim like a fish. When we got home, I let Paul shower first, and then I drained the hot-water supply. Paul had made coffee. We sat on the stools. He asked if I was still okay. Then, as if he wasn't convinced, he asked what I was going to do with the evening. I told him I'd water the tomatoes and try to anticipate the questions Fred Hogworthy would ask. Paul said, "You've got the job. They wouldn't have called on a whim." Unlike McClintock, where I'd been hired because Rachel liked the tie I was wearing when I dropped off my résumé. "The question is, " Paul said, "do you want it?" He stood up. He had hung our beach towels on the deck rail. He'd put our bags and hats in the closet. Those were the sort of chores that sometimes took me an entire evening. He finished his coffee, and I walked with him to his car. He waited until he was strapped in to say, "This is the way it is, right? We're together. I'm really happy. It's exciting, isn't it? And it only took us a couple of days to figure it all out—I mean, unless you count those ten years." He grabbed my belt and pulled me toward him. "Call me tonight, before you go to bed. I'll think up some hateful answers you can use in your interview. You don't want to work at Derby's factory. Don't take that job."

He beeped when he was halfway down the street and waved before he turned the corner. I went around to the backyard and watered the tomato stumps. I probably gave them more than they wanted, but I wasn't eager to go inside. I always felt let down when guests left. And it seemed predictably inept of Paul and me to be apart for our first night of living together. I wasted some time upstairs, measuring the prime spots for a second bureau. I had no messages. I avoided my computer. I didn't want to read the obituary Ellen had sent. My father had died plenty of times without any formal announcement. The telephone rang once, and I answered it. It must have been someone who knew me pretty well; I heard a gasp of surprise on the other end, and then the caller hmmmed and hung up. It was early evening. I figured the least I could do was to put away my father's books. They were still stacked on the trunk in the living room. They'd been arranged in descending order, with his last published book on top. Thomas must've done it before he left. Thomas. I felt disloyal; I hadn't thought of him since I'd got home, despite the tomatoes, and when I did, I didn't miss him. His being gone took no getting used to, like Paul's decision to move in. Maybe Thomas had known the ending from the start. He must have known he couldn't be my father forever. But he went ahead and made his approach anyway, and it was a successful graft, and when the time came, he had the good grace to cut out and leave me to enjoy the fruits of my life. *The Shaker Way* was the last book on my trunk because it was the first of my father's published collections. This was the one Thomas told me was a bad book, even dangerous. He'd kept it hidden while he was in the house, and before he left, he'd stuck something inside the cover. I knew it was a letter because there was a note taped to the book that said, "Mark, I wanted you to have this letter, which was your father's (inside). Thank you for the hospitality. Don't forget to water the tomatoes. Brother Thomas S." Inside were four folded pages of white stationery. The letter was dated 20 June 1959.

Mr. Sternum, I write to ask a favor I am not owed. I do not know if Sister Ruth has occupied any of your time on the telephone with our little tale of sadness. We are but three Sisters now at Hancock, and I think it will not be long before Eldress Fanny passes over to the Other Side. Sister Ruth and I will go North. It is hard to leave this home, but I left my home in the World as a child, and I left my home in Kentucky in 1910, and I expect I am getting rather good at leaving. But I do not like to think what will become of the round barn and the Dwelling and the other evidence of Shakerism in the Berkshires if the Biondi brothers are as wealthy as they are persistent. They are dangling a good deal of cash over our heads (so to speak, you understand), and the communities in Maine and New Hampshire must profit by our loss of Hancock. We Shakers are old. I think Sister Ruth will not ask you to return to the Berkshires, despite her desire to preserve our heritage. If she is right in her estimation of the mayhem your presence in Pittsfield might incite for your wife and children, then by all means stay away. It is the least you can do for Mrs. Sternum, to cause her no more hardship. Your children I cannot presume to speak for, though I cannot imagine you have been of much comfort to them in Ohio and Kentucky. If I speak too freely now, Mr. Sternum, we will have to agree it is my right, that age has its compensations. You owe me no succor. I have never strained my back on your behalf. And we Shakers have survived lo these two hundred years

*without your assistance. But, as I suspect you know, I do believe
you have an outstanding debt, something owed to the World. I
speak of your book, which Eldress Fanny refers to as "that damn
book." The Family has never published its opinion of your first
collection of photographs, and I trust Sister Ruth has never spoken to you about the many hours wasted by the Brothers and Sisters here in Hancock in vain discussions about the book and
schemes to counter its message. We do not blame you for our decline, even now. But when came you to us in 1941, under the
aegis of Allen Cuthbert, you proposed a series of Family portraits.
We thought it odd, and an embarrassment, when you asked us
Shakers to carry table lamps and lanterns through the room as you
worked. We had other occupations, and yet we accommodated
you. Do you contest my memory, Mr. Sternum? I record it here as
a reckoning. If I am wrong in my recall or my estimation of the
effect of your work, I pray you, advise me of my errors; I will, in
turn, advise our eldress to conduct the sale proposed by the Biondi
brothers, and we Shakers will leave quietly, as is our way. No one
has ever contested the beauty of our tables and chairs, nor of our
rooms. Equally, no man ever made such photographs of our things
as did you. Nor did anyone ever take so much time. Your method,
an antiquated one I have since learned, was painstaking. A young
friend of the Family who has made some pictures of us over the
years (in the normal way, with a momentary Click!), told me that
you had worked at excessively low speeds, which exposed the film
to the static objects for an inordinate amount of time, and thus
portrayed them in a fullness of detail the human eye itself would
not otherwise observe. It was not easy for us to take orders from
you, Mr. Sternum. For six months, you had us moving at your
whim, swinging our table lamps this way and that. Frankly, the*

others and I had to believe you were an artist. What choice had we but to trust that your finished photographs would portray us with dignity? You were gone long before you sent us a copy of your well-made book, which made you rich. We were as impressed as the World's people by the heartbreaking picture of our harvest table, the three chairs hanging by the bedroom window, the nested baskets, and the leaning brooms. I believe we paged twice through your beautiful book. We were not there. We Shakers had left no impression. Only the static objects were recorded. We had passed many times in the path of your lens, but we were nothing but light. You did not see us, did you? And when they were exposed to your brilliant pictures, the World's people could not see us. We were not there. Your pictures turned Shakerism into a perfectionist cult, Mr. Sternum. In your photographs, the Brothers and Sisters are represented by light alone, as if we were long-dead stars. You kept us in motion, and we were gone before we knew it. And now we are in motion again. We must leave Hancock. This Village is threatened with destruction. If you do not intercede, even the static objects will disappear. I trust you will speak to no one of my request. You will come to our aid or you will not. Tell no one of my plea. For if worse comes to worst, as it has so often for the Family in recent years, we will be bargaining with the Biondi brothers, and I would prefer to have them see no more of our weakness than is made obvious by our circumstances. Godspeed, Sister Celia, Hancock Center Family.

I knew the response that Celia's letter had generated; it was perfect. He swung by the stucco house and made my mother pregnant with me, which was his way of being my father and as close as he'd ever come to being a father to Ellen and the rest of the First Family. Then he whizzed around town, stirring up trouble, and when he was sure the round barn would not be razed, he turned away, and he just kept moving until he was out of the picture, which was as close as he'd ever come to being a Shaker. It was perfect. I wasn't impressed. I put the book on the shelf. I dined on cigarettes and coffee. I called Paul and told him I wanted to stay in town, with him, after I met with Fred Hogworthy at MCU. To prepare for that interview, I chose a dull tie from my small collection, which was what I figured Derby and his minions would be looking for—something standard, something Rachel Reed wouldn't look at twice.

MECHANICS
I and him? He and me?

When children are first acquiring the habit of English, they say funny things. <u>Me is lonely.</u> <u>Her is gone.</u> Kids don't know if they are the subject or the object of an event. Adults sound like kids when they pick up the phone and say, <u>This is her</u> (which means, <u>Her is speaking</u> since there is no other noun to perform the action), or when they say, <u>It's me</u> (which means <u>Me is here</u>, even though they mean to say, <u>I am here; it's I</u>). But in most other sentences with a single pronoun (<u>He</u> is going to the beach; wait for <u>him</u>) we don't say anything unintentionally hilarious. We quickly learn when someone is the mover, the doer (I wait, she turns, he leaves, you wonder, we survive, they disappear, who called), and when that someone is static, an object set in place by a pre<u>position</u> (<u>beyond</u> me, <u>for</u> her, <u>with</u> him, <u>between</u> us, <u>after</u> them, <u>to</u>

whom). We are not confused when we deal with one pronoun alone. But put a few of them together, and subjects and objects get confused. For example: <u>Please don't ask questions about (he/him) and (me/I). I don't know whether (her/she) and (him/he) can explain what happened.</u> Which pronouns do you want in each case? If you are confused, isolate them. (Sometimes people need to be alone to think.) You would never say, "Don't ask questions about he," as you would not say, "Don't ask questions about I." The proper agreement among these people is <u>Please don't ask questions about him and me.</u> Similarly, "her" and "him" are incapable of explaining anything. Given some time, after they've been isolated, it is clear that <u>she and he can explain what happened.</u> You will come to an agreement if <u>you</u>, <u>she</u>, and <u>he</u> spend time alone before <u>you</u> turn to <u>her</u> and <u>him</u> for their versions of the event.

The Future

Monday, 10 June,
and Beyond

perfect agreement

I GOT THE job. It seemed to be the least Fred Hogworthy could
do. Hiring me on the spot was easier than conducting a proper
candidate search, and he had to hire someone; none of the faculty at MCU wanted to waste his or her own time teaching students to read and write. I accepted the job because I couldn't
live without one. Paul thought I could live without a job, or at
least without the one at MCU, but he hadn't explained the eco-
nomic principles of his theory. We'd taken a break to read the
menu. We were at the Hot Kitchen, a filthy old bar and cafe-
teria; I was always relieved to get there before the health inspectors, who came by weekly to close the place down for
infractions of the Hair Net Code or the Bread Basket Recycling
Ordinance. I went there for five-dollar dinners. I was always
amazed they cooked at those prices; I certainly didn't expect
them to clean, too. And was it their fault that they couldn't give
away their dinner rolls? Paul ordered a Cheeseburg Special. At

the Hot Kitchen, the addition of iceberg lettuce and fries was still special. I ordered four eggs, sausage, two English muffins, and twice as many pan-fried potatoes as the cook typically dumped on a plate. The waitress's T-shirt had slipped off one shoulder, and she had a safety pin in her nose and no hair, all of which made her look very young, like a baby who'd tried to diaper herself. She said, "Sunny-side up, right? And I'll try to get him to grill the English." Clearly she'd taken my order before. I didn't recognize her. She returned with coffee and water, and then again with dinner. I couldn't remember who she was, but I was glad to be back in her neighborhood. Paul told me about his lunch with Peter Castle, and it was official: he wasn't going to the NIH. When I asked him how he'd explained his change of plans, Paul said, "I told Castle I'd made a stupid mistake. He agreed." I wondered if Paul had missed a chance to ask for more money or longer vacations. Hadn't he wasted his leverage? Paul looked a little embarrassed when he said, "Yes. I guess I did." He offered me a bite of his burger, a much needed palate cleanser before I dipped into the yolk of my third egg. My question had stymied him, and this surprised us both. I rarely had the upper hand in our discussion of practical matters. Finally, he said, "It hadn't occurred to me to bargain with him. I just wanted to be sure I could stay where I was, now that I wanted to be here. I mean, I already make more money than I spend, but I guess you can always use more." He helped himself to some of my potatoes. "I really can see your point. I've always been grateful to Castle for the job. Today more than ever. But you're saying, Why be grateful? They obviously want me to do the job. Why not turn that around to my advantage, right?" I was feeling a little less proud of myself, but I suggested that the two were not exclusive. Paul agreed, which made me nervous. He waited for the waitress to clear his plate, and then he said, "You're right. I could be a little less grateful and a little greedier. Of course, Castle could've offered me less money or extracted some other price. He didn't. The hospital has always acted decently; I thought I should, too. Or am I missing your point?" If I'd had a point, it had been ground down to something like the paprika on my potatoes. You didn't have to be Abel Nagen to understand this history lesson. I'd just accepted a job at a shamelessly self-serving university. I did not admire the way they treated students or the tenants of apartment blocks they bought. MCU was bigger and better known than most Boston universities; decent it was not. Like most privileged people who have the freedom to make fundamental choices, I'd squandered mine. Paul was one of the few people who would not congratulate me for doing so. When we got back to his place, we sat in the dark kitchen and stared at the park. It was late, and Paul was exhausted, a combination that always made me talkative. I wanted to end the evening on a judicious note. I said I thought maybe Agatha Kroll had been right to fire me. Paul said, "Just because you couldn't teach one student to spell?" I tried to explain that it had not been my classroom-teaching failure but something much more complicated. It was abstract, and it involved the apparent dichotomy of a private college trying to effect change in the public schools, and it had forced all of us to confront the limits of our morality. Paul hmmmed, and then he said, "Abstract moral dichotomies? I guess so. Or you could say you failed to teach Rashelle to spell. That was your job." I reminded Paul that he had to get up very early for a seven-thirty meeting. He said,

"You failed. Once. One out of how many? A thousand? It's a great record, Mark. Don't you see? You are the only person I know who could get himself fired under these circumstances." I told Paul he better go to bed. He said, "And maybe it could only have happened at McClintock. When I think about it, I cannot name a university in this country more committed to genuine education. And yet, after six months of meetings, what did the Administration achieve? Two deans and the president managed to turn a young woman who could not spell the word *juice* into a symbol for their college." Paul went to bed. I was wishing he hadn't gone to Korea just when the whole Spelling Storm broke. I was also thinking he ought to be in charge of more things, including my life. Then he came back to the kitchen. He asked me when I would be finished at McClintock; he wanted to clear his schedule for coffee and debriefing. I didn't know when I'd be free, but he pressed me for a time, so I guessed eleven-thirty. Paul's least admirable habit was working backward. He planned his days and our evenings from the bottom up. It didn't encourage spontaneity; a last-minute change of time or place rocked a day's worth of dominoes. Paul was so tired that he was basically sleepwalking, but before he went back to bed, he dug a bag of fat-free chocolate cookies out of his cabinet. There were only three left, but he wanted me to try one. He assured me they were "pretty good." I bit in. I think it involved egg whites and soil. I handed him the rest of it, and I decided not to hand my life over to him. As far as I will ever see, Paul is perfect, and he has his limits. Tuesday morning was gray, and Paul was gone before I was awake. When I got to Mc-Clintock, the campus was quiet. Summer school was not yet in session. A few of the pink azaleas had held onto their Commencement blooms, but everything else had gone green. I wasn't early, but I wasn't late yet, so I stopped and got a coffee to dribble on my tie as I walked to the vast Administration Building. From a distance, I saw Rashelle standing alone near the front door. I headed to the side entrance, smoked two cigarettes, and wagged my wet tie a few times, hoping the stains would pass as watermarks on hand-spun silk. It worked, but that made the rest of the cheap cotton look particularly drab. I went upstairs. A man I did not recognize was seated at the head of the table. I took one of the two chairs at the far end. The Three Furies were in their normal positions for a nine o'clock meeting in the conference room. Rachel was in her office next door. She was talking on the telephone to an indispensable secretary in the Graduate School who'd called to tender her resignation and would end up agreeing to take on additional responsibilities and send Rachel daily e-mails about her accomplishments. At the same time, Rachel was signing contracts for the adjunct summer faculty and reading her e-mail. Marie Bond was in Cambridge, having a coffee with a visiting scholar from Pakistan who was about to agree to teach a course at McClintock, though he didn't know it yet. Agatha Kroll was editing a two-hundred-page analysis of salary distribution among the professorial ranks that one of her secretaries had put together because the Faculty Senate had complained about equity for a year and never bothered to do anything with the numbers Agatha had made available to them. Once the report was distributed, it would be humiliatingly obvious that everyone was being paid about a thousand dollars for each day spent in the classroom. The senate would denounce Agatha for raising the salary issue again, then dig through their files, looking for a new agenda item. In September, they would rouse their colleagues for the umpteenth time with a run at the Holy Grail— reserved parking for so-called full-time faculty, just like other disabled people had. Faculty were always irate when they wheeled in at two in the afternoon in their shiny Japanese and German sedans and saw the jalopies of janitors, secretaries, and other eight-to-fivers taking up space. The man at the other end of the table introduced himself as Simon Dent, legal counsel for the college. He was big and yellow-haired, and it was hard to read his blank face. Was his brow furrowed by excessive earnestness or old-fashioned Yankee inbreeding? I was pretty sure I'd seen him walking around Harvard Square with a singles scull on his shoulder. Agatha darted in, followed by Rachel and Rashelle, who were laughing about something. Marie Bond was not far behind, and she nodded at Agatha and Rachel: it was a Go on the History of the Raj course for September. Rachel pointed in the direction of the Graduate School and smiled: resignation avoided. Agatha said, "As far as I can tell from the numbers, the Faculty Senate has compiled a compelling case against salary increases for faculty." We all shook hands and bowed, and then the seating began. As in the parking lot, there were no assigned places. This was the nature of the New Democracy at McClintock. Nobody ever knew who belonged where. Nobody ran or chaired meetings; they were free-for-alls. Politics at McClintock was "politics as usual," according to Abel Nagen, who said the New Democracy was, in practice, an ad-hocracy. Rashelle landed next to me, and I asked if we were waiting for her lawyer. "Nah. He didn't show. Les face it, Mark. Lawyers blow." Simon Dent took a note. "I ain't suin nobody." Heads turned our way. I thought maybe the meeting was over. Another note was taken. Marie said, "You okay, Rashelle? You sound tired." Rashelle nodded. Marie was watching me, smiling. She said, "Now that no one is going to be sued—" she nodded at Rachel—"what do you think we should do, Mark? Why don't you take the lead?" She meant "There's still a loaded pistol in the room. Rachel is out of harm's way. No reason to waste a bullet. The barrel is pointed at your foot. Wanna pull the trigger?" Simon raised his platinum pen and said, "What exactly is his role in the process now?" Rashelle looked at him and said, "*You* gonna teach me how to spell?" Simon made a note of that, too, which infuriated Rashelle. I think she considered it bad sportsmanship for the Administration to keep their lawyer in the game. She said, "How much that pen cost?" I don't know why, but I said it cost her and the other students two or three hundred bucks. Rachel laughed out loud, then coughed, but too late. Agatha slammed her hand on the table. Simon said, "I'll have you know this was a gift from my grandfather." Rashelle muttered, "His grandfather? Jeez, I wish my lawyer came. Coulda kicked this guy's ass." Marie reached out and clamped her left hand around Agatha's wrist. Rachel whispered something to Marie, who then used her right hand to pluck the pen from Simon. She laid it on his yellow pad and closed the cover of his leather portfolio. "All that is left is to plan your practice teaching in the spring, Rashelle. We won't need Simon for that." Simon stood up. Before he left, he shook hands with Rashelle and me. He could afford to be gracious, I suppose; he'd just add it to his bill. When he was gone, Marie said, "Before you leave, Mark, we want to congratulate you on the job at MCU." There were two notable facts embedded here. First, the three of them were "we" again, and maybe they always were. They worked like weather. Wind, rain, and thunder were separate in the sky, but on the ground, a storm was a storm, a force of nature. Second fact: word was already out about the MCU offer. I saw that I would be leaving through the same door as Simon Dent. I had arranged for my own compensation. Dent and I dealt in the same currency. Rashelle said, "So you really are quittin your job here?" I tried to respond, but Agatha said, "Rachel fired him." Rachel took the blow without flinching. She said, "Indeed, I did. I did it." I didn't want to leave her like that, so I said she'd made it easier than it might have been. Rashelle said, "She always makes ya feel better bout somethin bad." Marie added, "Well, Rachel's always nice. She's just graceful by nature." Agatha patted Rachel's hand and said, "It's true." Then the eulogizing was done. But Rachel sat up in her flowery casket; actually, she stood and walked to the window. Her back was to us, but I could see that she was crying. We all could. I remembered a story she'd told me after she'd observed my teaching during my first semester at McClintock. I was nervous the students wouldn't have anything to say, so I talked all the time. She told me she'd been nervous, too, but that her great fear was reading aloud from books she loved. She said she was scared to death that she would start bawling in the middle of *Middlemarch*. But then she finally worked up the nerve to read the first page of Eliot's amazing prose. And Rachel bawled. And so did most of the students, who already loved her and thus were ready to love the nineteenth-century novels she had taken to heart. Rachel had composed herself, but the rest of us were weepy or holding our breath. She said, "It's funny, but it really isn't in my nature. Most of my life, I was in a classroom, and there, teaching, I just did what came naturally to me. But up here, it's not always so safe. You're not there to make sure no one gets hurt, and by the time they come to us, people are hopping mad. And they start a chain reaction, and pretty soon Agatha is yelling, and somebody calls a lawyer, and where's the copy of the contract for the instructor who didn't show up for her class? Why don't faculty have private secretaries? Whom can I talk to about my roommate selling drugs?" She had been yelling, and she smiled. "When I first got here, I had no idea how to help. So I guess I learned to be nice to everyone. It's *second* nature to me. Isn't that lame? Whenever I'm positive I won't find that copy of the contract before a fight breaks out or I can't think fast enough to prevent your being fired, I make it my job to soften the blow." She turned around and looked out at the river across the street. Agatha, Marie, and I behaved like Shaker chairs—sturdy, stiff, strong; somebody should have hung us all up on the wall. Rashelle had the wit to say, "I'd hate to have your job, Rachel. I get pissed off when two kids wanna go pee at the same time." And I thought of Ellen and how she hated kids' questions. And I said, "You don't want to be a teacher, do you, Rashelle?" Rachel turned around. Rashelle looked at her. "I ain't cut out for it. I can learn to be nice, I know I can. But not with twenty kids who got no problem but whas for lunch in the caf and what kinda car your dad drivin. I can't care bout them. I can't." Rachel said, "You could care about a kid with no dad." Rashelle said, "Or a drunk for a father, sure. Who couldn't?" Rachel said, "Most of the rest of the world. That's who." Then Rachel pointed to Marie, who shrugged, as if she didn't get it, but she did, and she knew it was up to her to give it to Rashelle. Marie said, "If you wanted

to become a social work major, it would take at least three more
semesters." Agatha looked at the door, adding up the legal fees
the college had saved when Rashelle dropped her suit. But
Marie was better at this kind of math. She said, "There is some
scholarship money set aside for older students with children
who choose social work." Rashelle looked at me. "I still gotta
spell in social work, right?" I said she did but not on a blackboard. She said, "I had a buncha terrible social workers when I
was a kid." Rachel said, "They're still out there." Rashelle said,
"Ya mean somebody gotta least soften the blow?" Rachel said,
"Yeah, that's what I mean." Agatha sprang up from her seat.
"Done. Fine. Fine, fine, fine. Marie? Maybe you can figure out
how we can feed this story to the papers." It was not Marie's
job, but the vice president for public relations had resigned
soon after the Spelling Story broke and Agatha fired her. Agatha
held out her hand. "Rashelle, why don't you come back to my
office so we can look at the catalog together and pick out some
courses for the fall?" That wasn't Agatha's job, but it was summer, and all faculty advisers were resting up so they could do
battle with the Evil Administration in the fall. Marie stood up
and said, "Call me, Rachel. And use your second nature when
you do. Soften the blow, please. We have to hire a new director for the writing program. It's going to ruin the whole damn
summer. Comprenez-vous?" Agatha said, "I'm only going to say
this once—." Marie put her hand on Agatha's arm. "I already
said it. You gotta learn some French." Rashelle turned to say
something, but Agatha dragged her away to her office, and
Marie followed them, closing the door as she left. Rachel
looked at her hands. "MCU would be a real step up for you.
And they pay people better. And you deserve it. We'll never be

able to give you what you're worth." But she had, long ago, given me my worth. Paul was right; I belonged there. Rachel and I wasted an hour in the conference room. I don't remember what we talked about. It didn't matter. We had time. I finally went back to my underground office, a six-by-eight cell where I worked between Abel and Gillian. Oddly, they made good neighbors. I could always count on being mad at one of them, and they were fast friends who spoke almost every night on the phone and ended up not speaking to each other the following day. Every day on the job, I had a lunch partner and plenty of neighborhood gossip. I printed out my e-mail. I stuck the obituary from Poland Spring in a file of unsolicited applications for nonexistent teaching positions sent in by people I would never meet, where it belonged. I was still half an hour ahead of schedule, but I couldn't wait to tell Paul the news. He was in a meeting in a room with glass walls. He looked happy. I waited for him to look my way, and I used sign language to say, *You were right. I belong there. Now I need some coffee. I'll meet you downstairs when you're done. Why is everyone staring at me? Good-bye.* Unlike the decision to quit my new job at MCU and go back to McClintock, the decision about where to buy coffee was not easy. I was tempted, of course, by Bits and Chips, which I supposed was the haunt of my anonymous e-mail adviser. But for years I'd relied on the little pushcart espresso woman, who'd brought real coffee to Boston long before anyone in Portland or Seattle had invented mochaccino and frappé-latte and other caffeine-free blender drinks for people who'd given up coffee. I tried to sneak my triple espresso into Bits and Chips, but a teenager wearing a green paper hat said, "You can't come in here with coffee." You couldn't leave there

with coffee, either. I was happy to sit on the wrought-iron communion rail that separated Bits and Chips from the rest of the
World. Their few customers were playing video games. They
were expert. Watching those kids, anyone could see the bene-
fit of five impressionable years spent with educational TV. At
exactly eleven-thirty, Paul was at my side. He said, "I only have
half an hour. But I am coming up to Ipswich tonight. You got
the job, didn't you? Again, I mean. Your job. Oh! Are we having
lunch with her?" I thought he was referring to a girl with a braid
who was busy warding off an intergalactic invasion right beside
us. But he was pointing to the other side of the café, where
Agatha Kroll had a foamy drink and a few handwritten notes
she was transcribing for distribution on the World Wide Web.

MECHANICS
Despite what you've heard

Did any<u>one</u> lose <u>their</u> job today? <u>Neither</u> of the jobs <u>are</u>
perfect. <u>Each</u> of the administrators <u>have</u> <u>their</u> own <u>ver-</u>
<u>sions</u> of the story. Those three sentences sound fine to
most of us because we are unused to agreement. We tend
to disagree. Get used to agreement. All words in English
that end -*one* are singular; they work like *she* or *he*; so do
all words that end -*body* because there is but one body
per person. Before you use one of the -*body* or
-*one* words (some-, any-, every-, no-), try substituting *she*
or *he* to sound out the agreement. Listen again to those
first three sentences. Did any<u>one</u> (he) lose <u>his</u> (not their)
job? Similarly, *neither* and *either* mean "one," not "two,"
not "both." If there are two people or things in your sen-

tence, and you are talking about (n)either one, you are talking about a "she," "he," or maybe an "it." <u>Neither of the jobs</u> (neither it nor it) <u>is</u> (not are) perfect. <u>Each of the administrators</u> (each one of the Gang of Three; she, she, and she) <u>has</u> (not have) <u>her</u> (not their) <u>version</u> (not versions) of the story. When you want to achieve perfect agreement, you have to let each <u>he</u> speak for <u>himself</u>; every <u>she</u> must speak for <u>herself</u>; and then you have <u>it</u>, agreement. <u>They</u> are on <u>their</u> way.

p r e d e s t i n a t i o n

THE SHAKERS WERE right. Work is a Gift. For the longest time, I wasn't ready to receive it. I had learned reading and 'riting and 'rithmetic, but I wasn't prepared until I had taken the lessons to heart, where I now hold the stories of Rhea and Ruth and Rashelle, my three R's. Before I went home to my so-called tomatoes, I went to the Stellar Market. I circled the fresh food several times, just getting to know my way around. I wasn't ready to commit to this cooking thing, but I knew I'd be back. I scooted over to Frozen Foods. While I was pulling some ice cream sandwiches out of the cabinet, someone knocked on the frosty door. It was Janice, Janice of the plums. She was wearing a black T-shirt and jeans. "I made a fool of myself the other day," she said. "I'm sorry. The kids are at camp, and Dave was at work, and I figured it was summer, or almost." She closed the freezer door. "So, I almost . . ." She had a cart full of fresh things. "How's your father?" I said he was dead, and she said,

"My God, so fast. Was he sick for a long time?" That was a poser. I thought for a while. I said, "Just up and died. He was very old." She nodded, and she rubbed her face a few times, as if she couldn't quite believe it. Then she put her hand on my arm and said, "You live up the hill from us, I think. We're down on the flats, in that white place that looks like a barn. You know—the one that is a barn?" I knew the place. It was a romantic house, saggy and surrounded by reeds, one of those old wrecks everybody wants to live in except the people who live there. She was staring into my cart, multiplying. "Thirty-six ice cream sandwiches?" It was a dinner only Paul Pryor could love. I noticed that she had a precooked chicken in her basket; that was a meal I could prepare. I asked her where she'd found it, and she pointed to the deli. Then she said, "Listen, Dave and I gotta start making some friends. Why don't you and your pal come by some time?" I asked when. She said, "After dinner tonight?" Then we stared at each other. We'd both sounded a little too eager, as if we didn't get many opportunities to practice our social skills. Janice said, "Come by after nine. Is nine okay? We eat late." It occurred to me that we might not have anything in common except the roasted chickens we would have eaten for dinner. But I said nine was fine, and I wheeled away, working backward from nine o'clock to figure out what time Paul and I should eat. Then, from a ways off, Janice yelled, "Hey!" She ran my way. "Listen, I don't want to get off on the wrong foot again." She looked at her feet, as if to say, I only have two. "I want to have something you'll like. Juice or some special kind of water? I like wine. Do you drink?" This was a good omen. I was happy to tell her I did drink, like a fish. I went home. While I watered the tomatoes, I looked forward to drinks with our neighbors. Then I read Agatha Kroll's last bit of e-mailed advice. It was brief: "They are all our children, Mark, even the ones we shunt off onto social workers. She—Rashelle—needs, and they—the children she will serve—need, the basic skills. It's a funny job for a college professor, but no one else seems to be doing it. And it's not too late as long as it gets done. You have the summer. While you are out there on the beach, find a way to teach her to spell." When I'd had the chance to unmask Agatha, I had left her alone. I didn't think it was polite to intrude, even in cyberspace. It was enough to know that she didn't spend all of her time in the North Pole cracking her whip and yelling at the exhausted elves in her Third Floor workshop. She was bipolar, too. She went south, even if it was only for a few leased minutes of computer time. She didn't turn into someone else. She just got to her other side, where she wasn't responsible for making sure that everybody's salary package, or diploma, or classroom video monitor, or dorm room was wrapped and delivered on time. My anonymous adviser was the other side of Agatha: Agatha who had spent many years as a teacher; Agatha who was devoted to live music and modern dance, at the expense of many a night's sleep; Agatha, the Woman in the World, who predated the President of McClintock, a college that demanded that its president do just about everything except act like a president because that would be undemocratic. I was grateful to unpredictable Agatha for her good advice. I was impressed by her determination to maintain her other side and occasionally indulge it. And I was content to leave her alone to sip her cool drink—please God, caffeine-free.

SPELLING TIP
Prefixes

It's still true. Prefixes never change the spelling of the root word. This rule is as immutable as death and taxes, only more so as it turns out. But choosing a prefix is not an inconsequential act. *Mis-* will not change the letters of *spell*, but it will change the meaning. And to make meaning of our lives, each of us must deal with the pre-fixed things—that is, history. When we get attached to our predecessors (literally, those who died before us), our lives take on new meaning. And then we try to work it out. Air-traffic controllers and audio-interpreters de<u>scribe</u>; jewelers and stonecutters in<u>scribe</u>; doctors and herbalists pre<u>scribe</u>; clerics and parents pro<u>scribe</u>. Everybody has to have a job. But, you see, there is one basic skill at the root of them all, and we learn to do it by heart.

Printed in the United States
by Baker & Taylor Publisher Services